DRAW

GENTRY BOYS BOOK 1

CORA BRENT

Please respect the work of this author. No part of this book may be reproduced or copied without permission. This book is licensed for your personal enjoyment only.

This book is a work of fiction. Any resemblance to persons living or dead is purely coincidental. Any similarities to events or situations is also coincidental.

The publisher and author acknowledge the trademark status and trademark ownership of all trademarks and locations mentioned in this book. Trademarks and locations are not sponsored or endorsed by trademark owners.

© 2014 by Cora Brent
All Rights Reserved

Editing: C. Simone

Cover Design: © L.J. Anderson, Mayhem Cover Creations
Cover Photo: Artem Furman

 Created with Vellum

1

SAYLOR

We weren't friends.

That's the first truth to be acknowledged if anything can be understood about the chaotic passion that came later. Cord Gentry wasn't my friend and he sure as hell wasn't in my thoughts as I careened through the inky expanse of Death Valley in a dying Civic with my jaw still stinging painfully.

Night in the desert is otherworldly, preternatural. I breathed in the sweet perfume of it and reveled in the force of the hot wind on my face. All the windows of the car were wide open because the air conditioning had broken the summer after my freshman year at Oxy. Devin, in one of his falsely tender moments, had offered to foot the bill to get it fixed but I had learned to be wary of his offers.

Gingerly, almost without thinking about it, I brought my fingertips to my swollen face. He'd gotten me square on the curve of my lower right jawline. It was swollen. It would show a bruise tomorrow. I knew that because my fair skin was afflicted with a special sensitivity that marked easily. I also knew because it's what had happened before. The memory of it all brought a surge of rage over something I'd once thought of as love.

Until I knew it was the opposite.

The worst part was how I had fooled myself. At first he would just wrestle a little too hard. Devin would squeeze my wrist with a small, wicked smile until I yelped and then he would pull back, innocently insisting he didn't know he'd been hurting me.

But every violent ending has to begin somewhere.

"Look what you did, you asshole," I told him indignantly the first time my arm bore the distinct imprint of his crushing hand.

Devin was dismayed, or rather playing at it. "Oh, sweetheart," he'd said, kissing it and then slowly undressing me. He figured out early on how to sucker me in and I melted under his touch, squashing my own doubts. There was nothing bad about this, I told myself. Devin loved me. He said so. I'd always had so much disdain for certain other women, women like the ones I had seen lurching around back in my hometown of Emblem, the ones who would endure one terrible thing after another until it just seemed like that's the way things were supposed to be. But I wasn't like them. I could handle Devin.

The next time it happened he whined, "I'm sorry, Saylor," with the crumpled face of a boy as he held me tight, too tight.

Then, after he slapped me hard because I'd disagreed with his assessment of the MLB draft picks, it was "Aw Say, I just love you so fucking much."

I was angry. I held my face and called him a lousy prick as he wheedled his way back in, murmuring things he knew would break my stony silence.

"Say," he whispered, running his lips over my neckline and up to the place where his hand had done damage. "I love you."

I remained furious but still I let him bend me over and ride me how he liked even though I couldn't come that way. He was rough and I was dry, unready, but I took it just the same. As Devin grunted his claim on my body, I stared at the beige-colored wall two inches from my nose and bit the inside of my cheek to keep myself distracted. That moment was exactly when it occurred to me there was something very wrong with it all.

Devin Berlin was absurdly hot. He was rich. His father was a

Silicon Valley overlord who'd invented one of the backbones of personal technology; motherboards or modems or something. I always forgot the specifics. Devin's arrogant grin landed on me one classically sunny southern California day when I carried a latte to the table where he sat alone.

It had been a desolate semester, nothing but studying and waitressing. My mouth ran dry and I tried to fend off my own nerves as his smile lingered on me. "Can I get you anything else?"

"Some company," he'd said, sipping his latte and pulling a chair to his side, secure in the knowledge that I would sink right into it.

Devin spent a lot of time building the features of his suntanned body. He knew the effect was as addictive as sugar. I'd seen him around campus, full of conceit and muscle. It was a little sick really, to think I'd grown into the kind of woman who got so wet over the combination she didn't care about anything else.

That finally changed when he broke my nose.

It happened on Valentine's Day. Jesus, you could piss yourself over the irony; the imaginary holiday of love and chocolate topped off by a swift blow to crack your face in half. I don't even remember why. An argument in the car, something mundane and silly like couples clash over and then forget about.

"Holy fuck," he'd whimpered as I held my face in stunned agony, feeling the blood drip between my fingers. "Saylor, I'm a monster. I can't even fucking believe I just did that to you. I'm going to drive you to the police station, baby. You need to file a report on me. Oh, honey. Sweet Say. I ought to be put in jail for what I just did to you."

But through the pain I just shook my head. The only thing worse than the pulpy mess that was now my nose would be telling a roomful of people about it. Besides, I knew he had no intention of allowing me to press charges against him. "No. But you'll damn well never do that to me again, Devin. I mean it this time. That's it."

He'd started to cry. "No, shit, never. Saylor, I love you. You know I love you."

The car rolled to a stop at the next light. Devin reached over and put his hand under my skirt, snaking between my legs. I didn't stop him. I looked out the window. It wasn't quite dark yet and the low rider beside us held a quartet of men who peered curiously at my bleeding face. They were rough men, gangbangers by the grim, tattooed look of them. I wondered if they hit their women too.

We lived in a posh beachfront condo financed by Devin's father and by the time we got there he was fully immersed in the role of loving boyfriend. He cleaned me up, helped me into a robe and then let me know how hard he was. Even as I cursed the betrayal of my body I let it happen; I let him ease me onto the bed and spread my legs as he rolled on a condom. I watched his face as he grimaced through his orgasm and felt nothing. Finally, my heart had begun to harden. I welcomed the detachment.

The next day I peered soberly at the raccoon-like bruising under the garish light of the bathroom vanity and balled both hands into fists. Couples fought all the time. I remembered the howling battles between my parents. It was a vicious back and forth of verbal stabs that was painful to hear. It did not surprise me when they separated. But there were no sounds of fists hitting flesh. There were no bruises the next day.

My eyes narrowed in disgust at my own reflection. How the hell could I allow this and still look myself in the eye every day?

"Skateboarding," I explained with a ridiculous laugh to anyone who asked. "Rolling full speed through a parking garage after four Jello shots." Then I laughed again, a moronic giggle that sounded repulsive even to me. Then whoever had cared to ask in the first place would smile with polite doubt and turn away.

The truth was too humiliating. I worried more about what those bruises said about me than what they said about Devin. Only Brayden knew. But my cousin and lifelong best friend was nearly three hundred miles away in Arizona. He repeatedly threatened to drive out and confront Devin but that sounded like a nuclear-level disaster. Devin worked every day at being strong. Brayden hadn't thrown a punch since he was pummeled on the school playground by one of the Gentry brothers. I begged my cousin not to come.

"Saylor," he pleaded and I could hear it in his voice; the fear, the resignation, the disgust. I couldn't blame him. No one was more disappointed in Saylor McCann than Saylor McCann. I made Brayden swear that he wouldn't tell my parents. They knew nothing. They were still living their separate lives in Emblem and working at the prison.

"You deserve better," he coughed. He ended the call before I could answer.

Really, I had no answer. Not for Brayden, not for myself. 'Better' had proven to be an elusive concept where the male factor was concerned, starting with the high school scumbag who'd sweet talked his way into my pants and through my virginity. There was a reason for it, a reason far worse than sixteen year old hormones. Cord Gentry had made a bet. And then what did that son of a bitch do? He laughed about it uproariously and all the people I'd known my whole life bent themselves in half trying to be first to sit on the gossip train.

I suppose everyone has a pivotal story of painful adolescence and that was mine. I'd known what the Gentry brothers were. A set of fraternal triplets born to a depraved family, they were rough, sexy and wild as wolves. Together they comprised a powerful triumvirate that ruled the youth of Emblem. I tried not to be among the girls who fell unreservedly for their golden good looks and broad shoulders. Until Cord Gentry noticed me one day and crooked a finger with a sly smile. It didn't take much at all for me to unlock my knees and lie down on the floor of a dirty garage for him. I'd felt awful enough about it two seconds after it was done. Then it got worse. It turned out to be all a game, some sort of sick Gentry boys challenge to see who could pop the nerdy McCann chick.

That was a bad time. Through it all I only had Brayden to hand me box after box of tissues as we hunkered down on the floor of my lilac bedroom and played grunge music from the early nineties with religious intensity. My cousin, a sweet kid who endured high school hells of his own, wiped away the snot-encrusted tendrils of my brown hair and gazed at me sadly. He said the same thing he would sigh into the phone six years later.

"You deserve better."

As soon as Devin walked through the door tonight I knew he was drunk. I also knew the violence was in him again. He'd been tiptoeing around me since the Valentine's Day punch but I often sensed he was biding his time, like a cat. I was graduating in two days and already looking for an apartment. It would have been nice to find a good job to go with it. Waitressing didn't pay well and, shockingly, it turned out employers weren't clamoring for English majors with a concentration in creative writing. But I knew I had to get out. Soon, before he pounced again. He would, I was sure of it.

When Devin spotted me sitting on the couch with my laptop he smiled. My heart stopped. Oh, that sounds so cliché, and I dearly loathe clichés but there is no more appropriate term. When you meet danger eye to eye, your heart really does stop. And then it resumes beating again, furiously.

"Who the hell you talkin' to?" he slurred.

I closed the lid of the laptop. "No one, Dev. I'm writing."

He threw his keys on the breakfast bar and held out his hand. "Gimme it."

I held my computer against my chest. I was telling the truth. I had rewritten three chapters of my novel but hadn't saved them yet. "No," I told him, standing.

I should have felt inadequately prepared, standing there barefoot in my tank top and shorts while Devin Berlin coiled strength into his considerable muscles. He was drunk, slow, but still dangerous.

"You think I don't know," he growled, "about all the fucks you get on the side, Sweet Say?"

I closed my eyes. *Sweet Say.* His nickname for me. Once it had been endearing. Now it only sounded lethal.

"I haven't been with anyone but you since we met. You know that, Devin. Now why don't you go sleep off your liquid paranoia and we'll talk in the morning." My voice fought with my nerves, trying to stay casual. Something more than my nose had already broken in me. And as I watched Devin's mind sorting through the rage of this imaginary betrayal, I realized it would always come back to this. There was no way out but to leave. There was no time other than now.

I held my computer tighter and tried to smile at my boyfriend. I had no intention of talking to him in the morning. The reason was because I had no intention of even being there in the morning.

He reached me so quickly I didn't even have time to flinch. I could smell the mix of smoke and liquor on him. It used to make me hot, just like it used to make me hot when Devin would push his hand crudely between my legs and inside my panties.

"Tell me a bedtime story first," he grinned, fingering me rudely and roughly. It wasn't a request.

Repulsed, I twisted away. There was nothing erotic about any of this. The feel of his fingers groping inside my body was vile. But as I saw his eyes glaze with fury I knew I had waited too long. I should have left sooner.

Devin grabbed the laptop out of my arms. I cried out as he held it over his head and slammed it into the marble floor. It landed with a cracking thud and I lashed out, pushing my palms into his hard chest.

"Asshole!" I screamed.

When Devin clocked me in the face he was clumsy. Otherwise it would have been worse. Still, the blow stung and left me off balance so that I toppled face first into the buttery leather sofa. Devin was immediately on top of me, all hands and hot breath as he ripped my shorts off. I struggled mightily but he pinned my arms and I felt him growing hard, pushing relentlessly against the soft flesh of my backside.

I twisted my head, saying his name, trying to get him to hear me. "Devin. No. Fucking stop it, Devin."

"Filthy slut," he groaned, getting harder as I tried in vain to kick him off. "How many boys you give it to, Sweet Say?"

I thrashed. I was wild, desperate. The feel of his dick trying to pry me open was revolting. "I hate you. Sick bastard! I hate you! Get the fuck off me!"

"You love me, Say. Aw shit, you're tight."

My mind screamed. All the times he'd been abusive he'd never done this. I'd realized some time ago how it was all bound together with him, the violence and the sex. But I was always willing. Perhaps if I hadn't been he would have done this brutal thing sooner. The thought unleased a primal ferocity that coursed through my blood like fire.

I'd always heard stories of people in extreme circumstances who find themselves, just for a moment, endowed with superior strength. A soccer mom pinned under her overturned SUV. An elderly man fighting off a pack of attacking pit bulls. As I writhed under Devin's cruel violation I became that surge of adrenaline. I rolled my head into my chest and reared back with a great gasp of power. The back of my hard skull caught him under the chin and he wavered, dazed. One swift elbow in the gut later and he'd fallen on the floor, his dick flopping around idiotically.

Naked and furiously wronged, I stood and calmly picked up a beach-weathered end table. I'd never been a strong girl and Devin was twice my size. His hideously handsome face held something close to surprise as he watched me raise it above my head. I wasn't Saylor McCann formed out of a shitty prison town in the desert. I was powerful, a goddess of vengeance. I brought that thing crashing down on top of him with the strength of five angry women. Just then the most satisfying sound in the world was the impact of wood cracking over flesh. As he screeched like a pig I even found myself smiling.

"Fuck!" he howled. "You broke my goddamn arm. Bitch," he spat.

Devin was floundering at my feet, still drunk and now with his right arm bent at a cruel angle. A leg of the table had broken off and I grabbed it, holding the thing like a baseball bat and enjoying the way he cowered at the sight of me.

I tapped his sweaty forehead with the table leg. "I'm leaving," I told him plainly, "and if you try to stop me I'll break something else. Something more important."

Devin glared at me hatefully. I could almost read the disjointed outrage churning behind his dark eyes as if he'd spoken the words aloud. *Sorry ass bitch lucky I stuck it to her all this time should have tossed her snatch out months ago.*

I stood and felt oddly clear headed. I needed to get out. Now, before he was done stewing in his pain.

With one eye on my sprawling ex-boyfriend and the other feverishly packing a duffel bag, I warily held the impromptu bat in case Devin got a burst of adrenaline to call his own. With breathless haste I pulled on a pair of sweatpants and grabbed a shoebox of my most treasured possessions; a small army of thumb drives holding everything I'd written since the age of ten. I'd always meant to upload it all to a more secure location. As soon as I figured out where I was going, that's what I would do.

I paused in the living room with my bag over my shoulder. Devin seemed like he was beginning to sober up. Amid the splinters of the ruined table, he appeared to be struggling to pull his phone out of his back pocket.

"Devin, you are a cruel bastard," I told him coolly. "And you are going to have a miserable life." It felt good to say that to him. He gave me an uncomprehending look. "Goodbye." I left.

When I sat behind the wheel of my ancient Civic I breathed a quick prayer for it to start. Then with a sigh of weak relief I pointed it east. I wanted to get the hell out of California. The entire state seemed wrapped up in Devin. Wrapped up in the worst things I thought about myself. I wasn't at all the confident, successful woman I'd planned to be. I was a weak-willed girl.

Worse, I hadn't learned a thing about who not to trust.

2

CORD

I hate dreams. My mother used to be one of those crystal-wearing Tarot-reading types who saw every twitch of the subconscious as a message from the universe. At least that's how she would talk when she wasn't fucking high. And she was high most of the time.

No, dreams were the useless leftovers. It was shit that had been shoved to the back of your mind for a reason. It was the nightmare of constant childhood hunger. It was the agony of watching your brother get the tar kicked out of him by a madman who was your blood too. And it was the knowledge that you would be next. Dreams were the place that made you and the place you hated most. They were heat and dirt, sometimes with blood and screaming. Worst of all, dreams were isolation because you had to walk them alone, without the two people who were a part of you since the moment you existed.

Creed and Chase knew I liked to wander after a fight so they let me be. We all handled it differently. On the rare occasions Creed did the work he would lapse into a dark place, grumbling about our bastard father as he drank himself into a blackout. It wasn't good for him to be in that place and anyway he was better at the agent role, making deals and getting the action set up. People looked at him and were reluctant to pull any bullshit. Chase was different; he needed to exercise his dick until he ran out of juice or ran out of women. But on my nights I only wanted a few hours of quiet.

"Damn good fight," Creed said, slapping my shoulder.

"Hell yeah," I agreed, picking the last of the tape off my knuckles and rolling it into a sticky ball. My knuckles had impact cuts anyway; they would be stiff tomorrow.

"Three G's, bro," hooted Chase, fanning himself with the cash. Creed made a face and grabbed it from him

"You takin' the truck?" Creed called as I started to walk away.

"Nah," I answered, pulling on a frayed old flannel shirt with the sleeves cut out. Chase liked to tease me about my Goodwill pickings. He shouted that 1993 called and wanted its fashion sense back. He laughed when I flipped him off.

We lived in an apartment complex less than a mile from the university and the place was crawling with students. I hadn't been in a classroom since the last bell rang in the dusty hallways of Emblem High. These college kids seemed like a different species; sleek, shiny and groping their way through the best days of their lives. Finals had ended and parties oozed out in every direction. The two girls nudging each other ten feet to my left were cute. I knew they were whispering about me. They looked like expensive types though, the moneyed daughters of Scottsdale who were looking to roll with the rough stuff for a night or two. Another time I might have taken them up on the nasty offer in their heavily lined eyes. A glance down at their shapely, tanned legs was enough to get me rising. But my head still wasn't right and I didn't want to deal with any of it.

I got all the way to the north side of the complex before finding a building that wasn't the site of some wild orgy of a party. Stepping on the stucco frame of a dark patio, I hauled myself onto the second floor balcony and from there hopped up to the flat roof. I knew a guy who lived there, an owlish kid from Emblem named Brayden. The first time we'd run into one another at the mailbox, I'd read his loathing. I couldn't pretend not to know why. But the years we'd spend in the same shithole of a town seemed to cement a nameless bond. He struck up a conversation one day at the pool and we'd been something like friends ever since. I asked him that day why he didn't just spit in my direction and walk the other way. He would have been justified. Bray McCann dangled his skinny white legs in the pool and looked thoughtfully over to where his hot little taste of a girlfriend was toweling off.

"Everyone should have one chance to remake themselves, Cord." Then he peered at me with a green-eyed intensity that reminded me uneasily of someone else. "Don't you think?"

Yeah, I did think so. Creed hadn't wanted to stay in Arizona but Tempe was a far cry from Emblem. And Chase just wanted to go wherever there was a diverse selection of ass. A college town was just his brand of pretty. We scraped by for the first few years, finding work where we could and hitting the after-hours scene pretty hard. Everything was lively here, clean. In that way it was worlds different from the place we'd come from. Emblem was seventy miles away but might as well have been the far side of the moon.

Here, in the shadow of one of the nation's largest universities, we didn't have to be 'those Gentry boys' and everything the curse of our last name entailed. All the men in our line went rotten at some point and everyone in Emblem just knew we would follow suit. After a while we gave them reason to believe it. We weren't good kids. We were tough and mean, terrorizing our peers and running roughshod over any authority figure who tried to give a damn. And when we grew a little older, we were the nightmare of every man with a daughter.

But there was a world of hurt none of them knew about. Even the ones who lived out in our neck of the grubby outlying desert would have been shocked to see now we hunted ground squirrels to fend off the hunger pangs. It was a rare cloudy day in the desert when our mother emerged from her fog of addiction long enough to notice she had children. Our father, Benton Gentry, was the lousiest piece of filth who ever walked. In a long life filled with heinous acts the worst thing he ever did was beat his pregnant wife to a pulp, throwing her into premature labor. She almost bled out in surgery, taking the three of us with her. Her jaw still pained her and she was never able to have any more children, although that might have been a blessing. Benton could have killed us all and sometimes I thought he would. Although he wasn't much nicer once we were on the outside, eventually we learned to fight back.

Chase, Creed and I were always surrounded by a shifting collection of motley relatives. Family lore said that Gentrys found themselves out Emblem's way in the 1930s. A pack of forsaken Okies who chugged west in their jalopies en route to the golden country of California, one of them glimpsed the wide irrigation canals and figured they must be closing in on the Pacific Ocean. And so they stayed. Most of their descendants were shells of something less than humanity, strung out and useless. It was best to keep wide of them. But when Uncle Chrome visited for a stretch we clung to him like a life preserver. He'd done time for some of the worst things a man could do to another man, but he knew shit. He knew how to hit and where a body was softest. He would spend tireless afternoons with the three of us under the brutal sun. He had scars everywhere and most of them he didn't like to talk about. He met a bad end, Uncle Chrome did, spread out all over the road three years ago when his bike took a drunken tailspin on a freeway outside Flagstaff. I still grieved over that. Uncle Chrome was one of the only adults who ever seemed to really care in a way that was honest.

The surface of the roof was hot under my back. I removed my shirt and lay flat, letting the day's heat soak through my skin while I stared up at the sky. I always looked for the Three Kings even though they were harder to find out here amid the city lights. They comforted me, a reminder of my brothers and the unbreakable entity we made together.

Creed was right; it had been a good fight. My challenger was just another frat boy but quicker than most. Stakes were higher this time. For us, it might mean the difference between eating well for a few months or scraping together lousy pennies for backbreaking labor under the summer sun. He'd gotten me good in the ribs twice. I fingered the firm, muscled skin covering my ribcage and pressed. Yeah, I'd be feeling that tomorrow.

Frat Boy backed away after he'd gotten in those shots and I circled, taking shallow breathes to fend off the pain and gauging my opponent more carefully. The way he kept glancing back at his cheering fraternity brothers told me a lot about him. Almost as much as the scuffed combat boots he must have scored from an army surplus store.

Creed had set things up with this crowd before. They were wealthy, arrogant, as were most of the boys who gravitated to this sport around here. But anything they'd learned had been taught to them in sterile safety. They couldn't fight for crap. This dude was different though. He wasn't really one of them, no matter how desperately he wanted to be. The frat probably pledged him for this purpose, so they could throw him out here and test what value he had. If he failed they would probably toss him away like a bony fish.

The venue was an abandoned warehouse on the other side of the Salt River. It was adjacent to an old bread factory that hadn't operated in decades, yet somehow the yeasty smell of the dough lingered. The only light was from a few old camping lanterns. The only noise was the bloodthirsty yells of men who had money riding on the fight's outcome.

My opponent had gotten cocky pretty quick under the hooting praise of his buddies. He parried and feinted in a show that began to irritate me. Some of these guys were fucking dancers. I wasn't. This was about beating the man in front of you. It didn't need to look pretty.

The guy's crooked-tooth smile was centered on me but I could tell he wasn't really focusing. I could feel the rising fire in my blood, the pulsing rush that would end his night. I didn't need to glance back to know that Creed and Chase were there. My brothers were always there.

I continued to circle, slowly, ever so slowly. The frat boy took mistook it for fear and decided to talk trash.

"You had enough?" he mocked. He had one of those naturally

pinched faces that gave him a beaten look no matter what expression he wore. I kept quiet.

"Yo boys," he yelled. "I think this little poodle needs to be taken for a walk. What do you think?"

He'd looked away, just briefly enough. When he returned his gaze to the ring his beady eyes showed alarm as I advanced. I got him in the jaw and he stumbled, spitting a line of bloody saliva. When he righted himself I saw he was no longer unfocused. I also saw hate in his narrowed eyes. I was standing between him and whatever reward he'd been promised by those fraternity shits.

Gabe Hernandez watched us on the sidelines, his hand at his chin, a mild look on his face as if he were watching something no more compelling than a dull sitcom. He was a major player, the guy to deal with when the stakes got into the four figures and beyond. Of course, that was still small potatoes in the world of underground fighting. Creed had told me that even in the dusty belly of Phoenix there were six figure fights. But the higher the payout, the more brutal the action. At least that was the word.

Frat Boy turned out to be a kicker too. He let fly with his left leg and I jerked back. I was quick but still caught a glancing blow off my shoulder. I spun and landed a tight fist in his solar plexus. He staggered backward, his face a sick blend of pain and fear. But with all the men yelling behind him he clenched his jaw and found some more scrappiness, plenty to take another swing.

It wasn't enough. I ducked his aim with ease and crushed the bone under his right eye. My hands were already swelling and I glanced back at my brothers. They soberly nodded in unison and I heard them as clearly as if they were on either side of me, speaking in each ear.

Finish it, Cordero.

I pulled back and gave him a clean cross to go out on. His eyes rolled back into his head and he fell to his knees as the loud mouthed little twerp who'd done the announcing tonight counted to ten.

Frat Boy didn't get up again and my brothers and I were three grand richer. It would pay rent and more for the next few months. I held out a hand to Frat Boy but he didn't take it. He wobbled to his feet and someone tossed him the beaten shirt he'd been wearing. I saw the shame in his posture as he returned to his suddenly unfriendly companions. I felt a little sorry for him.

Money changed hands and the place began to empty out. I found myself eye to eye with Gabe Hernandez. He gave me a cold smile.

"You Gentry Boys should consider upping your game," he said.

Creed answered. "Nah. We like our bones intact, you know?"

Gabe nodded as if he didn't really care anyway. "Well, I can appreciate that. But if any of the three of you ever change your mind, you know where to find me."

"Hey," I coughed. "Sorry, you know, if you lost some change here tonight."

Gabe smiled. "I didn't. My bet was on you. Good night, gentlemen."

When he was out of earshot Creed spat on the floor. "Fucking snake," he swore, glaring after Gabe.

"Maybe," agreed Chase. "But he probably ain't sharing an old Chevy with no bumper."

Creed scowled. "You think some fresh wheels is worth getting your neck broke?"

Chase waved a hand. "Hell no. I got such a pretty neck."

Creed nodded at me. "What do you say?"

I shrugged. "I like all my shit where it is too, but damn man, it'd be nice not to scrape the bottom for once. It would be a hell of a payout."

Creed looked away and Chase grinned at me. We were three pieces of a puzzle but no one would mistake one of us for another. Creedence had always been the biggest. He'd grown into a serious man prone to episodes of crushing darkness that were better left untouched. I'd seen so many willing girls try to break through that gruff fog but none had even chipped a dent. I think out of the three of us he was the most wounded by the terrors of our childhood, although he would have popped me a good one if I'd said so out loud.

Chasyn played the foolish playboy but he was a lot smarter than he let on. Back in Emblem he was always the one who scored outrageously high on any test thrown in his direction. Teachers had tried to push him into the smart classes but he balked and made a nuisance of himself until they sighed and sent him back down to us.

As for me, I was somewhere in the middle of all that. When we finally reached the age where we could leave Emblem and not get chased down by the law, there was no question we were in it together. As we always had been.

The events of the night played out casually in my head as I lay there on that roof. And when I stared unblinking at the Three Kings, the stars of Orion's Belt, those distant balls of fire blurred together in my sight until they seemed to be one unbroken line. If I had been the only one born the day Benton Gentry assaulted his pregnant wife, I doubt I would have survived this long.

The stars moved an inch across the black sky and the restless fury that still sometimes threatened to devour me was quieted.

3

SAYLOR

As I made my way to the I-10, that thick manmade artery cutting through the continent, I knew where I was going. I plucked my phone from my purse and dialed my cousin.

"Brayden," I choked, hating my own rambling distress. "I did it, I left him. He's-fuck, it's bad. It's about ten o'clock right now. Damn, I really need to talk to you. School's finished. Me and Devin are finished. California tastes like shit. I can't stay here. And Bray, I'd rather swallow acid than face the Emblem peeps right. So I'm heading in your direction. Call me back. Please Brayden, call me back."

A curse escaped my lips as I threw the phone down. Brayden was notorious for failing to answer his cell phone, or even keep proper track of it. I had no idea if he would receive that message.

Southern California sped by and I bid it a bitter good riddance. As far as I knew, my dad had been planning on driving out in two days to attend my graduation. Somebody would need to tell him it wouldn't be necessary unless he wanted to sit there and watch everyone else's kid walk across the stage. It didn't matter, the ceremony. It was a bunch of preening and photographic flashes. It was the culmination of a long journey that for most would end in crushing debt and disappointed hopes. I kept telling myself that. My father would certainly be happier to have the obligation removed. Instead he could remain in Emblem for the weekend, ensconced in the flabby arms of whatever big breasted bimbo had attached herself to his shiny Dodge rims. As for my mother, well, she was in the throes of a new love substitute anyway. She had sighed with happy relief when I said, "No ma, don't sweat it. You don't have to be there."

I pictured her with a cigarette dangling out of the left side of her mouth as she gushed. "So proud of you, Say. I sent you a Target gift card."

"Oh god, Target. I love Target," I had told her, trying to sound not at all bitchy. "They undoubtedly have the best toilet paper selection."

If you had an ounce of enterprise in you, then Emblem, Arizona wasn't a place you wanted to stay. As long as I could remember, my desire to leave the bowels of my desert hometown approached zealotry. Of my peers, a third would end up working at the nearby state prison complex and perhaps live stilted, unhappy lives like my parents. Statistically, another third would succumb to the pull of drugs and other turmoil, perhaps winding up incarcerated themselves and poignantly guarded by former classmates. The final third would move on to college and something resembling brighter futures. But even most of them would choose to remain in the state. Brayden was enrolling at ASU. My whole life had been spent in that scorching prison town seventy miles south of Phoenix. I wanted out, way out. Years of diligent, single-minded work vaulted me to the top of my class and the scholarship to attend Occidental College was the sum of my dreams. I didn't even offer Emblem one final, affectionate backwards glance the day I left.

The landscape of California was an improvement over the landscape of central Arizona. I felt immediately liberated from the oppressive heat and from the cast of tiredly familiar characters who had populated my world from birth. I didn't like to be reminded where I came from. My new peers all appeared to live breezy lives atop pairs of three hundred dollar shoes. I spent summers immersed in work study and piloted my sputtering vehicle to the beach every time I could scrape together ten dollars for the gas.

As for my parents, they seemed to grow immediately accustomed to a child free existence. My mother dated more than any free spirited twenty year old. I visited them in Emblem a few awkward times a year. We talked on the phone sometimes. It was enough.

The only sore spot was Brayden. I missed him. I missed him a lot. Over the last few years I felt like distance had cost us some of the closeness we'd always shared. He had a girlfriend he seemed serious about and one more year left at ASU to complete a graduate program in mechanical engineering. I still thought of him as my best friend.

Another sad surprise was that boys on the coast were still boys. Dating was a routinely disappointing endeavor punctuated by the occasional orgasm. When I met Devin the spring semester of my junior year he seemed too good to be true. He *was* too good to be true.

Somewhere in Riverside County I considered pulling over and giving Brayden another try, perhaps messaging him through Facebook. After all it wasn't really fair to descend on the guy's game with no warning. I was a bruised bag of ruin with no plan. Bray had a life of his own out there in Tempe. He had, what's-her-name…Millie. I'd seen her pictures on Facebook; a pretty Asian girl with long black hair and a dazzling smile. She wore white dresses a lot and majored in one of those high concept disciplines, like Anthropological Social Economics or some shit.

My hands tightened on the steering wheel as I crossed the border from California back to the state of my birth. It was nearly midnight and I should have been exhausted but I wasn't. I felt as if I had spent years in the black oblivion of a nightmare and I was finally awake.

I shifted and focused on the blackness ahead. I swear the loneliest stretch of road in the United States has to be the I-10 between the California border and the fringes of western Phoenix. Academically I knew that wasn't true. There were whole swaths of empty country in those vast states of the far north. But just then, beaten and quietly praying to something I didn't think existed past the glittering stars, it seemed there was no other surface of the earth quite as bleak.

About fifty miles outside of Quartzsite I realized I had to pee pretty desperately. I passed two desolate rest stops that had been boarded up for whatever reason and I cursed the whims of local bureaucrats who evidently cared nothing for the bladders of distressed women.

Finally, the tiny lights of the west valley were near enough to touch. I pulled over at a QT station within sight of the nuclear power plant. When I breezed through the doors, hunting for the bathroom, the counter attendant gawked at me. At first I thought it had to be because of my swollen face but when I sat on the toilet and glanced down I saw my left nipple playing peek-a-boo with the low neckline of my tee shirt.

"Hot mess," I grumbled, shoving it back where it belonged, thinking about how helpful it would be if I had a bra on.

Once my bladder was empty I inspected myself in the mirror, wincing as my eyes shrank under the piercing ceiling lights. It seemed whoever had decided on those industrial bulbs was either hoping to inflict mass blindness or else root out a few covert vampires.

So my jaw was swollen and yes, it would be bruised. I pushed my hair behind my ears and filled the sink with cold water. As I bent over and bathed my face I remembered the disgusting feeling of Devin's violation. I wondered if it counted as rape if the guy couldn't finish because someone hit him with a table. As I blotted my face with a paper towel I decided that it did.

"Fucker," I muttered, startling an elderly Hispanic lady who was just coming through the door. She smiled at me nervously and it occurred to me that with my damaged face, mismatched clothes and wild hair I could be taken for a prostitute. Or one of those meth heads whose PSA posters serve as cautionary tales in public transit stations.

I rooted around in my purse and found a comb. As I sorted through the tangles in my hair I tried not to listen to the tinkling sound of a stranger peeing. The woman didn't look at me when she emerged. She washed her hands and exited, leaving a five dollar bill on the cracked vanity. I almost chased after her to return it. I wanted to tell her I wasn't hopeless. I was a goddam college graduate with an adequate body and a novel in progress that somehow was going to amount to something. Convenience store charity was wasted on someone with my prospects. Yeah, I *almost* said all that.

Then I changed my mind and used the five to buy a cherry Icee and a bag of Doritos. It was a good meal.

While my car was filling up I called Brayden again.

"Jesus, Bray," I said to his voicemail, somewhat exasperated that he was the only twenty two year old in the world who didn't stay connected at all times. "Anyway, I'm slightly less fragile than I was the last time I left you a message. But I'm still on my way with the handful of things I could carry in the trunk of my half dead vehicle. It is midnight now and I can see the lights of the nuclear power plant. Know what that means? It means I'll be in Tempe in a little over an hour. Christ, I need a shower. I hope you're not out of town or something because I have no other friends here and if you're not around I'll have to find a nice Walmart parking lot to cozy up in until morning. Love you, man."

The Phoenix metro area is huge. Perhaps not Los Angeles kind of huge, but still. You've got to drive an awful long time to get from end to end. After gliding forever through the west valley, I saw the towering structures of downtown Phoenix and then, finally, the fringes of the east side.

I had already plugged Brayden's address into my phone and as I passed the bold outline of Sun Devil Stadium I knew I was getting close. Arizona State University was a shining beacon of liberty to Emblem kids.

The area surrounding ASU always has been and probably always will be a circus of apartments and fast food dives. As I drove hesitantly through the Palm Desert Apartment complex it looked like Mardi Gras. People hung off balconies and meandered about in lurching, intoxicated glory. I poked my head out of the car window and called out to a quartet of blondes.

"Hey, do any of you know where apartment 2163 is?"

"BWAHAHAHAHA!" they responded and then one of them bent over and vomited into an oleander bush.

"Thanks," I waved. "Thanks a lot!"

You'd think an apartment complex roughly the size of the city of Buffalo might have a map posted somewhere. But if it existed then I couldn't find it. Nor could I clearly read any of the building numbers as I rolled passed and squinted. Finally I gave up, parking the Civic in a far flung corner that looked as good a place to start as any. In an act of sheer futility I called Brayden again. Of course he didn't answer. Of course.

Warily I watched a pair of hulking men prowling around, drunk out of their gourd. I wasn't eager to risk being manhandled so close on the heels of the Devin encounter. After fumbling around in my backseat I found a dark hooded sweatshirt and pulled it on. Though it was easily ninety degrees outside, I was aiming to look like a tough guy who might be up to no good in the dark. It might keep the creepers away. I tucked my hair under the hood and hunched my shoulders as I started to make my way through the maze of dwellings.

After about five minutes of aimless wandering I concluded it was impossible for anyone to find anything in this labyrinth of stucco. I sank against the nearest wall with a dejected sigh. When I looked up I saw the numbers 2163.

My Hallelujah moment was, however, short lived when I banged on the door for a solid ten minutes and no one answered. I leaned my head against the door, feeling every bit of energy drain away.

"Don't cry, Saylor," I soothed myself. I hated to cry. "Don't do it."

After several moments of blank staring in which the meaning of the universe eluded me, I decided I should try to break in As I peered into the dim living room I glimpsed several framed pictures of Brayden and Millie so I knew for sure this was their place. I yanked on the window frame. Brayden was the forgetful sort. He might have left it unlocked. I yanked harder.

I expected the window might be locked after all. I did not expect to be abruptly tackled to the ground by a mountain. It was all too reminiscent of Devin's attack. Even as I landed on the sharp gravel I let out a raging shriek and kicked out with all my might.

"Shit," swore the mountain in disbelief, "you're a girl."

I felt myself being pulled up by strong arms attached to a body. And my, what a body. It had a chest with something tattooed in Latin across the muscled expanse. It also had shoulders with more ink that were glued to strong arms. "Are you okay?" it asked me and I nodded mutely, staring at the eruption of maleness that I could appreciate even in my trying circumstances. Then I blinked in disbelief when I saw that the body also had a face. It was one I recognized.

"Out of the frying pan and into the fire," I muttered, shaking my head. I crossed my arms and looked him in the eye. "Cord Gentry. What the hell are you doing here?"

4

CORD

I heard a scuffling noise underneath me and was cheered by the idea that Brayden might be home. There was something wholesome about hanging around Bray and Millie, his girl. Sometimes I got to feeling a little disconnected from the wider world apart from my brothers.

After climbing down to the second floor balcony it was an easy jump to the ground below and I pulled it off without a sound. But when I straightened out all I saw was a dark, hooded figure trying to pry open the lock on Brayden's window. A skinny high school punk by the looks of him, he was just begging for a lesson in good manners.

I didn't know if he was carrying anything more lethal than stupidity. I decided to chuck him to the ground and sort the rest of it out along the way. He fumbled too much, meaning he didn't know what the hell he was doing. Piece of cake to take him down. I didn't really want to hurt the kid. I just wanted to scare the living crap out of him and send him on his way to think about being a better person. That's all. And if he pissed his pants in the middle of it, so much the better.

He was a featherweight and went down with barely a nudge. It was a good thing I didn't handle him harder because the yelp of pain and surprise knocked the wind out of me.

"Shit, you're a girl," I said, shaking my head. Okay, so the would-be intruder had a vagina. It didn't mean she was off the hook. But still, I couldn't ever justify hurting a female. That was the path to being as big a bastard as my old man.

"Are you okay?" I asked as I pulled her up. Her hood fell away and a cascade of wavy brown hair spilled onto her shoulders. She was sputtering somewhat indignantly, then gave me a hard look that stopped me cold. I think she was even more shocked, though she managed to gather her wits enough to speak first.

"Out of the frying pan and into the fire," she grumbled and glared at me hatefully. "Cord Gentry, what the hell are you doing here?"

I swallowed. "Hey, Saylor. Nice to see you too. What's it been, four years?"

"Not long enough and I didn't say it was nice to see you for god's sake. I asked what the hell you're doing lurking around Tempe like Jack the fucking Ripper."

I just stared at her. Saylor McCann was one of the few things I've ever truly felt bad about. Sometimes I meant to ask Bray what she was up to now but I never had the guts. Wherever she was I was sure she hated the shit out of me.

"I was catching a prowler," I muttered, then narrowed my eyes. "You know, you looked suspicious as fuck out here." Saylor let out a hiss and turned her head, as if she were hoping I would just dissolve into the atmosphere. She pulled her sweatshirt off and I found myself noticing the soft curves of her body. She wore a tight shirt and no bra. Then I realized from the way she crossed her arms and shuffled dejectedly that she was trying not to cry.

"Hey," I reached for her but then backed off. I could read her icy look well enough in the dark. "So what, you're here to visit Brayden?"

"What the hell do you know about my cousin?"

"I know he's not home."

"Wow, you're a real Sherlock goddamn Holmes."

"Shit, stand down, okay? I don't know where the hell he's at but you're welcome to come back to my place for a while if you don't have anywhere else to go."

She gaped at me in disbelief. "Your place?" she echoed. "Thanks Cord, but I think I'd rather run my tongue over some hot charcoal for a few hours."

There was a flood lamp overhead. Her face was bathed in the brash yellow light and I looked at her more carefully. "Jesus, I didn't do that to your face, did I?"

Her shoulders slumped. "No. His name's Devin. He's an asshole."

"Obviously." I began to simmer with a slow boil towards this unidentified Devin prick.

Saylor sighed and stared miserably at the ground. "You're an asshole too," she finally said.

I chuckled. "Never said I wasn't. But you can still come hang out with me and the boys for a while, unless you prefer crawling around in the dark. You know, the next guy to come along might not be as nice as me."

"The boys," she frowned. "What boys?"

"Creed and Chase. You might remember them."

"You Gentry brothers are fairly unforgettable," she said witheringly.

I didn't care for the sound of that. I was a mighty dick when I was sixteen and she had more than enough reason to despise me. But she was acting as if I should be squatting a step below the gutter. The fine folks of Emblem had always shaken their heads over the white trash Gentrys. We were violent, shiftless, hopeless. They even made up stories that we were inbred.

"Fine, I guess you don't need a damn bit of help, Saylor, great judge of character that you are." I was being mean, running a finger across her swollen jaw as she cringed. "You obviously know a good man when you see one."

I'd hit her below the belt there. Her face collapsed and she leaned against the side of the building. "Just leave me the hell alone," she muttered and I felt a jolt of remorse. She'd apparently been through the wringer tonight already. No need to make it any worse.

"Look," I told her. "I made you an offer, one Emblem reject to another. You can stay here alone and nurse your old bitterness if you'd rather do that."

Saylor didn't answer. She didn't even look at me. I shook my head and started to walk away, no longer in the mood to deal with some cranky chick and her angst.

"Cord," she called.

I turned around. She looked lost. She looked like she did when she was sixteen and found out the guy who had just popped her cherry was more of a shithead than she had imagined.

"Bray never told me you were here."

I raised a sarcastic eyebrow. "I wonder why."

She offered a vague little smile. "He didn't know I was coming and I can't get ahold of him." She stared down at herself and made a face. "God, what I wouldn't give for a shower."

I waited. "Offer stands, Say."

Saylor nodded tiredly and coughed once. "Okay. Look, I'm just going to grab my bag. I left it in my car."

I joined her. "All right, I'll go with you. Never know who or what is hiding out in the dark."

Her sidelong glance had a wry quality. "No kidding."

Saylor's car was the same battered Civic she'd had in high school, except it had California plates now. She reached into the backseat and grabbed a purse and a dark duffel bag. I tried to take the bag myself but she waved me away.

"I got it," she said tersely.

I rolled my eyes. "Of course you do."

The silence between us was painfully awkward as I led her back to the three bedroom apartment I shared with my brothers. When I held the door for her she hesitated at the threshold and looked up at me with uncertainty. I tried not to openly wince at the sight of her bruised and swollen face. It didn't matter who she was; shit like that just turned me inside out.

I pointed to the first door on the left. "Bathroom's right there. I cleaned it today so it's not too disgusting. Help yourself to whatever you need."

She nodded and said nothing, dragging her bag inside the room and closing the door behind her.

Creed was intensely playing Xbox, one of those militaristic games where everybody shoots everybody else in a drab post-apocalyptic setting. Chase was lounging on the couch as a slinky blonde climbed all over him.

"C'mon," she purred as Chase put his hands on her tits and smiled. He noticed me standing there but didn't take his hands from the girl's tits as she squirmed impatiently.

"Did I hear you roll through the door with some company?" he asked.

I grabbed an apple from a bowl on the kitchen table and perched on an arm of the couch.

"Sort of," I shrugged.

Creed tore his gaze away from the game and glanced around. "Where'd you put her?"

As if on cue the shower blasted to life.

"Aw shit," said Chase, kneading the girl's tits more enthusiastically. "You didn't bring home another homeless dude did you?"

I took a bite of the apple and watched my brother's date straddle him, moving back and forth over his crotch as if there was no one else even in the room. Chase reached under her halter top and she moaned.

"That guy was all right," I said, staring at the girl's face. Her lips were thin and she wore gobs of makeup. "He was a musician. Just needed a place to recharge."

Creed didn't agree. "He pissed in the shower. He stunk up the place for a fucking week." He threw down the game controller and began to stalk down the hall. I could tell he was planning on barging right into the bathroom and hauling our guest out forcibly.

"Hey," I grabbed his shirt. "Don't, okay? It's not what you think. It's a girl."

"A girl?" Chase asked with interest as the blonde threw her head back and began to move more urgently while making all kinds of noise about it. Maybe that was her thing, getting off in a room full of people. Chase had probably plucked her out of a nearby party and not bothered to ask her name.

"Not that kind of girl," I said, pointing. Then I lowered my voice in case she could hear anything beyond the spray of the shower. "You're not going to fucking believe this, but it's Saylor McCann."

Creed let out a low whistle and Chase laughed out loud.

"Yeah right," he howled. "If you were dying in the street, bro, Saylor McCann would dig a heel into your neck to end you quicker. So really, who's the chew toy you got in there?"

I threw the apple at his head. "Quiet, I'm serious. She was trying to get into Brayden's apartment but he's nowhere in sight." I glanced down the hall where the shower was still running. "Look, don't give her any shit, okay?"

Creed had backed off the notion of charging into the bathroom but he was frowning doubtfully. "Didn't she hate your damn guts? Didn't she hate all of us?"

I shrugged. "Probably still does. But I couldn't just leave her there sniffling in the dark with nowhere else to go."

Chase seemed to have lost interest in the subject. The girl had let him push her shirt up until her bobbing tits were shamelessly exposed. She continued to writhe in his lap and let out feline cries of ecstasy.

Creed returned to his video game, shooting up a bevy of digital people in an imaginary world. I looked down the hall again, suddenly wondering what the hell I'd gotten myself in the middle of.

Of course I'd known Saylor since kindergarten because Emblem was like that. She was a snooty girl who stuck close to her cousin Brayden and was part of the smart crowd, the kids who were going to make it. Maybe that's what made her such a tempting target. She wasn't shy about her snub-nosed disdain for us, the dirty Gentry boys, and one night, drinking stolen wine coolers over a fire pit as we camped way out in the desert, her name came up.

"I could hit that," Chase had said with confidence.

"Bullshit," Creed sneered.

I tossed a bottle into the fire where it cracked and sent up a furious lick of flame. "I second the cry of bullshit."

Chase reached over and shoved me hard. "I know a hungry chick when I see one. Now Say McCann might think she's worlds above us, but I'll telling you, any one of us could get in there."

Creed was suddenly thoughtful. "Maybe."

I smiled. "Should we make it interesting?"

Chase held up another bottle. "Two cases of these?"

"Come on," I balked. "That's a challenge worth at least five."

"Done," nodded Chase.

Saylor was suspicious when I hailed her in front of the library the next afternoon.

"What do you want?" she scowled, averting her pretty green eyes and nervously toying with the end of her long braid.

I gave her my most dashing Gentry smile and slyly ran my hand down her arm. "Just wanted to say hi, Saylor."

After a reluctant moment she smiled back. She was thinner than the girls I usually liked. But she was cute in a repressed, geeky sort of way. Most of all, I could tell right off the bat that Chase was right. Her eyes wandered over me and she blushed. She was hungry as shit.

Saylor had never really been in my line of sight much. She wasn't the party type and never hung around looking for a good time. Now and again I saw her with some of the upper crust assholes who I didn't have much to do with.

I stowed her books under my arm and walked with her in the direction of her house. She lived in the close knit neighborhood between the high school and the prison, mostly populated by families of correctional officers. It was tree-lined, clean and the rank opposite of the shithole I lived in two miles away. On the walk I said all kinds of things I didn't mean. Saylor giggled a lot.

We were passing an old bench where something historic had supposedly happened. No one knew exactly what though, since the plaque next to it had long ago faded into smoothness.

"Sit down," I told her, pleased when she did so without question.

We were in the shade of a towering mesquite tree. She looked at me a little nervously.

With a flourish I withdrew a sheet of notebook paper from her books and pulled a pen out of my back pocket. I felt her eyes on me as I sketched rapidly.

"Here," I said, passing the paper over.

"Cord," she breathed, her eyes wide. I knew I was a decent artist, especially when it came to people. I could take an okay looking girl and make her seem like a supermodel. It came in handy sometimes, particularly when you were trying to get behind a locked door. I watched her face as she stared at the sketch I'd made of her.

"It's beautiful," she frowned. "But it doesn't look like me."

I tried not to roll my eyes. I smiled instead. "It looks just like you, Saylor. You're beautiful." And then I leaned in.

I knew right away this was going to be easier than even Chase thought it would be. She was eager to be kissed and it was obvious she hadn't been kissed much.

"Saylor," I whispered, running my hands up and down her arms as she trembled. "I want to be alone with you."

She chewed on her lip and looked away. I thought she was going to push me and tell me to fuck off. That would have been the smart thing for her to do and she was a smart girl. But she wasn't being smart just then.

"Okay," she said softly.

On our short walk she had mentioned something about her parents going through an ugly divorce. I wasn't really listening to that though. As we reached her brick ranch-style house she got nervous and said that her dad was home. He was on third shift at the prison and slept during the day.

I pulled her to me and played my tongue across her lips, noting with satisfaction the impatient way she pressed her body against mine.

"You got a bedroom?" I asked, massaging her waist until she just about purred. Her pale cheeks were flushed and she was looking cuter by the minute. I couldn't wait to climb underneath her clothes and get to business.

She hesitated. "Yeah, but...I mean my dad's asleep and all but he wakes up easy."

"Oh," I frowned. I didn't want to get on the wrong side of some crazed father defending the virtue of his princess. I'd already been there, done that. Then I noticed the detached garage. "That thing empty?"

She understood and nodded. I grabbed her hand and pulled her through the service door into the dark interior. We kissed again and I felt her all over, getting myself really worked the hell up. She was getting hot too, I could tell, kissing me like she was starving and I was the only meal in sight. I smiled at the thought of how pissed Chase was going to be.

"What's wrong?" Saylor asked, noticing my smile and getting confused.

"Nothin'," I told her, reaching under her shirt. "Just happy to be here with you."

She relaxed and didn't stop me. She didn't stop me at all. I found an ancient orange blanket and spread it on the grease-stained floor, easing her down that way. I had to show her what to do but she caught on quick. By then I wanted her pretty fucking bad. I pulled her soft panties away and slid my pants off as I took a condom from my back pocket, the last of a pack I'd stolen from Ace Market about a month earlier. I saw the way her green eyes widened when I settled between her legs. It gave me a moment of doubt.

"You sure you want to do this?" I asked her, ready to back off in a heartbeat while I was still able to.

But Saylor only nodded and slipped her arms around my neck. "I'm sure, Cord."

I was kind of outside myself after that. I wasn't gentle because I wasn't thinking about Saylor. Suddenly what I was doing became a sick sort of payback. I was avenging every crappy thing anyone had ever said or thought about a Gentry even as I was proving what a piece of shit a Gentry could be.

White trash. Vicious. Heartless. Soulless. Lazy. No good. Fuck their own cousins.

Then, when it was over, I didn't feel a shred of tenderness as Saylor shyly covered her body and tried to smile at me. I didn't feel a goddamn thing at all. I casually lit a cigarette and said the most awful thing I could think of.

"Well that sucked," I breathed coolly and watched the shock register on her face. "But it was still a bet worth winning."

"A bet?" she squeaked.

I smiled. "Sure. You were as easy a fuck as the three of us figured you would be."

I smoked and watched her go through the emotions of horror, grief and finally anger. Yeah, she should have known Cord Gentry wouldn't have latched onto her out of nowhere. She stood up with tears of shame and rage already falling.

"Get out," she muttered and then screamed it. "GET OUT!"

I took a big drag, blew smoke in her face and laughed. Then I ran all the way home to tell Chase he better pay up. And Chase, who couldn't keep a secret for love or money, told everyone else.

For the next two years, until we all graduated and scattered, I could never look her in the eye again. I never thought I would have to. Until today.

Mercifully, Chase had taken himself and his blonde to his bedroom. I could still hear them going wild in there but at least it wasn't happening in plain sight. I was relieved. Saylor was the type who might make a big deal out of shit like that.

"Hey," said Creed, and I realized he'd been watching me.

"Yo," I answered.

My brother nodded soberly. Sometimes he had some sort of supernatural triplet sense when either me or Chase was bugged by something. "It was a long time ago."

I shrugged, trying to play it off. "Gentrys have done worse I guess. Hell, I know they have."

Creed didn't blink. "Shit's different now, Cord. We ain't dirty, hopeless boys running around the desert, hoping to god no one's conscious enough to break wood on us when we get home."

"That was no excuse," I grumbled. "I know it. She knows it."

Creed dropped the game controller and stood. He looked at the closed door of the bathroom. The shower had squealed to a halt but there was still no sign Saylor was coming out soon.

"Well," he finally yawned. "I'm hittin' the sack."

I stuck out a thumb towards Chase's room where the sound of energetic bouncing reigned. "It'd be nice to hit it *that* hard."

Creed smiled and stretched. "Nah, it's a beat my own meat kind of night."

I sank into the couch and waited. The noise of Chase and his lady friend eventually died down but Saylor hadn't emerged from the bathroom. I hoped she wasn't in there doing anything weird. She'd always been kind of an intense girl and whatever had happened to her tonight had obviously rattled her cage.

I crept to the door and listened but didn't hear anything. When the door abruptly creaked open I had to jump back.

"Jesus," she gasped, dropping a bunch of shit on the floor.

"Sorry," I said, getting hit by a wave of steam from her long shower. "I started to worry you were in there cutting yourself up or something."

"No," she glared. "I wasn't." She gave me another hard look, as if she'd forgotten that I would even be around. She had combed out her wet hair and let it hang loose. Apart from her swollen jaw, her complexion was creamy and flawless, her green eyes luminous. She wore the same t-shirt as earlier but had changed to a pair of gym shorts. "Are you going to move so I can get out of the doorway?"

I hadn't realized I was blocking her. I backed off and headed to the living room, hoping she would follow. "Chase and Creed headed in already but they said to tell you hi. You want a beer or something?"

"No," Saylor said shortly, sitting delicately on the couch and cradling her purse in her lap. "I mean, no thank you, Cord." She withdrew her phone and scowled at it, cursing lightly.

"He's always losing the damn thing," I commented. She looked at me questioningly. "Brayden and his phone."

"Oh," she nodded. "I know." She looked around with obvious confusion. The place was a mismatch of whatever furniture could be conveniently carried away from Goodwill when we needed it. "You guys been living here long?"

I got a beer for myself. "About a year in this apartment. Before that we bounced around like pinballs for a while." I took a drink, watching her rub her hands on her bare thighs. It was probably a nervous habit but it got me looking at her legs. They were nice. "So, how's California?"

Her expression immediately darkened. She pushed her long hair behind her ears. It made her appear younger. "I loved it. Until I hated it. My graduation's in two days. I'm not going."

I was beginning to realize what she meant. "So this isn't just a visit." I pointed to her bag. "Those all your worldly possessions?"

Saylor stuck her chin out. "No, it was all I could grab. I had to get out of there quickly."

"Because of him?" I pressed. "Dylan?"

"Devin," she corrected me and then shuddered.

"Bastard. This the first time he did something like that?"

She took a full minute to answer. "No," she said in a soft voice.

I stretched, feeling a twinge of soreness from the effects of the fight. "You know, Saylor, when a guy belts you in the mouth it doesn't mean 'I love you.'"

"Well thank you, Dr. Phil. But you know what? You can sit on your platitudes and rotate."

"I might," I considered. "If I knew what the fuck a platitude was."

She glared but it wasn't the furious kind. It was a look of hurt. "Think what you damn well like about me, Cord. Yeah, it happened more than once and I stayed and I took it. I told myself I would get out and then I didn't. I know how that sounds. I know what it makes me. But it was the first time he…" Saylor couldn't finish her sentence. She sank into the couch and buried her head in her arms.

I had to ask. "What?"

"He raped me," she whispered, then raised her head. The look in her eyes was like a punch in my gut. "Okay? Now you know the whole ugly, sordid, disgusting truth."

"Ah, shit," I said softly, as it dawned on me that there was a painful reason she'd wanted to shower so badly. "Goddamn, I'm sorry, Saylor." I handed her a napkin and she blew her nose into it while I downed the rest of that beer. Inwardly I was seething. For Saylor, for my mother, for every woman who'd ever suffered the harsh hand of a man who wasn't worth two fucking cents. To my shock, she burst out laughing.

"Christ, I'm sitting here in the middle of the night pouring my heart out to Cord Gentry."

"Yeah, I'm feeling a touch of the surreal with Saylor McCann blowing her nose in my living room."

We eyed one another for a long, uncomfortable moment before I broke the silence.

"You know," I said uneasily. "I was thinking about it and Bray mentioned something about going camping up at Four Peaks with his girl."

"Oh," Saylor exhaled, looking defeated. "That would explain why he's not sitting in his apartment waiting for his basket case cousin to drop by unexpectedly." She started to stand and shoulder her bag. "Listen, thanks for letting me hang out here for a while."

"Well, where are you gonna go now? Emblem?"

She laughed hoarsely. "Hell no. I'll just find a motel for the night and see how things look tomorrow." She rubbed her eyes. "I think I can handle it all after a night of sleep."

I made a decision. Creed might grumble but the hell with it.

"Stay here," I said.

Her head jerked up and she opened her mouth to say something, then closed it again. "No," she finally said in a soft voice, sighing tiredly. "No, I can't, Cord."

I stared down at my bruised hands. I didn't want to be the asshole she thought I was. I may have been a lousy fuck once but Creed was right. Things were different. I'd done everything to best the curse of being a Gentry from Emblem. It seemed like a bad idea to let a beaten girl from my hometown go wandering around Tempe in the state she was in. "You can take my room. I swear no one will bug you in there. Really, it's no big deal. I crash on the couch half the time anyway."

"Cord," she said and I heard some pain in her voice.

"Well, you take the couch then. It's a comfortable couch. Look at it."

She looked. "It *is* a comfortable couch." She dropped her bag to the floor and managed a watery smile. "All right."

By the time I returned with a thin blue quilt I'd ripped off my own bed, Saylor was already curling up.

"Thanks," she whispered with soft gratitude as I covered her. She looked so sweet and vulnerable that an actual lump rose in my throat and I shook away the feeling. Saylor was just some chick crashing on my couch for the night. She didn't mean a thing to me.

Then she propped herself up on one elbow. Her shirt slid carelessly off her shoulder and showed the top of her right breast, which caused something else, something a little harder, to rise.

"You're welcome," I said tersely, turning to leave.

"No, really, Cord. Thank you."

I stared at her for a few more seconds as she pulled the blanket over her body and closed her eyes.

"You're safe here, Saylor. I promise. Good night."

5

SAYLOR

I woke up to the Steve Miller Band singing and Gentry brothers grinning. At first I thought I was having one of those odd dreams where I was back in Emblem, trapped for eternity in the midst of all the faces I never wanted to see again. But when I blinked they were still there. Then I remembered yesterday.

And Devin.

And Cord.

"You look like crap, kid," Chase Gentry told me cheerfully as 'The Joker' played in the background.

Creed kicked him under the table. "Don't be a dick." He looked at me seriously. "Forgive my little brother. Emotional maturity hasn't found him yet."

"Little?" Chase scoffed. "When are you gonna let it go? You're what, ninety seconds older than me?"

Creed stood and stretched his fingertips to the ceiling, displaying his intimidating physique. "Yeah, little. You'll always be smaller than me, boy."

My lower jaw felt like it had been packed with gauze. I was sure Chase's description had been accurate. I expected that when I found a mirror the image that stared back at me wouldn't be too pretty.

Chase shoveled mouthfuls of brightly colored cereal while Creed started fiddling with the coffee pot. I cleared my throat and the brothers glanced at me. They weren't identical, but they looked alike in a way that was disconcerting. They had the same dark blonde hair and wore perpetual tans that might have been a result of running wild in the desert from toddlerhood. Their forms were all powerfully muscled paragons of masculinity. If I hadn't known who they were, if they'd just been men I passed on the street, I'm sure I would have stared.

"He'll be back," Creed said and I realized he was talking to me.

"Cord?" I asked, pulling the quilt around me. It smelled freshly washed.

"No. Jesus Christ," Chase teased, snorting over his own humor.

Creed poured a cup of coffee. Surprisingly, he brought it straight to me. I accepted it thankfully.

"He just went to see if he could hunt up that cousin of yours."

I took a sip of the coffee. It was strong. It felt good going down my throat.

"So, Saylor," Chase said, peering at me with curiosity. "Who fucked up your face?" I saw Creed toss him a hard look but he didn't pay any mind.

"My boyfriend, well, *ex*-boyfriend, beat me up," I said. It was the first time I'd spoken the words aloud. It felt oddly liberating.

"No shit," said Chase mildly. He didn't seem shocked. "And so you left?"

"Yes. After I broke a table over his head."

Chase grinned. "You really broke a table over his head?"

"I did. It made this awesome cracking sound. Sort of like that scene in *Titanic* when the ship broke in half. I'm sure his arm was broken."

"Whose arm was broken?" Cord asked, poking his head around the corner. I hadn't heard him come in. His blue eyes fastened on me. I didn't like the look of pity in them. I was beginning to feel like the human equivalent of a stray dog.

"Devin the Dick," I said.

"Oh," he nodded, scratching his head. "Bray's still not around. Since he doesn't like to answer his damn phone I wrote him a note and shoved it under his door."

"A note," Chase cracked up. "What is this, 1985?"

"What happened in 1985?" Creed asked.

"The Delorian hit eighty eight miles per hour," Cord answered.

"I think Madonna was born," Chase piped up good naturedly.

"The three of you would look good with mullets," I said. The brothers all stared at me for a second and then the three of them busted up laughing.

"Hey," Cord looked around, poking Chase in the arm. "Where's your little friend?"

Chase talked with his mouth full. "She took off after a sweet exchange of head. I think she stole my fucking wallet."

Creed sighed and grabbed something from the top of the fridge. He threw it on the table. "She didn't take your damn wallet. There's your wallet."

Cord approached the couch. I shifted to make room for him but he sat as far on the other end as he could and still be on the same piece of furniture.

"So," he said with some awkwardness. "How are you doing?"

"Okay," I shrugged. "I don't know. Maybe I'll have a better answer in a few hours."

Cord's face was serious. I drank my coffee and watched him covertly through my eyelashes. He was definitely something to look at, but then he always had been. Manhood had filled him out, hardened his features. A faint scar cut through his left eyebrow.

"You're different," I said. I hadn't meant to speak the words. It had been running through my mind that Cord Gentry wasn't exactly as I remembered him. But then, I supposed I wasn't as he remembered me either.

He mulled the words. "I'll take that as a compliment."

I sipped my coffee and listened to Creed yell at Chase for leaving his dirty dishes in the sink. For as long as I could remember, the Gentry boys had been callous hellions who rode roughshod over anyone who dared to challenge them. But as Chase cuffed his brother affectionately over the head I thought about how I'd never seen them like this, as siblings who obviously cared for each other. I knew they'd had a rotten upbringing. There was always a shifting population of hood-eyed Gentrys staggering around Emblem. It must not have been easy to make it out of the violent poverty that they'd been born to.

Cord watched his brothers absently as they wrestled like overgrown lion cubs, Creed finally getting the upper hand and beating his impressive chest in victory.

Chase pouted and shoved him away. "Keep pounding the drum, King Kong."

"Sore loser," Creed retorted. "You reek of cheap perfume by the way."

"Whatever. I'm gonna go shower the stink of that girl off. You know, she asked if you boys wanted to take a turn. Christ, she was nasty."

Cord laughed. "You want a nice girl, you gotta be a nice guy."

Chase paused next to the couch and raised an eyebrow in my direction. "You're one to fucking talk, Romeo."

I winced into my coffee cup as Cord shot me a quick glance.

"Guess I asked for that," he muttered, shaking his head.

He drummed his fingers on his lap and for the first time I noticed the cuts on his broad knuckles. The skin appeared somewhat bruised as well. I pointed. "Did you get in a fight?"

Cord smiled vaguely. "You could call it that if you want."

"What would you call it?"

"Work."

"I don't get it."

"Do you need to?"

"Well, were you in a fight or weren't you?"

He glanced at Creed, who was listening to us with interest. "Sort of," he said cagily.

I felt oddly annoyed. "Sort of? Did you 'sort of' ball up your fist and hit someone with it or not?"

His eyes flashed with irritation. "None of your damn business, Saylor."

I almost answered with a smart remark but stopped. He was right, it was none of my business. And who was I to judge when I'd stuck around in the bed of a monster?

"You're right," I swallowed.

"Hey," he reached a hand out and lightly touched my knee. I was embarrassed to realize that a brief touch from him did something to me. "I'm sorry, Say. Look, I didn't mean to come off like such an ass."

I rose stiffly off the couch. "Cord, you've been really decent. But I think I need to get out of your way now."

He didn't argue or protest that I wasn't in the way at all. As I neatly folded his quilt I saw where his eyes were looking and glanced down. In the harsh light of morning my nipples were plainly evident through the tight t-shirt. I hunched over, feeling a tad humiliated.

Cord smiled at my discomfort but didn't redirect his gaze.

"Nice," I scolded, pulling on my sweatshirt.

"I agree," he shrugged with infuriating coolness. "But the temp is already ninety in the shade. Might be easier to do like other girls and wear a bra."

"Crap," I said, thinking of something. I grabbed my duffel bag and rifled around for a minute.

"What's wrong?"

I kicked the bag. "I don't have any."

He looked at me blankly.

"Bras!" I shouted. "I packed about sixteen pairs of panties and no bras."

Creed chuckled from the kitchen.

"I was in kind of a rush," I grumbled, finding a black tank top and pulling it on right over my shirt.

"Well then," grinned Cord as he crossed one leg over the opposite knee, "I guess you're up shit's creek, honey. I mean it's not like we have any stores around here."

I glared at him. "Give me a fucking break, would you?"

He watched me quietly for a minute and then went to the kitchen. He pulled something out of the freezer and brought it to me.

"It's meat," I observed.

"I should have thought of this last night," he said. "Stop moving. Just hold this to your face for a bit. Even all these hours later it might reduce the swelling a little."

"Oh," I said weakly, sitting down with a frozen New York strip against my jaw. "Does it really look that bad?"

"It doesn't look good," he said honestly.

Creed spoke up. "I'm glad you broke the son of a bitch."

I smiled but Cord looked troubled. He took his phone from his back pocket and pointed it at me.

"Put the meat down for a second."

I was confused. "Why?"

"Because if you really broke his arm he's liable to file assault charges on you."

"What?" I exclaimed. "*He* is going to file charges on *me*?"

"Don't be surprised," Cord muttered, snapping a series of photos of my damaged face. "If he does, you'll need to prove it was self-defense."

"Self-defense," I shook my head. "Yeah, that's what it was."

Cord put his phone down. "Saylor?"

I looked at him. He seemed hesitant to say whatever he was thinking.

"Do you need to talk to someone?" he asked. "You know, about what happened to you?"

"I did. I told you what happened."

"No," he sat down next to me. "I mean someone who can maybe help you deal with it all."

"I'm dealing," I muttered, holding the icy meat against my skin again.

"Are you?"

"Yeah, Cord. I can handle it. I'm not the first girl to wind up beaten and raped by a guy she thought loved her. I don't want to sit on a couch and surgically extract all the psychological horrors. I don't want to write bad poetry about it and revel in my fear. A few minutes ago you told me something was none of my goddamn business. Well, this is none of yours."

I didn't realize how shrill I'd become until I heard my own gasp of hysteria. I took a deep breath and tried to calm down. Creed was still in the kitchen, standing at the counter and looking for all the world like he'd rather be anywhere else. Cord was quiet. I snuck a glance at him and couldn't read his stoic expression.

"You never told me," he finally said in a mild tone, "what you majored in."

I exhaled, feeling calmer. "No, I didn't. English. Creative writing."

"Yeah," he said with a slow smile. "I remember that about you. You were always scribbling in notebooks and shit."

"And shit," I agreed.

The knock on the door was jarring. I suppose I was still a little uptight because I jumped half a foot in the air.

"Come in," Cord called. "It's open."

After all these hours riddled with pain, anger and uncertainty I hadn't shed a tear. But the sight of my cousin's face crumbling when he saw me sitting there with a swollen jaw caused me to burst into wracking sobs.

"Brayden," I cried, jumping up. As I felt his warm arms around me I was home. We'd been born two weeks apart and had always been an inseparable set. Say and Bray. He was the protective brother I never had, the only true friend I ever needed.

"I'll kill that mother fucker," he swore. As I pulled back and looked into his eyes I saw that he meant it.

I hadn't fully realized how much I'd missed my cousin until he was right in front of me. He was the same he'd always been; wiry and slight with huge green eyes behind thick glasses.

"I'll be fine, Bray." The tears fell unchecked. "God, I should have listened to you."

He hugged me again, patting my back as if he were a comforting parent. "It's all right now. It's over. It is over, right Say?"

"It's over," I confirmed. "I'm not going back to him."

The flash of white material in the background caught my attention and I looked at someone I recognized from pictures.

Millie smiled at me. "Hi, Saylor," she said as if we were long acquaintances who were simply meeting again. She had the glossiest black hair I'd ever seen and the warmth of her character was written all over her face. She reached for my hands and I took them gently.

"Nice to meet you, Millie. You're even prettier in person." I touched my face self-consciously. "Bet you wish you could say the same about me."

Millie smiled and then looked carefully at my face, the smile disappearing. She touched my cheek with a maternal kind of tenderness. "At least you got out," she said quietly.

"Yeah. Took me longer than it should have, but yeah."

Brayden had begun to look around the Gentrys' living room. I didn't know what Cord had or hadn't said in his note but it seemed to finally occur to him that it was startling to find me here. I could see him noting my makeshift bed on the couch and he looked at Cord with a question in his eyes.

For his part, Cord had retreated to the kitchen and was talking quietly to Creed. He noticed Brayden's confusion and stepped up.

"I ran into Saylor last night when she was looking for you." He shrugged. "It was late. She crashed here on the couch."

"I was in sorry shape," I told my cousin. "It was actually pretty cool of Cord to look out for me."

Brayden was visibly surprised by this piece of information. I could hardly fault him for the shock. It was still a little unsettling even to me. Yesterday I couldn't have imagined spending ten minutes in any room belonging to Cord Gentry. Once, when I was mildly drunk and feeling particularly dramatic, I had described him as 'the nemesis of my formative years.'

The former nemesis was staring at me from several feet away. I found myself wondering what was going on behind his blue eyes then shook the thought away, figuring I might not want to know after all.

My cousin had apparently decided to take it all in stride. He slapped Cord affectionately on the shoulder and I remembered that they had actually already made peace before I showed up.

I cleared my throat and took Brayden's arm. "Anyway, cuz, it seems I'm quite homeless right now. I can't imagine going back to Emblem and being that-"

"Stop," he raised his hand. "Just stop it, Saylor. Of course you're going to stay with us." He hugged me and again I felt the blissful relief of being with family.

"You might want to ask Millie," I whispered.

Millie came around and squeezed my waist. "Millie says she wouldn't have it any other way."

Brayden grinned at her and she winked, pulling me away a little. She had the slightest of accents and I wondered where she was from. "You, my dear, are the most prominent fixture in Bray's recollection of his tortured youth in the scorching dungeon of a small town. It was all 'Me and Saylor, Saylor and Me.'" Her laughter was like the peal of a silver bell. "I can't believe it's taken so long for us to meet."

"Yeah, well," I blushed. "I was lucky. He's always been there for me, as much as any brother could have been."

She squeezed my arm with affection. "Well, I'm glad you're here, although I wish the circumstances were different."

My mood darkened as I thought of Devin back there in California. I wondered what he would do with the rest of my things. I had the uneasy feeling I hadn't heard the last of him.

Chase wandered in just then wearing nothing but a towel and the ink on his chest, similar to Cord's. He stretched, smiling at everyone.

"Well," he yawned, "it's a goddamn Emblem High reunion."

"Go Scorpions," I said ironically, referring to the absurdly ugly mascot.

"'You sting, we sting *harder!*'" Cord and Creed shouted in vulgar unison. It was Emblem High's rather inane motto, more a source of derision than a cheer.

Chase offered a sweeping salute and blew a lewd kiss in my direction. Then he disappeared down the hall as he simultaneously removed his towel, exposing a notably firm, bare ass.

"Jesus," Cord shook his head, but I could see him grinning. Our eyes met and held for what seemed like a long time but was likely only a few seconds. I looked away first.

Brayden grabbed my duffel bag and looked around. "This all you got or is there more in your car?"

"No, I'm afraid that's it. Everything else I own is probably being burned in a beachside bonfire."

Bray slipped his other arm around my shoulders. "It's all right. We can always get more stuff. We can't get another Saylor."

"True," Cord spoke up, "there's only one."

I glanced at him sharply, but he didn't seem to mean anything by it. He'd already started to wave us out.

"Bye, Cord," I said quietly and that got his attention.

"I'll see you, Say." Then he smiled. "See and Say."

"Yeah, you're the first one to come up with that one. Anyway, here's your meat back."

His eyes flickered. "I *will* see you, Saylor."

"Maybe," I told him, and then followed Bray and Millie out the door.

Even though every instinct told me not to, I looked back anyway. Cord was staring after me. Aside from accidentally knocking me to the ground and unwittingly staring at my breasts, he hadn't done a single improper thing since we'd collided last night. He'd been civil and even considerate. But as our eyes met one last time I saw a more penetrating version of the look he'd given me on the couch. Maybe the power of lust followed a man like Cord everywhere he went. Or maybe there was an ancient connection between us that was difficult to erase. Because even with memories old and new, I felt it too.

But I took care to keep my face neutral as I closed the door behind me.

6

CORD

When I really felt like I needed to slide inside of someone or fucking burst I knew where to go. After all, we were living in a college town fairly drenched with hot young bodies. When the three of us hit the night together, women crawled out of nowhere and glued themselves to us as if we were magnetized.

I could use the release. I'd been feeling all charged up as of late. Which was why I surprised myself by staying behind when Chase and Creed decided to hit Mill Avenue. Sure, it would only be the summer crowd but the pickings would still be something worth sorting through.

Chase was perplexed. "What are you gonna do, sit around here and watch Netflix all night? C'mon, Cord."

"I don't know," I shrugged. "Maybe I'll go for a walk or something."

"A walk?" Chase sputtered. "A walk!?"

Creed seemed amused. "You planning on walking anyplace special?"

"Should I be?"

"I saw her last night, you know."

"No, I didn't know that. Wait, who? Where did you see her?"

Chase caught on. "Yeah, she was down at the pool. Looked pretty fine." He rubbed his crotch and grinned.

I glared at him. "Fuck you, man."

Creed sighed. "Why don't you just go talk to her?"

"Why? Because I nailed her in her dad's garage once upon a time and then described the feel of her pussy to everyone."

"Remind me," Chase said, "just how *did* her pussy feel?"

"Shut up, asshole. Besides, she's on the heels of some shit. She doesn't need me hanging around."

Chase was suddenly thoughtful. "Maybe she wants you hanging around."

"No, she doesn't. Wait, you think so?"

Chase laughed. "No." His blue eyes twinkled. "But maybe she'll want *me* hanging around."

I sneered. "You and Saylor McCann?"

"Why not? Maybe I'm tired of all this trash. Maybe, like you said, deep down I want a nice girl."

"The hell you do," I muttered, kicking the front of the couch like a moody kid.

Chase grinned at me again. "If you say keep hands off, I'll stay hands off."

I just glared at him in response.

Chase shrugged. "You got it."

"You sure you won't come out?" Creed asked.

"No," I sighed, sinking into the couch.

Creed and Chase glanced at each other but left me to my brooding. It had been nearly two weeks since I tackled Saylor McCann in the dark and I couldn't stop thinking about her. The first few days I just chalked it up to some residual remorse over shit that happened when we were kids. But when I caught sight of her the other day, dreamily staring into the distance as she sat on the edge of Bray's patio and played with her long hair, I knew it was more than that. Even though I'd walked over to pay a polite visit I reversed course immediately before she saw me.

Instead I got a day pass at the gym and pounded on a bag until my knuckles felt like chopped meat. But she was still in my head until I worked it out later, beating off and guiltily picturing her warm body underneath me. Or on top of me. I wasn't picky. I just wanted to ram myself into her until we both crashed into fucking ecstasy.

As I sat there staring at the quiet apartment, nothing jumped out at me as a decent way to kill a few hours. Last week I got to talking to a guy who said he could get me in as a bouncer at Apex, a club on Mill Ave. It wouldn't be the windfall of a fight, but it sounded pretty good right now. Mostly it sounded like a way to pass the time and I could end every night getting off with some girl who wasn't the one I'd ill-treated years ago. I was starting to regret not tagging along with Chase and Creed.

"Fuck it," I said to the empty living room and jumped off the couch. I wasn't doing anyone any good here. Mingling with the horny crowds still didn't sound terribly appealing but I needed to find some answer to the hard restlessness that grew stronger every minute.

As soon as I was outside I started running. I didn't know where I was going but the shriek in my chest quieted everything else. I skirted all the way around the apartment complex and out towards University Drive before doubling back. The sweat was pouring off me by that time and I took off my shirt, wiping my face with it. It still wasn't very late. The last of the day's sun was only then ducking behind the horizon, giving the world a briefly muted quality before it would melt into darkness for a while.

It couldn't have been an accident that I ended up in front of Brayden's building. I didn't approach the door, instead choosing to circle around at a distance. The lights were on and I saw shapes moving behind the blinds. Several times I would take a few steps forward, intending to knock on the door, but then I would fall back, chickening out. I was sweaty and it was nearly nighttime. It would seem weird if I dropped by.

Making a decision, I turned around. Maybe I should catch up with the boys and see what the hell else was out there tonight.

"Cord."

Her voice wasn't surprised. It didn't sound particularly friendly either, only curious.

I turned around. "Saylor, hey."

She looked me up and down. "What are you doing out here?"

I wiped my forehead. "I was just out for a run. Thought about swinging by, but, you know…" I shuffled, keeping my eyes on the ground like a moron.

"No," she said. "I don't know."

I thought I detected a note of amusement in her voice and when I looked up she was smiling. She also looked damn good.

"You going swimming?" I asked. It was rather an unnecessary question, given the fact that she was wearing a bikini and carrying a towel.

Saylor nodded, making her way down the path. "Yeah, I like to swim at night. People are off doing more interesting things and I usually get the place to myself."

I figured she was giving me a hint that I ought to bow out and leave her be. I was about to tell her to have a good one when she surprised me.

"You look like you could stand to cool off."

I reconsidered. "Maybe I could."

She waited until I was beside her before she started walking again. Her hair was wrapped in a lime green headband that matched her bikini. She pulled the headband off, shaking her hair out, and I could caught wind of the fruity scent of her shampoo. That's all it took to get me going. Well, that and the sight of her creamy skin, close enough to lick.

Saylor, however, seemed oblivious. She pulled a blossom off a nearby citrus tree. "I love the way these smell."

"Reminds me of the orchards outside of Emblem. Got many a breakfast off those trees."

"They're not there anymore, I heard."

"They're not," I confirmed. "There's a new trailer park in the spot instead."

She peered up at me with a quietly appraising expression. The bruises on her face had faded. "You know, I thought I'd see you sooner."

I opened the pool gate. "Well if I would have known you were waiting I might have shown up earlier."

She pushed an index finger playfully into my chest. "I didn't say I was waiting."

Saylor dropped her towel onto a lounge chair and kicked off her flip flops. "You're not going to get a suit?"

I pulled my jeans down and raised an eyebrow. "Boxers."

"Oh," she murmured, fussing with her headband again. I could tell she was blushing and it make me hard as a fucking rock. I looked at her, really looked at her. She'd always been a cute girl and she'd filled out nicely since high school. Those breasts, those hips, they were barely there back then. All that wasn't it though. There was something else about Saylor. Something wistful and sweet that I badly wanted to bury myself in.

But I'd burned that bridge a long time ago. I took a running leap and dove into the deepest part of the pool.

When I surfaced I saw her at the other end, casually sitting on the steps. I ducked under and swam over to her.

She was lazily circling her feet in the water when I hauled myself up to the concrete.

"So how have you been, Say?"

She smiled into the mini whirlpools she was making. "Better than when you saw me last. It's weird, this void of inactivity after four years of classes, papers, finals and work study. I got a job though. Waitressing, but it's something."

"Oh yeah? Where at?"

She laughed. "Cluck This. The bartenders wear chicken hats."

"Hey, don't knock it. A job's a job. Anyway, they do have pretty good chicken. You been writing at all?"

She looked surprised. "Not really. I've been using Millie's computer since mine met with an unfortunate demise."

"Just be glad you didn't follow."

It might have been the wrong thing to say. Saylor's clear green eyes fixed me with rather a stern look. I wanted to snatch those words back, damning myself for forcing her to remember shit she probably spent a good deal of energy trying to forget.

"I am glad," she said without smiling.

I had to stop myself from looking at her body. It was doing all kinds of nasty things to me without trying. She stared down at her long legs as they lightly kicked the surface of the water. I wanted them around my waist as my swollen dick prepared to plunge inside her.

"What do you write about?" I asked with forced coolness.

"Fantasy romance."

I didn't know what the hell to say to that. Saylor looked at me and grinned. "I've been working on the same thing for the past year. It's my own personal universe, bizarre and unpredictable as those who populate it. "

"You said it's romance?"

She sighed. "Yeah. That's the heart of it. A clandestine story of lovers from different worlds who began as enemies."

For some reason listening to her talk about this imaginary shit got me even harder. "Why are they enemies?"

"Born to it. She's a human living in one of the carefully guarded cities of the realm. His race are fierce outliers who cannot be tamed, creatures what have fallen between the cracks of human and beast. They're seen as a threat." She looked far away, as if she were busily picturing the characters who were alive in her head. "Sometimes they are a threat." She paused and pointed to my arm. "Kind of like those guys."

I looked down the tattoo covering my right bicep. "The centaur?"

"Yes. In mythology they were usually savage. Wild and lustful."

"And strong," I reminded her, having heard some stories from Chase when he was going through a mythology phase. "Sometimes even wise."

"Sometimes," she acknowledged.

Saylor had a lot of passion for her work. It was in her voice. I found myself envying her for that reason, wishing I felt that way about something too.

I cleared my throat. "I'd like to read it, your book."

She wasn't buying it. "No, you wouldn't. And anyway it's languishing in a hopelessly unfinished state." She frowned, staring at her reflection in the water. "I don't know how it ends."

"Doesn't it just end however the hell you decide it ends?"

"Yes. But it's tough to write about love when life tells you it might not be real."

I thought about that for a minute. "I think it's real for some people."

She didn't seem to want to stay on the subject. "I guess. I mean, there's Millie and Bray. They've got a good thing. Once I thought that was how stories usually ended." She stepped down so that the water was up to her navel. "You never told me what you do."

I thrash the shit out of guys for money and hope my body doesn't break in the process.

Somehow I didn't think a girl who had been used as a punching bag herself would appreciate my line of work. "A little of everything. I get by."

Saylor took the hint and didn't ask anything else. I jumped back in the water, hoping to god it was dark enough so she wouldn't see the thick outline of my massive hard on. I wanted to tear that flimsy green bikini off her with my teeth. "You been back to Emblem yet?"

She shook her head. "Nope. I talked to my dad briefly. I think he was suspicious but he didn't ask too many questions." She sighed. "Which was a good thing because I didn't have too many answers." She swam to the side of the pool and rested against the side. "You go back often?"

"Not if I can damn well help it," I answered, thinking regretfully of my mother still there with that sick fuck. She never had any interest in leaving though. Or in much else except scrounging for her next fix. The last time we visited, about a year ago, it had been when the old man was on one of his thirty day vacations. My mother, who had once been a beautiful woman, grabbed at the cash Creed offered her and gave us a ghoulish, toothless grin. Then she turned around and hobbled back inside the rusted single wide while we watched her solemnly, knowing she'd already forgotten we were there.

"I don't go back," I told Saylor.

"I see," she said. She rested her elbows on the concrete and looked up at the sky. "He keeps calling," she said quietly.

"Your dad?"

"No." She suddenly dove under the water and swam all the way across the pool. So she was talking about *him*; that dipshit who got his rocks off hitting his girl. And more. A sick wave washed over me as I remembered her admission about what else he'd done to her. It made me feel like a lousy bastard for the raunchy thoughts in my head.

Saylor touched the far end of the pool, surfaced briefly, and then headed back.

"You're a good swimmer," I observed when she came up again. "Better than I am actually."

"The ocean," she nodded. "I was in there every chance I got. Fighting your way out and then fighting your way back in builds up your endurance."

"Kind of like life."

She laughed. "So now Cordero Gentry is a philosopher?"

"Cordero Gentry is a lot of things."

"Tell me," she said, shaking out her hair.

It had grown completely dark. I heard the bustle of people coming and going from the apartment complex but we were still alone in the pool. I joined her on the side. "You want to hear how I learned how to swim?"

"Sure."

"Well, my dad decided one night when we were about eight that we were going to learn or die trying." I paused, thinking about being yanked out of bed by the cruel hand of Benton Gentry. "I'm sure you know the community pool, over on Main?"

Saylor nodded.

"Well it was about midnight so the place was closed. Shit like that never stopped my father though. He cut through the padlock on the gate and hauled us inside. I have to say, I was piss scared. We all were. Chase was even crying a little. You see, we knew well enough by that point that if old Dad thought it was a good idea, then it was likely to hurt in some way. And we'd only even been near a pool a few times."

"Where was your mom?" Saylor asked gently.

"Passed out," I shrugged. "High. Who knows? Anyway, there were no lights on anywhere. I stared down into the black place where I knew the water waited and wondered if I was going to die." My voice grew hoarse with the memory. No one knew this story but my brothers. I cleared my throat. "Benton threw us in one at a time. Creed was always the quickest, the strongest. He managed to get to the side first and climb out. I could hear my dad yelling at us to get our lazy asses out of there. Chase was thrashing beside me and the old man was laughing his goddamn head off. I kept going under but every time I did I pushed my brother over to where I knew the side was. Creed was reaching out for us, shouting that we were almost there. Then I went under again and couldn't get up. I opened my eyes and saw nothing. There was nothing. I knew I couldn't hold my breath for more than another few seconds. And I knew when I did open my mouth, it would be over. When some hands grabbed me I thought it was already over. Then I broke through the surface, dragged there by my brothers. Creed had anchored himself to the side and held onto Chase as he caught me and pulled me up."

"My god," Saylor shook her head. Her voice was pained. "Cord."

"Hey," I nudged her. "No, I didn't tell you that so you would feel all sad for me. I just wanted you to know that rotten shit happens. It just happens and even if you survive it can twist you in a way that's tough to undo. Saylor, I'm sorry that bad shit happened to you." It was hard to say the next words. "I'm real sorry for what I did to hurt you. I think about it a lot. I'm deeply ashamed. I'm worried it might have fucked up your life and I can't forgive myself for that."

She sighed thickly. "You think the reason I ended up with a guy who beat the crap out of me was because of you?"

I wasn't explaining it right. "Not exactly," I told her. "But the things that happen to us can affect the direction we go later on."

Her face was sad. "You messed me up pretty bad back then. I'm not going to sugar coat it. You know, I'd never even really been kissed before that day. I'll even say that I hated your goddamn guts." She sighed and clasped her hands in front of her. "But what happened later, with Devin? I allowed it. I conjured every creative excuse there was and I stayed. So I can't lay that on you. That's on me." She swallowed. "I don't hate you anymore, Cord. We were sixteen and I believe you when you say you're sorry. I know there are a lot of people out there who would hold a grudge like that forever but I don't want to be one of them. If they think that makes me weak then so be it, but I don't agree."

"I don't agree either," I told her. "You're anything but weak, Saylor."

I wanted to hold her more than I wanted my heart to keep beating. She leaned her head against my shoulder and I impulsively kissed her forehead. I knew that was as far as it could go right now.

Saylor looked down and, with the lightest of touches, ran her fingers across the stark black words written in script on my chest.

"Vincit qui se vincit," she read aloud.

"Know what it means?"

Her nose wrinkled as she tried to puzzle it out. "Something about winning," she guessed.

"Close. 'He conquers who conquers himself.' Chase has a thing about Latin."

Her face was inches away from mine. "Have you? Conquered yourself?"

"Sometimes," I told her honestly. She seemed to accept that.

We hung around the pool for a little while longer, not really saying much. With her, it seemed all right to be that way. As I watched Saylor carefully wrap a towel around her body I stopped feeling guilty over how much I wanted her. I'd boned from here to the sky with a huge collection of girls and I'd rarely given them much thought. Even the ones who stuck around for a while were always on borrowed time. I couldn't seem to find a single one who mattered. But Saylor had gotten to me in a way that hurt.

"I'll walk you back," I offered.

She bowed her head and fell into step beside me. "I'd like that."

We heard shouts here and there, drunken laughter. The night was nice though. People who didn't live in the desert often didn't realize what a dramatic temperature difference could exist between night and day.

"So what's going through that head of yours?" I asked her, afraid of the answer, afraid she was thinking of the first time she'd taken a walk with me and what had happened after.

She grimaced. "I need to drive back to Cali."

I tensed. "Why?"

"Because that's where all my stuff is. I mean, I can't go living off Millie's wardrobe forever."

"I'll get you some money to buy more fucking clothes."

She thought that was funny. "What? No. Cord, come on. Devin won't try anything. In fact he says he's getting help. I told him that was good because he needed help. He said I could drive out anytime and take whatever was mine. Bray will come along."

An alarm went off inside my head. "You shouldn't go."

She looked at me. "How come?"

"'Cause I may not have many talents but I can usually sense when things are bound to go foul."

She rolled her eyes. "I don't believe in premonitions."

"Do you believe in common sense? Don't fucking go, Saylor." She glanced at me with some irritation. "Please," I said quietly and she softened.

"I know how this must seem to you. But believe me, the next man who tries something like that isn't walking away with his balls intact."

"Well, okay. Good. But I still don't think you should trust him any further than you can throw a pickup truck." My mind was working rapidly. "When are you planning on driving out?"

"I have off on Monday so I was thinking of going then."

"I know Brayden takes some summer classes, right?"

She nodded.

"So I'll go with you. I'll drive out there with you to California, help you get the rest of your stuff and let that Devin fucker know he's not going to get the chance to hurt you again."

"You don't have to do that," she said softly.

"I know I don't. That's why I'm offering."

She smiled. "You might change your mind when you hear my car doesn't have air conditioning."

"We'll take my truck."

I couldn't read the look in her green eyes. She might have just been trying to figure me out. Or she might have been recalling the snotty little delinquent she'd grown up with.

"Why?" she shrugged.

"Because my truck may be an ugly pile of metal but at least it has air conditioning, a necessity if you're driving through the desert in summer."

She twisted her mouth. "No, I mean, why do you want to do this? Why do you want to insert yourself in the mess some girl has made out of her life?"

"Would you believe I'm on a mission of personal redemption?"

Saylor bit her lip. "No. I already told I don't hate you anymore. And you shouldn't feel sorry for me."

"I don't feel sorry for you. But the thought of you going out there to face that psycho alone will keep me up at night. You don't want me to lose all kinds of sleep, do you? Makes me cranky. And then I start doing weird shit, like tackling pretty girls in the dark."

"No," she laughed. "I guess we can't have that. All right, Cord. If that's really an offer I'll take it. I'm sure Bray will be relieved that he doesn't have to do the honors himself."

We were in front of Brayden's apartment. I saw something flicker in the window and figured we were being watched.

"So, Monday, right?"

Saylor nodded. "Yeah, let's leave early. I just want to get it over with and be back here by evening."

"Works for me. I'll be around to get you at seven am. That okay?"

"That's fine." She shook her head and laughed lightly.

"Now what?"

Her grin was playful. "I've spent a lot of hours wishing you'd get your testicles mauled by a rabid squirrel."

"That would have been upsetting."

"Well, I'm glad it never came to pass."

I glanced wryly down at my crotch. "I appreciate that."

Saylor pulled her towel around her shoulders. "Unfortunately, it seems my malice has been wasted. You're a different guy than you were then."

"I'm the same guy," I told her soberly. "It's just the mechanics have changed a little."

She cocked her head slightly. "Well, I'm glad," she said. "I'm glad you're here and that we're, what are we? Friends?"

"I think so. Sure."

"And we're not in Emblem anymore."

"No," I agreed. "We're not in Emblem anymore."

Saylor nodded to the apartment door. "Bray and Millie are home. You want to come in for a few?"

"Yeah, I would, but my boxers have soaked through my jeans. So now it looks like I've pissed myself."

She looked at my wet pants. "Well, I hinted for you to get your suit."

"Next time I'll listen to you, Saylor."

"And next time I'll remind you of that."

A lock of brown hair had fallen across her face. Without thinking I reached over and pushed it back. If she were any other girl I'd move in and grab her, haul her back to my bed. But Saylor wasn't any other girl. She turned around and started walking to the door.

"Say," I called, "you working at Cluck This tomorrow?"

"Noon till close."

"Maybe me and the boys will drop by. I meant it when I said their chicken was the shit."

She nodded seriously. "It's good for you, too."

"Fried chicken is good for you?"

"Yeah, they only use cage free chickens fried to a crisp in buckets of fair trade organic lard."

"Well then, I'd be a fool not to eat there every day."

"And you wouldn't want to be a fool." Her hand was on the door.

"We're on for Monday?"

"We are. Thanks again for the offer."

"Well, thanks for agreeing, I guess."

"Naturally." I thought I caught a flash of naughtiness in her eyes. "After all, I wouldn't want to keep you up at night."

Baby, if only you knew.

7

SAYLOR

Bray and Millie were pretending they hadn't seen a thing, that they never twitched the window blinds to watch me standing outside with Cord. They sat on the couch together with their hands intertwined and smiled at me with artificial surprise.

"Did you have a nice swim?" Millie asked with a sweet smile.

Brayden was more pointed. "Find any fish in the water?" Millie elbowed him in the side.

I smiled. "God, you guys are cute." They were. My cousin had always been the kind of quietly sensitive guy girls didn't pay much attention to until they were old enough to learn the value of a thoughtful soul. In high school I always used to tell Brayden that someday he'd meet a gorgeous, awesome woman who would treasure the kind man he was sure to become. He used to shuffle with embarrassment and tell me to cut the sentimental crap.

As Brayden absently circled his arm around Millie's thin shoulders I felt some triumph in the fact that I had been right. It also did me good to see the way a man could be; not cruel like Devin or indifferent like my father.

"And Cord?" Millie grinned as if she were reading my thoughts.

I was defensive. "What about him?"

"You were with him, right?"

"It's a free apartment complex; he has the right to use the pool too."

Bray slapped his knee and laughed. "Jesus, you're into Cord Gentry!"

My face grew hot. "I didn't say that. Really, you of all people know how impossible it is for me to look at Cord."

"I looked at him," Millie teased. "He's not half bad."

"Hey," Brayden protested with a small frown but Millie kissed him quickly on the lips to show it was all in fun.

"You know I only love you, my darling one."

"Do you think they'll get married?" Brayden mused as if I wasn't even in the room, "Maybe produce a bevy of little golden Gentry babies?"

"I'd say it's a virtual certainty," Millie answered.

I plunked down on the edge of the couch, not caring if I got it wet. "Very funny, assholes."

Brayden wagged a finger at me. "Don't pout, Say." Then his face grew serious. "You know I'm just smartin' with you. After everything you've been through, it's better if you just take it easy for a while."

"Listen to you. What are you, my dad?"

"No. Would you like me to call him?"

"Please do. We can all listen to him pretend to care for about five minutes before getting distracted by the latest excuse for bosomy female companionship."

Brayden stood and walked over. When I looked into his eyes I always saw my own. Those green eyes were a McCann trademark. "Bitterness doesn't suit you." He paused and sighed deeply. "I just want to see you take care of yourself first."

I met his eye. "I think I'm trying."

"All right," he nodded, then felt in his back pocket for his wallet. "Listen, I'm going to head around the corner and grab some pizza. Sound good?"

"Yeah, Brayden. That sounds good."

He smiled at me, kissed Millie softly and then left. I pulled the towel around my middle and sighed theatrically while Millie headed to the kitchen to set the table.

"He just worries about you," she said in a gentle voice. Having emigrated from Malaysia when she was ten, Millie still had the slightest of accents.

"I know," I said. "I worry about me too."

Millie shot me a sly look. "So what of this Cordero? He comes by to see Brayden sometimes but I don't know him or his brothers very well."

"Bray ever give you a history lesson on life in Emblem among the Gentry boys?"

Millie carefully avoided looking at me. "Yes. He told me about them. They used to scare him to pieces. And he told me about you and Cord."

"Me and Cord," I scoffed. "Yeah, I spent a few years despising the air he breathed. If the earth swallowed him whole I wouldn't have minded. I do believe it was considered justified loathing." I chewed on my lip, considering everything that had happened since then. "But it's different now. There's more to it than that. More to him. It's a lonely feeling actually, to think you have everything all neatly bound up and branded. You know, this is a good guy, that one's a bad guy. Then you find out it's not true, that maybe it was never true. Maybe sometimes decent-hearted people do crappy things and there's nothing deeper to it than that." I didn't realize how I'd begun twisting a linen napkin in my fingers. I let it go and smoothed out the wrinkles. "So what do you think?"

Now she looked at me. Without a waver she said, "I think you're right, Saylor. There are a million mysteries wrapped up in every heart. It would be foolish to believe they can be easily sorted."

I couldn't even articulate what was going on in my own heart. "There's something there, Millie. I knew Cord from about kindergarten I guess. First he was this dirty little kid who I avoided. Then he was this brutally hot guy I secretly crushed on and then finally just a cold jerk who hurt me..." My voice trailed off and Millie stared at me.

"And now?" she prodded.

"I don't know," I said honestly. I thought about Cord telling me a terrifying story from his own painful childhood. And about the way his blue eyes would squint for a second when he focused on me, as if the sight of me was surprisingly unfamiliar. I also thought about the way his muscled body looked in his wet boxers and felt a delicious little shudder roll through my core. Then I remembered Devin and how for a while I'd thought I loved him.

"Maybe," I considered, "I just don't quite trust my own judgment right now."

But Millie scolded me with a light tap on the arm. "That's one thing you should *never* doubt, girlfriend."

"Do you ever feel that way?"

"No," she answered immediately. "No, I don't."

Being around Millie was like being around Brayden. I felt a surge of affection and impulsively I hugged her. She wasn't startled. She merely hugged me back and then broke away, laughing that I stunk of chlorine.

"Well, think I'll go haul my stinky ass to the shower," I said.

I always turned the water as close to blistering as I could stand it and stood under there for an eternity. When I'd done that at Cord's apartment he'd gotten worried that I was in there breaking open my wrists or something. That thought never crossed my mind, though. When the hot water cascaded over my skin and the steam hung so heavy it was like a cloud on earth, all the sorrow and unpleasantness of the day's hours were blotted away. I didn't have to think about the reflexive clenching of my jaw whenever Devin called with his wheedling promises. The uncertainty of my employment prospects seemed, for a short time, inconsequential. The memories of Emblem didn't intrude, nor did the people I would have preferred to forget.

Cord.

His face found me anyway. I grimaced and turned the spray on full blast, letting the tiny knives of hot water pound my back. When he'd told me that awful story about his father and the pool, my heart had hurt for the boy he was. For all three of them, actually. It was a sorry lot to be born to. My father and his poker buddies used to have their own Gentry punchline.

"How do you know a Gentry has been in your house? Your cat's in the oven and there's shit in the sink."

The Gentrys. They were a running joke in a town where no one was really living high. Maybe that's what made it worse though. Emblem existed in the shadow of a place where men were locked up after they did terrible things. It was a curious symbiosis between the town and the nearby prison, which was overwhelmingly the largest employer in the area. Without the prison, Emblem would likely wither away, eventually becoming one of those half remembered ghost towns that littered the west. Maybe that's why the bruises of three unruly boys didn't cause too many eyes to bat.

Cord Gentry's bruises weren't all in the past though. Uneasily I recalled the way his knuckles had been all swollen and cut up the night I crashed on his couch. He'd clammed up when I questioned him about it and even put me in my place a little. Battered knuckles didn't just materialize out of nowhere though. Obviously, he'd been in a fight. But what of his vague smile and the way he called it 'work'?

The thought of Cord's bruised hands prompted a curious tug in my belly, similar to the way I'd felt as a child when my old cat, Nancy, had limped home with her leg swollen from a scorpion sting. I was surprised at how much I hated the idea of him being hurt.

As my mind wandered to the jolting recent memory of his nearly naked body in the pool and the obvious strength in his powerful hands, my thoughts turned to a less wholesome place. Yes, I'd recognized the look in his eyes for what it was, even though he hadn't done a thing about it except for that sweet forehead kiss, which seemed born more out of companionship than passion. It went without saying that Cord could have any girl he wanted. He'd proven that long ago. And though he'd had rotten intentions that spring afternoon when he waved to me in front of the Emblem Public Library, I had wanted him too. As I wanted him now.

An inner voice kept screaming at me, *It's Cord Fucking Gentry, you idiot!* I knew that. I also knew I shouldn't want any guy fresh on the heels of the Devin Disaster. A big piece of me was still an open wound and I didn't know when it would heal. But I wanted Cord just the same. I told myself the thought was harmless, that it didn't mean a thing. I wouldn't act on it.

My hand travelled unwittingly between my legs and just like that I was lost in the fantasy of my steamy desire. I hadn't felt much like indulging in the days after Devin's assault. I was as surprised as anything to find that Cord Gentry, the boy I'd detested, was the man I now pictured between my legs. In my reverie, Cord's strong hands were stroking my body, his smooth muscles rippling under my palms as he bent his head to maul my breasts. I remembered the tattoos on his chest and how they had made him seem even wilder. I brought myself closer to climax and imagined how his hard organ, scarcely contained by those flimsy boxers earlier, was sliding inside of me...

"SAYLOR!" my cousin bellowed, banging on the door. "Pizza!"

He might as well have blasted me with an arctic spray. The mood was killed and I finished my shower feeling supremely idiotic. By the time I got out to the kitchen Bray and Millie had polished off half the pizza. I took a slice and nibbled idly while they made cow eyes at one another and talked in that intense couples' babble that only people who are in love can stomach.

"Hey?" Brayden kicked me under the table and raised his eyebrows over his beer. "Are you okay?"

I tried to smile. "Say is okay."

Millie offered me a pitying look and glanced at Brayden. I concentrated on chewing my pizza and tried to forget my bathroom daydream. I didn't need a bout of wild sex to complicate my life. I needed a better job than serving chicken at Cluck This. I needed to find my own way.

"Cord Fucking Gentry." I hadn't realized I'd said it out loud until Millie and Bray gave me twin looks of bafflement.

"Cord Gentry," Brayden said and raised his beer in a mock toast.

8

CORD

Chase wasn't going to let me off the hook easy. "What happened to the thrift store wardrobe?"

I frowned, shifting the truck into park. "What the hell are you talking about?"

Creed laughed from the back seat. "Yeah, you're all pressed and shit. Got your Timberlands on. You even shaved today."

The door made a violent screaming sound when Chase threw it open. "Jeez man, you're makin' us look bad."

"Just behave your damn selves, would you?" I grumbled.

"Hey," argued Chase, "if you didn't want to risk abject mortification why did you invite us?"

"'Abject mortification?'" I parroted, shaking my head. "Anyway, I didn't invite you fools. You just sort of attached yourselves to me."

Creed pounded me on the back. "Can't help what began in the womb. Anyway, we like chicken too."

"That's right," Chase grinned, giving eyes to a leggy redhead. "We like chicken too."

The place smelled like the recesses of a deep fryer. My brothers made a beeline for the bar while I took a table in the back and stared at a menu. It was Sunday evening but the place was crowded, although I had never seen Cluck This when it wasn't crowded. The restaurant enjoyed a prominent location on University Drive and the sheer number of people who wandered around Arizona State University night and day ensured its success. Out of the corner of my eye I saw Chase and Creed take interest in a pack of cackling sorority girls.

"Hi," said a perky voice. "My name is Saylor and I will be your waitress tonight."

Goddamn, she looked better every time I saw her. Her cheeks were flushed from bustling between tables and her long brown hair hung loose and shiny.

She smiled sweetly and cocked her head. "Can I get you anything to start?"

You, honey. In my lap. Grinding the hell out of this fresh boner.

"I'm just here for the health food you promised me," I told her smoothly.

"Well," Saylor said, clicking her pen with mock efficiency, "we offer fried chicken in a greasy wire basket, fried chicken between starchy bread with a pickle, and gourmet-style fried chicken with the bones of the bird intact."

"I'll take Greasy Basket Chicken and a Coke."

She jerked her head over to Chase and Creed as they simultaneously downed shots at the bar. "You the designated driver?"

I held her eye. "Something like that."

She stared back at me, all wide green eyes and creamy skin. She started to say something, then stopped with a troubled look on her face. "You want to order for them too?"

"Baskets all around."

"How cute," she grinned. "You'll match."

When I stood up abruptly it startled her. She took a step back, a wary look in her eyes.

He had done this to her, I realized with a stab of rage in my soul. He'd made her afraid. I wanted to kill him for that alone.

I lowered myself back into my chair. She was looking at my hands.

"No work tonight?" she asked.

"No," I said flatly, "no work tonight."

She hesitated. "I'll put your order in and be right back with your drink."

"Hey, Saylor?"

She turned around, her head tilted in the most sweetly curious way. "Yeah?"

"Your name tag is on upside down."

She looked down. She let out a soft chuckle. "I did that on purpose," she lied, fixing it. "To confuse all the rabid lechers who proposition me."

I tried not to sound too interested. "Are there many of those?"

She laughed again and shook her head. "Don't worry about it, Cord. In spite of some evidence to the contrary, I can take care of myself."

I watched her go, not bothering to distract myself from picturing her bare ass in my hands as I hauled her body back and forth to suit my needs. But it wasn't the night for that and so I tried to think the boner away by internally reciting the Pledge of Allegiance.

Chase kicked a chair over as he approached the table. A trio of skinny guys two tables over gave him a hard look but he narrowed his eyes at them in a silent dare and they returned to their nachos.

I looked for Creed. "Where'd your brother go?"

"Ladies Room," he grinned. "Lucky bastard. Took a tight mouth with pretty hair in there with him."

I rolled my eyes. "Are you serious? You know you can get arrested for shit like that. It's public indecency or something."

Chase laughed. "I've seen you do worse, man." He slugged me. "Quit looking worried. Saylor ain't listening." His expression grew thoughtful. "This is different, huh? It's not your plan to just hit it and walk away."

I leveled my gaze at him. "You're the smart one, Chasyn. You tell me."

Chase glanced over toward the bar. Saylor was over there, grimacing as she tapped a touch screen monitor. "I think," he said with a rare note of heartfelt consideration, "that girl right there is the one who might be able to turn you inside out." He kneed me playfully under the table. "Nothing wrong in that, Cord. Hell, if I found something that kept me up at night and made me want to keep my dick in one place I'd go for it, too."

As Saylor laughed at something one of the bartenders said, she tossed her hair and her gaze happened to land in my direction. When she saw me watching her she blushed and looked away.

"More to it than that," I said softly, "there's a history there."

Chase scoffed. "So what? I mean, there's baggage attached to everything, bro. Maybe you connect with her *because* there's history, rather than in spite of it. Great writer named Pearl Buck once said 'If you want to understand today, you have to search yesterday.' You get what that means?"

"Hmm. Careful, Einstein, your brain is showing. I know how you hate that."

"Fuck you, I'm being serious."

"Anyway," I told him quietly. "I get that. We are what we are because of all the shit that's already happened. I even said something like that to her last night."

Saylor chose that moment to breeze by with my drink. While she was bending over, setting a napkin on the table, Chase took the opportunity to check out her ass with a grin.

"I see you," she said without pausing as she set the glass down.

"I see you too," he answered cheerfully.

Saylor's mouth twitched with amusement.

"Thanks," I muttered, taking a sip.

She glanced around. "So where's your counterpart?"

"Creed has a rotten case of the shits," Chase deadpanned. "I wouldn't go near the restrooms if I were you."

"Noted," Saylor shrugged, handing me a straw. "Your chicken will be out in a few."

Chase stared at her unabashedly. He was never one to skate around a subject. "You know, Saylor, you've gotten pretty fucking hot."

She glanced at me, looking confused. I kept my face bland and after a moment she laughed. "Thanks, I guess."

As she turned around she nearly collided with Creed. He collapsed in a chair, panting slightly. "Hell, that hit the spot. Worked up an appetite though."

Again, Saylor seemed a little perplexed, probably because Chase had led her to believe that our absent brother was off taking a dump. But she didn't say anything as she headed for the kitchen and Chase winked at me, licking his lips meaningfully.

"She swallow?" he asked Creed in a mild voice.

Creed was nodding to a pretty brunette who actually looked slightly like Saylor. "Some things are sacred, asshole," he answered in a grumpy tone.

Chase chuckled. "Yeah, totally sacred. Some chick you'll never see again sucks you off over the dirty toilet and it's a goddamn moment of religion."

Creed elbowed him. "Shut up, junior."

Chase sighed and addressed the ceiling. "I don't know why I put up with such abuse from this gorilla."

Creed grinned slowly. "Cause I'll kick your ass if you don't."

"Bullshit. You've gotten fat and slow."

Creed pulled his shirt up, displaying an impressive set of muscled abs that caught a few appreciative female glances. "I'll give you a few seconds to revise."

"Fuck that."

"Guys," I pounded my fist on the table a little too hard. My brothers stared at me. "Can we just *try* to pretend we're not a pack of savages?"

Creed snorted and played with his lighter. "What crawled up your ass?"

Chase gestured to Saylor, who was walking our way with a trio of greasy-looking baskets. "Nothin' yet. That's what he's all bent out of shape about." He offered Saylor a brilliant grin. "Thank you, sweetheart." He picked up a strip of fried chicken and took a savage bite. "Say, Cordero wants to offer you a ride later."

Saylor looked at me. "Thanks, but I've got my car." She started to walk away.

"Not the kind of ride I meant," Chase muttered under his breath and she turned around.

"I know what you meant," she retorted with a hint of sharpness and then stalked back to the bar.

I shoved my brother. "Do I look fucking amused?"

"No," Chase smiled. "But then you rarely do."

Creed was scowling into his phone. "Can it, kids. We've got stuff to talk about."

I stared down at my basket of fried chicken strips. Suddenly I wasn't hungry anymore. "What's up?"

Creed tossed his phone in the middle of the table. "Text from Gabe. He's short a fighter tomorrow night. Wants to know if we're interested."

"What's the payout?"

"Decent. He'll flat out give us two grand on a win." His eyes turned steely. "Here's the rub though. It's not our usual crowd. These guys are from South Phoenix."

I grimaced. "That means gangs. Trouble. Bad idea."

Creed considered. "Maybe."

"Definitely. They'll have a ton of iron cocked at our heads while we stand there with nothin' but our dicks in our hands."

Chase laughed. "Yeah, but our collective dicks are pretty potent." He shrugged. "I'll take it. Where's the venue?"

"Some shithole off Van Buren. Ten o'clock."

I saw Saylor bringing food to another table. A piece of hair fell in her face and she tried to nudge it back with her shoulder. She had soft hair. When I'd briefly brushed it back from her face I'd wanted to keep going and touch every inch of the rest of her.

"I'll be back long before then," I said, still staring at her.

Chase tilted his head and played dumb. "Back from where?"

"You know damn well where. We just talked it about it on the drive over."

Creed was skeptical. "You really think it's wise to get in the middle of some chick and her psycho ex?"

"Yes," I answered flatly. "I do."

Chase wiped his greasy fingers on a napkin. "Maybe we should all go. A Gentry boys road trip. You know, we've all scarcely been out of this oven of a state. I like the beach."

I thought about being captive in a vehicle for hundreds of miles while Chase and Creed issued competing vulgar comments that were sure to disgust Miss Saylor McCann.

"Hell no," I said.

Chase pouted. "I'm disappointed. Had my heart set on going to the shore and building sand castles."

Creed joined in. "Me too. I was planning on going surfing. Plus that girl don't look half bad in a bikini."

The memory of Saylor's tender, scarcely-clad body got me instantly hard again. My brothers thought it was funny when I shifted in my chair. We knew one another too well.

"'*He conquers who conquers himself*,'" Chase toasted, laughing. "Maybe you should go use the restroom, Cordero."

When I tapped Saylor on the shoulder on the way out, her responding smile appeared genuine.

I jerked my head to where Chase and Creed were bullshitting by the door. "Sorry about them."

"Don't be. They mean well."

"Sometimes."

"I'm glad you showed up," she said. "Broke up the evening a little."

"I like looking at you," I said without thinking and then nearly bit my own tongue off when her eyebrows shot up.

"Well, you'll have your fill tomorrow. I mean, we'll be in the car together for a total of about ten hours. You sure you're still able?"

"I'll manage."

She smiled quickly. "Thanks Cord. Seriously. Now that push is coming to shove I'm glad I'm not headed into the lion's den alone." She looked at the ground. "I'm nervous."

I reached for her, touching her arm in comfort. "Don't be. I know that dickhead's type. He's not going to mess with anyone who looks like he might hit back harder." My voice softened. "You think I'm gonna let anything happen to you?"

She stared at my hand as it lingered on her arm. I removed it, feeling like a jackass. She was probably figuring she'd just gotten away from one shitty guy and didn't need another one clinging to her.

But when Saylor leaned over on tiptoe and gave me the briefest of soulful kisses, I realized I was lost where this girl was concerned.

She didn't say 'Good night' or 'Goodbye' or anything at all. She just spun on her heel and walked back to the kitchen. I liked that she didn't say anything. I joined my brothers outside and the three of us parried roughly in the parking lot under the light of the moon.

9

SAYLOR

I awoke the next morning with a zoo full of butterflies in my stomach. The light filtered in through the window blinds and I tried to calm my mind as I watched the palo verde tree outside bending lightly in the morning breeze.

I didn't want to see Devin. Ever since the night I left I'd only felt a vague disgust for him, but that was just part of the problem. I thought about the other night in the pool with Cord, talking about the past and about regret. I'd never figured myself to be the kind of girl who would stay in an abusive relationship. It was a tough truth to acknowledge about yourself, that you weren't strong and decisive like you'd assumed.

And what of Cord? I rolled over on Millie and Bray's couch, pulling a blanket around myself. I believed he was more surprised than I was by that quick kiss last night. I'd been thinking about him all day by that point, trying to reconcile a hot-blooded troublemaker with the serious man who seemed intent on protecting me.

Really, I might have meant little to him. He'd made a comment once about redeeming himself and he'd given hints that he'd suffered a few moments of guilt over what happened between us years ago. Of course I also saw the way he looked at me, as if he could stand to have me in his bed. But such was the nature of the beast in most men.

Just the same, if Cord had put his arms around me and his hands on my body last night, I would have gone with him anywhere. Instead he had just stared at me, mutely unreadable, until there was nothing else to do but walk away and leave him to his night.

Brayden was up early, as usual. He usually spent a few hours in the library before his classes began. Millie was always a late sleeper. She was spending the summer interning at a shelter in Phoenix and didn't have to be in until ten.

My cousin wordlessly passed over a cup of coffee and I wasted no time becoming acquainted with it.

"It's hot," I winced.

"It's coffee, Say. It's supposed to be hot." Brayden ran his fingers along the rim of his mug and looked worried. I put my hand on his arm.

"I'll be fine today."

There was a lot of doubt in his face. "Maybe I should go with you."

"You think you're going to scare Devin more than Cord Gentry will?"

Bray gave me a vague smile. "No, I don't think anyone would scare him more than Cord."

"Look, I'm just going to get my stuff and get the hell out of there. Devin said he probably won't be there anyway. I don't think he's eager to see me either."

"Well," he sighed. "Call me if you need anything."

"Why? You never answer your phone."

With a flourish he withdrew it from his pocket. "I keep it on me all the time now."

"That's a good idea. You never know when desperate relatives will need you."

Brayden sighed. "Be careful today, Saylor."

"I will. Believe me, I've learned my lesson. Seriously, I've got to go hose myself off before Cord shows up."

Since I was short on time I couldn't luxuriate in my usual marathon shower. As it was, I heard Cord's voice chatting with Brayden as I dressed. I pulled on a comfortable maxi dress I'd picked out at Kohl's a few days earlier and applied my makeup with care, telling myself it wasn't for Cord.

"Liar," I scolded my reflection and rolled on some lip gloss.

My anxiety wasn't all due to Devin. The excited feeling in my gut was caused by the notion of spending so many hours close to Cord. I recalled the brief feel of his lips and shuddered at the bolt of desire that shot through me.

"There she is," Brayden said, quite unnecessarily, as I entered the kitchen.

Cord looked me over coolly. I had to fight the urge to squirm. His blue eyes seemed capable of a mental strip search. After a moment he smiled. "Ready, Say?"

I grabbed a few bottles of water from the fridge. "I'm ready."

Brayden leaned in close to Cord and nudged him softly. "Take care of her, man."

Cord kept his gaze trained on me. "Damn right I will," he said.

Bray raised his eyebrows a little at that but he seemed a tad bemused as he looked from one of us to the other. "I'll see you tonight," he told me and waved as I closed the door.

Cord drove a Chevy extended cab truck that looked as if it had seen better days. He explained that he shared it with his brothers and held the door open for me as I climbed into the passenger seat. The interior smelled heavily of aftershave and smoke, a heady combination which advertised the fact that this vehicle belonged to men alone.

As Cord started the engine I felt suddenly very shy and the truck seemed very small. I found myself staring at his hands, marveling at the obvious strength of him. It wasn't just passion that coursed through me, it was a defining feeling of safety, of security.

Then my eyes traveled up to his face as he squinted into the rising sun. I'd nursed a secret crush on Cord Gentry, on all three Gentry brothers really, long before they made a pact to deflower me. It was almost a rite of passage among the teenage girls of Emblem, to fall crazily for the volatile Gentry boys. But I was always determined to be a step ahead of the crowd. I pretended I didn't even see them.

"What?" Cord asked with a touch of irritation.

"Huh?"

"You're staring at me like I've got snakes crawling out of my mouth."

"Oh," I flushed. "You don't."

He swiveled slightly and appraised me. "You look pretty."

I didn't flinch. "So do you."

He glanced down at himself and grinned. "Cool. That's just the look I was going for."

I shoved him lightly. "Shut up. You know you're hot as shit."

Cord looked pleased. "You think so?"

I crossed my arms. "Is there a reputable female who doesn't?"

"What about the disreputable ones?"

"They're not real choosy to begin with."

Cord laughed. "You've got an answer for everything, don't you, Saylor?"

"No," I mumbled uneasily, smoothing my hands on my dress and trying to quiet the conflicting emotions at war in my head. "not everything."

"Hey," he nudged my knee. "I didn't mean to kill the mood. Here," he turned up the radio, "listen to this song. It's impossible not to be all kinds of happy while listening to this song."

I listened. "It's Tom Petty."

"It is," he confirmed. "Did you ever see that Tom Cruise movie where he's flipping the stations in his car and looking for something to match his enthusiasm? Well, when he gets to *'Free Fallin'* he has this big YES moment and he starts howling the lyrics at the top of his lungs. Now he can't sing for shit, but it doesn't matter because everything he's thinking and feeling at that moment is all wrapped up in that song so he belts it out anyway."

I laughed. "You can be pretty wordy when you want to be."

"Only when I have something important to say." He pointed to

Sun Devil Stadium as we passed it. "You know, they filmed that movie over there."

"I think I remember it. *Jerry Maguire,* right? My dad used to watch it all the time."

Cord began singing along to the music. It shocked me to hear the smooth timbre of his voice.

"You're good," I told him.

"At many things," he boasted.

"Maybe. But I was talking about singing."

"Nah, you should hear Creedence. My brother could be a superstar, if he would only let people listen to him."

I gave a short laugh. "Creedence, Chasyn and Cordero."

"That's us," Cord said, somewhat somberly, as he turned onto the Interstate.

"Unusual names. All three of them."

He laughed hoarsely. "Okay, *Saylor*."

"Yeah, that was my mom's bright idea. While she was in the hospital waiting to be induced she read a magazine article about what ladies' footwear was going to look like for Fashion Week."

He was confused. "Did I miss the trend of Saylor shoes?"

"No. That was the last name of the article's author."

"Ah. Well, I can't throw stones. I'm named after a fucking soap opera character. Creedence, of course, is because of that old rock band. Chasyn is from some fantasy novel, the name of a king who tamed dragons or some kind of crap."

"It suits you," I told him. "All of you."

He glanced at me questioningly. "Why is that?"

"Unique names for a set of unique boys."

"Men now," he reminded me.

I stared at his muscular arms. "How could I forget?"

And then I saw it again in his eyes, the expression of raw desire. I wondered if he had any idea how much I'd thought about him since that dark night when he'd found me, a ruined mess, and shown a level of kindness I would never have expected from a Gentry.

We talked easily as the miles passed, mostly about Emblem,

about the limitations of being raised in a prison town, about the tired people we knew who remained there with resignation. We paused in Blythe for a rest stop and to grab a quick bite to eat.

As I leaned against the truck, sipping a mammoth forty four ounces of Styrofoam-clad caffeine, I watched Cord carefully wash the truck's windows. Something was still troubling me about him.

"So you had the day off today?" I asked mildly.

He froze for a second and casually resumed his window washing. "I might have some work to do tonight."

"That's evasive."

He didn't look at me. "Intentionally."

"All right, all right. I can take a hint." I started to meander around to the back of the truck when Cord suddenly caught my hand.

"Saylor?"

His touch elicited a sensational shock that traveled straight to my libido. He held on to me and I didn't jerk away.

"Look," I told him, "I'm sorry if I came off as prying. It's really human of you, giving up your day for me like this. You don't owe me a thing, Cord."

He smiled and shook his head, finally letting go of my hand. "I was just wondering if you'd mind running inside and grabbing me a pack of gum while I finish gassing up."

"What flavor?"

Cord allowed me to pay for the gum but he wouldn't accept any cash for the gas. It made feel a little guilty, given what a guzzler the truck was. It also made me wonder what exactly he expected in return. And if I would give it to him.

The closer we got to the coast the more restless I became. Once, a seeming lifetime ago, I'd traveled this way as a fresh faced teenager full of hope and promise for the future. I'd intended to never return to the searing desert.

"So this is smog," Cord observed, peering into the haze surrounding the greater Los Angeles area.

"This is nothing. It's not bad right now. You've never been to California?"

He ran a hand through his short hair and his face turned troubled. "Twice. First time was a disastrous road trip to Coachella with Benton. He said he was visiting some old friends. Only they turned out to be a pack of burnouts who went on a three day bender with our father while we slept in a filthy shed."

"And the second time?"

He broke into a dazzling smile that stabbed a hole in my heart. "Chase woke up one morning and decided he had to see the ocean. It evolved into something of an argument with Creed since we were so low on cash were living off Ramen noodles. But Chase can be rather theatrical when he wants to. Said he was going to see the goddamn ocean before he died and since you never know how a day is going to end, now was the only time." He shrugged. "So we went. Laid on the beach for hours, got drunk and swam in the ocean. It was a good day."

"'We'," I nodded. "You guys do most everything together, huh?"

We were heading into some traffic and Cord had to slow down. He took the opportunity to pause and give me another penetrating stare. "Not everything."

I blushed, once again at a loss over what to do about being on the receiving end of his riotously sexy gaze. I had to look out the window so he wouldn't guess how he was tearing me up inside.

When we reached the beach, Cord raised his eyebrows at the spread of luxury condos and let out a low whistle. "This guy a movie mogul or something?"

My hands had clenched involuntarily as he pulled into a parking spot. "Daddy's money."

"So how much stuff you got to get in there?"

"Not much. Just clothes and personal crap. Devin said he threw all my shit in some boxes by the front door. All the furniture, everything heavy or expensive, belongs to him."

"Okay." Cord started to open the door.

"Wait." I held him back. "Look, I think you should stay here for a few minutes. Let me just go up there, scope things out and get Devin to make himself scarce."

He was incredulous. "You've got to be shitting me. You think I'm just gonna hang out down here and think pretty thoughts while you confront that prick by yourself?"

"I just don't want there to be a scene."

"There's already been a scene," he reminded me, touching my healed jaw.

I had to make him understand. "Cord, Devin is rich and he's violent."

"He's also a runny batch of chicken shit. Which is why I need to go with you."

I pulled at his arm. "Five minutes. Please, Cord."

He stared at me. "Right outside the door is the best I can do, Saylor. And believe me I'll bust it right the fuck down at the first sound of trouble."

I swallowed, noting how his fists were clenched. Devin would never be a match for Cord, even without a busted arm. "I believe you."

"All right. Let's go."

The tension in Cord's muscles was almost palpable as he walked beside me. When we reached the door of the condo it looked exactly as it had the night I left. Somehow this made me more uneasy. I knocked and waited as Cord leaned against the wall next to the door. The sharp ring tone on my phone told me even before I looked at the screen who was calling.

"Devin."

My former boyfriend's voice sounded tired. "Just use your damn key, Saylor."

I reached into my purse and withdrew it. Cord's eyes narrowed as I gave him a final pleading glance and walked through the door, shutting it softly behind me.

Devin was sitting on the couch with a laptop. His right arm was heavily bandaged. He saw me and grinned ruefully, rising from the sofa.

"Fractured in three places. The x-ray was quite spectacular."

"I'm sure it was." I crossed the room, watching him warily, and tossed the key onto the breakfast bar.

"So what did you tell people?"

Devin glanced at his arm and laughed a little. "Said I was skateboarding." His smile dropped and he looked almost apologetic. "Isn't that what you used to say?"

"What did you tell people about me?"

He frowned. "Hardly anyone asks about you, Saylor. When they do, I just tell them you got a job out of state and we've opted not to do the long distance thing."

I crossed my arms. "Well that saves you some face I guess."

He rubbed the back of his neck with his good arm and scowled. "What the hell do you want me to tell people, Saylor?"

I shook my head miserably. "I don't care." I really didn't. People would believe or not believe what they wanted, and see or not see whatever suited them.

He took a cautious step towards me. "I wasn't lying when I said I was sorry."

I coughed. It felt suddenly cold in the room. "You're sorry. You're sorry, that's good."

"It's also true that I'm getting help to deal with the way I-"

"Repeatedly beat the hell out of someone you said you loved?"

He winced. "Yeah," he nodded, sighing. "There's just all this shit in my head, Saylor. With my dad and with what he and everyone else expects of me-"

I laughed meanly. "You've got to be fucking kidding."

His dark eyes flashed with a warning I was quite familiar with but I pressed on anyway.

"You live in the lap of luxury, scarcely having to work for a thing. The good life was handed to you and you still can't be decent, for god's sake. You didn't crawl out of the bowels of a hellish childhood desperate to make a good man out of yourself."

Devin stared at me. "What the fuck are you talking about?"

I knew exactly what, or who, I was talking about. But I didn't care to discuss him or anything else with Devin.

"Never mind. Those all my boxes? I just want to get the hell out of here."

His voice was rising. "You don't need to be a bitch about it." Devin held up the laptop. "You know, I got you this as an apology for the one I broke. And then I thought we could go have dinner or something and try to be friends."

"Dinner?" I spat incredulously. "Funny thing is I've turned over a new leaf and no longer wish to dine with men who assault me. And you're wrong, Devin, I do need to be a bitch about it. So take your laptop and shove it straight up your waxed ass."

His mouth hung in the shape of a comically surprised O for a moment as the hand holding the laptop wilted. Then the familiar wrath flashed in his dark eyes and he smashed the thing on the hard floor, as he had done before. I started to back away as he came for me. This could be bad.

At the crack of the door being kicked open I whirled around to see Cord barreling through. The look on his face was madness. I said his name, desperately trying to deflect him. It didn't work.

10

CORD

"*Please, Cord,*" she'd said and I couldn't refuse her.

So I did as she asked and stayed on the other side of the door as she headed in to confront her nightmare alone. I leaned close to the door and listened, hearing Saylor's voice. There was no yelling, not yet. God help him if he hurt her. I didn't care how rich or connected he was; if he even brushed against her elbow too hard he would be wearing his own blood for a suit.

I didn't walk the edge like Creed did. My feet were firmly planted and I knew, always, when to lash out and when to pull back. It was why I took more than my fair share of the fights. I was evenhanded, cool.

But as I heard the sound of his voice, this unknown prick who'd damaged that sweet girl, I was up on the railing and staring into the abyss. All he had to do was make a wrong move loud enough for me to hear and I would jump into the dark hole that awaited.

And then it happened.

He yelled and she yelled. Then there was a loud crash and that was all I needed to launch into action. The door was easy to break and though I vaguely heard Saylor calling my name in shock I went for him anyway.

He was exactly what I'd expected; groomed and soft, the product of money and gym equipment. One of his arms, the one Saylor had broken in desperate self-defense, was bandaged stiff. But it was his eyes that were least surprising. They shone with real fear and I wouldn't have been stunned to look down and see him pissing himself. Men like him, whether they came from a shiny tower by the ocean or a crappy trailer in the desert, were all alike. Hitters who were fucking terrified of being hit.

His throat unleashed an incoherent gargle as I grabbed him by the hair and let loose with a cracking punch, splitting his nose. He waved his broken arm in the air as if to complain of the unfairness but when had the son of a bitch ever been fair to Saylor?

As I hit him again and again, he wasn't some sorry rich bastard with a streak of cruelty. He was worse. He was my old man and he deserved to be fucking maimed for the agony he'd wrought.

"CORD!"

She was yelling, sobbing, throwing her body against mine to pushing me back and stop me. I blinked.

Saylor was still clutching at me. Her head was lowered and her long brown hair hid her face. At my feet was a sniveling shit pile who called himself a man. I bent close to his ear. I was aware that I was speaking but didn't even recognize my own voice.

"Listen to me, asshole," I hissed. "You touch her again, I'll kill you. You try and pull any bullshit with the law over this and I'll kill you just the same. Nod if you understand what the fuck I just said to you."

He held his hand over his nose and moaned. But he nodded anyway.

Saylor was still holding on to me. But it wasn't because she wanted to be close. She was trying to head off whatever move I made next. I pointed to the boxes by the door.

"This your stuff?" I asked her.

"Yeah," she managed to say. She raised her head and looked at me. What I saw in her eyes made my mouth run dry. I had terrified her. When she saw me she saw a monster.

Calmly I stacked the boxes on top of one another and lifted them.

I wasn't sure whether she would follow me out. In her head it might have been a pretty awful choice; me or Devin.

Saylor said nothing, even when we reached the truck and got back out onto the road. She was done crying; I glanced at her a few times and saw her staring straight ahead with a look of baffled shock. She didn't speak again until we were closing in on the windmills outside Palm Springs.

"Do you want to tell me now?"

I tightened my hands around the steering wheel. "What?"

She stared at me evenly. She was no longer horrified by the sight of me. But rather than the shy warmth I'd gotten used to, her expression was distant. "Why were your knuckles all bruised the night we ran into each other, as if you'd been ramming your fists into walls?"

"No, not walls," I told her.

"People?"

"Yes."

"Why?"

There was no point in skating around the issue any longer. But I didn't want to talk about it while careening down the Interstate. Saylor waited while I pulled over on the next freeway exit. It was the most intense part of the afternoon and the sun was brutal. I messed with the air conditioning setting while she sat quietly.

"My brothers and I earn cash winning fights."

"You mean illegal fights?"

I shrugged. "Underground fights. I guess it would be illegal if someone decided to see it that way. What's the difference?"

"Why do you do it?"

"Because it pays better than minimum wage and I'm damn fucking good at it."

She looked out the window and played with a piece of her hair. Her voice was small, sad. "You used to fight a lot."

"Used to? You mean back in Emblem? I thought we already had a history lesson. You going to rehash every bullshit thing I ever did?"

"You and your brothers were terrible. You beat the crap out of Brayden more than once, just for existing. He wasn't the only one."

"Is he still pissed about that?"

"No."

"Then why the hell are you bringing it up?"

She made a face. "That's how I remembered you, all of you. Hit first, ask questions later."

"So that's it, huh, Saylor? I can't win with you. No matter what I say, no matter what I do, you'll see me as the trashy kid who likes to pick a fight."

"Cord." Her lip trembled a little, but she stayed on the other side of the cab.

"No, the hell with that. We're just the tacky Gentrys. Good for nothing but fucking and fighting, isn't that what all you clean living folks always said? Well, now you've had the privilege of witnessing both of my talents." I rubbed my crotch, being purposely crude. "You want another demonstration, Say? We could make some time here right on the side of the road."

She turned away in disgust. "Stop it."

I opened my zipper. "Come on, Saylor. I've seen you looking. I know what you want."

Her face lost all color. I closed my zipper and opened the window, pushing my head out into the heat and breathing deeply.

What the hell was wrong with me?

"You've conquered nothing," she said in a voice full of loathing, flinging open the door and jumping out onto the side of the road.

"Hey!" I called to her. She ignored me, walking determinedly on the shoulder of the road in the direction of a derelict gas station.

I pulled the truck directly in her path. "Saylor!"

"Fuck off, Cord!"

Shit, I'd never just drive away and leave her here in the middle of nowhere. "Look, I'm not gonna touch you, okay? I swear on the lives of my brothers. Just get in the truck and let me drive you back to the valley."

She looked away, shaking her head and biting her lip. But she also stopped walking. I turned the engine off, intending to sit there as long as it took her. She looked me in the eye and I could read how much she despised me. But she still pulled the door open and got in.

I restarted the engine and rolled the truck back to the freeway. I could have told her there would never be anything for her to worry about. She'd defeated the most hardboiled place in my heart. I would rather slice the skin off my palms one millimeter at a time than do anything to hurt her.

But...*FUCK*. I didn't know how to hold her hand and beg her to see me for who I was.

The fury that had overcome me earlier hadn't left. In a sudden fit of wrath I punched the steering wheel. Saylor gasped and then glared at me, finally facing away to scowl out the window.

For the rest of the drive back to Phoenix, there was nothing else to talk about.

Icy silence still reigned when we reached Tempe. I pulled up to Brayden's apartment, unloaded Saylor's boxes and left them in front of the door. She stood a few feet away, watching me in silence.

Her face was so miserable that for a split second all I wanted to do was cradle her in my arms.

"That's everything," I said curtly.

"It is, isn't it?" She wasn't just talking about the boxes.

"Bye, Saylor."

She didn't come after me. I wasn't sure I even wanted her to. There's too much bad history between us and I wasn't capable of redeeming myself with her. Likely she would run off with another rich fucker who treated her like used furniture.

No way was I going to stick around and watch that.

As I took the handful of sharp turns through the parking lot and back to my apartment I knew I wasn't done tonight. The most vicious part of me, the piece that originated with Benton Gentry, demanded satisfaction. I tore into the apartment, hunting for my brothers. If the fight was still on I wanted to take it. I needed to take it.

11

SAYLOR

I kicked my boxes through the front door and then ran out of energy. So I sat on the couch and cried. It wasn't a redeeming, cleansing cry. It was the sort of gasping, heaving ugliness that bubbles out of a dark place and refuses to be contained. It was the cry of heartbreak and despair.

Since Cord Gentry had returned to my life, I'd thought about him more than he ever could have guessed. The sight of him was initially a reminder of everything I'd disdained as a kid growing up in Emblem. I don't recall the moment I figured out that the world was bigger than the dust and trailer parks of my hometown but it seemed I'd always wanted out of there.

There was also the matter of how intertwined people were with memories. I couldn't think of Cord without remembering the stink of the Gentry name in Emblem. Even as they were scoffed at they were still feared. Cord was at the center of that malevolent aura.

But the Cord I'd remembered was a world away from the one who had chastely covered me with his bed quilt and choked out his painful memories. That was the man I now grieved for. When he broke Devin's door down he didn't even see me. He was a machine of incoherent rage. If I hadn't stopped him he might have kept hitting Devin until there was nothing left to hit.

Millie found me still curled up in a sobbing heap and dropped her purse in alarm. "Saylor," she soothed, searching my face and pushing the hair out of my face as a mother might. "What happened?"

And for a moment I just clung to her like a child. A few deep breaths later I was able to speak again.

"Let's just say things didn't go well in Cali."

Millie's luminous dark eyes looked me over. "Dammit, what did he do to you? Wasn't Cord there too?"

I closed my eyes. "Cord was there. Devin and I started arguing and Devin came after me. Cord was outside and when he heard the commotion he broke the door down."

Millie's mouth hung open. "Oh my god."

"Yeah." I swallowed and grimaced. "Jesus Millie, you should have seen him. Cord was out of his head. He went for Devin with no humanity. For a moment I thought I was about to watch a man die."

Millie folded her hands in her lap. "But you didn't."

"No. I kept holding onto Cord and screaming while he kept hitting but he couldn't seem to hear me. And then suddenly he did. He looked at me as if he was surprised to find me there. Crap, do you have a tissue?"

Millie handed me a small package of tissues from her purse and looked at me expectantly.

"Then what, Saylor?"

I blew my nose and recalled the sound of Cord's voice in that moment. It was deep, guttural. It meant the words that came out. Those words were tough to repeat. "Then he told Devin he'd kill him if he called the police or came near me again."

"What do you think this Devin character will do now?"

I had given that some thought on the drive home as I looked out the window and silently watched one state turn into the next. "I don't know. Honestly I doubt he'll do anything. See, that's the thing about

Devin. He's got the heart of a coward and he's not going to risk himself even for revenge. Cord had him pretty well figured."

Millie frowned. "Where's Cord now? I get the feeling there was a bit of a showdown between the two of you."

I pulled a pillow into my lap, feeling desperately unhappy. "There was. I don't know, something happened to me when I saw him lose it like that. Then he tells me he earns a living by fighting in some kind of underground blood ring."

Millie nodded vaguely. "Yes, Brayden had mentioned something like that."

I was surprised. "Bray knew? Might have been nice if he'd shared that speck of data with me."

She shrugged. "Maybe he thought you knew. Or maybe he figured it shouldn't make much of a difference."

"Shit, Millie, how could it not? You know what it was like growing up watching those guys? Seeing them violently bowl over anyone who got in their way? Everyone knows what the Gentrys are like."

"I don't," she said simply. "What are they like?"

I exhaled raggedly. "Sexy as hell and scary as shit."

"Saylor, are you afraid Cord would hurt you like Devin did?"

"No," I answered immediately. "No, Cord wouldn't do that, not to me."

"But you don't trust him."

I shook my head. "I don't know," I said sadly, "I suppose I don't. I mean, at the end of the day he's still the guy who fucked me as a joke and beat the shit out of anyone who ever disagreed with him. Maybe it's not his fault. Maybe there's no getting away from what you were born into. And Cord was born a Gentry."

Millie looked away. She seemed unhappy. "I've seen you judge yourself harshly, Saylor. It seems you've decided to judge everyone else harshly too."

Her words stung a little. The tears threatened to return. "I know. It's pretty shitty of me, huh? What business do I have judging anyone? There's not a whole hell of a lot I can point to with pride. God, I wish I could be like Bray, you know? There's a bald, simple truth in the way he sees the world and everyone in it. It's like those thick glasses give him a crystallized view into everyone's soul."

She gave me a faint smile. "Brayden doesn't care what other people think. He lets his heart tell him where to go."

I nudged her and tried to offer a watery grin in return. "I'm glad it led him to you. I love you for making him happy. You two are the archetype for the perfect couple."

Millie didn't appear to be listening. Often, when a person wrestles with something that is painful and complicated, the internal struggle is evident on her face. Millie wore such an expression now.

Finally she took a deep breath and spoke. "After I came to this country my parents chose the name David for me." She tilted her head and looked at me evenly. "That was the name people knew me as until I graduated from high school."

I blinked. "And then you became Millie?"

She smiled. "I was always Millie."

I didn't understand. Yet, suddenly I did. Millie watched my face and when she saw the comprehension dawn on me she nodded and began explaining. She told me what it was to be trapped in a body that felt alien to you from the time of initial self-awareness, an identity which was fundamentally mismatched with your soul. Even worse though was the stark insistence by everyone in your life, everyone who was supposed to love you, that you were wrong. They claimed to know you better than you knew yourself. *Look in the mirror,* they told you. *Look, here is your name written down. You are mistaken. You are confused. It will pass. When you grow into a man you will see.*

"Do you talk to them?" I asked. "Your family?"

Her mouth twisted, illustrating her pain. "They don't wish to talk to me. They are very traditional, my family. They say Millie doesn't exist, that I have violated nature, and that the boy they raised has forsaken them."

I took her hand. "I'm sorry."

Millie hugged me. "Why are you sorry? I still have hope that someday their minds will change. The world gets bigger all the time. And I am happier now than I have ever been."

"You're still the perfect couple," I told her. "You and Bray."

"Brayden is the first man who looked frankly at all my complexities and loved them. The first time we made love he told me he didn't care *what* I was, only *who* I was. He's rare, your cousin, but then you know that."

"I've always known that. It makes me happy to hear someone else say so. You know, his dad, my uncle, is a real piece of work. Used to drink a lot and tear him down for not being tough and naturally combative, as if that's the only way men ought to be." I shook my head. "Asshole. I don't exactly connect with my folks either, although I wouldn't compare it to what you've gone through." I paused and let everything sink in. "We're all adrift in a way aren't we, Millie? You, me, Brayden."

"Cord," she prompted. "His brothers too."

"I suppose that's true," I said slowly, thinking of the Gentry boys back then and the Gentry boys now. "One time I remember they got in trouble for breaking into the elementary school after dark. They stole food from the cafeteria and for a long time I didn't realize it was likely because they were hungry. My dad used to say those boys would wind up no better than their father, who was in and out of lockup." I shuddered, picturing the Gentry patriarch. "That guy was a scary son of a bitch. Once he cornered my mom in a grocery store and groped her before she belted him with a chuck roast, grabbed me and ran away. I can still hear the sound of his gruesome cackle following us. She made me swear not to tell my dad because any confrontation between my dad and Benton Gentry was bound to end in blood."

I stopped talking and stared at my hands. Cord wasn't his father. I'd been unfair to him today. I'd seen how it pained him when I shrank back, regarding him as something less than human. And the fact remained that if he hadn't busted through that door, then I would probably be in a California hospital right now.

Millie knew what I was thinking. "You should go to him."

"I'm not sure how I feel. Or how he feels."

She cocked an eyebrow. "Well, isn't part of the fun finding out?"

"I don't know, it might be too soon. Maybe I should just concentrate on me for a while, read a bunch of self-help books, finish my novel, and perhaps befriend some battery operated satisfaction in the absence of the real thing."

Millie laughed. "Is that what you want?"

"No," I said with rueful honesty. "What I want is for Cord Gentry to take me apart in ten different ways."

"Well that sounds more interesting than your first plan."

"It does," I said softly, suddenly awash in the steamy vision of Cord's strong hands insistently exploring every part of me. He wanted to, I was sure of it. Although he might have revised his intentions after the day's debacle.

"I can't win with you."

He'd said that in defeat. Maybe it was true. Or maybe it was never about winning. Maybe it was only about stumbling through the dark until you found someone who just might be a perfect match.

Millie embraced me again. I hugged her back and thanked her for being family, loyal and kind, the only sort that mattered.

I retreated to the bathroom and looked at myself in the mirror. My skin was red and blotchy so I ran a sink full of cold water to bathe my face in. The image in the mirror waited patiently while I inspected it. I had my father's green McCann eyes and my mother's chestnut hair. I hadn't seen either one of them since I'd returned to Arizona. Suddenly it irked me a little, that there was so little connecting us that they were not the ones I chose to run to when I was in trouble. But I had Brayden. And now Millie too. I'd begun to understand something; that if you found even a few people to cling to in this sorry mess of a world then you were terrifically lucky.

Millie was right. I should go to Cord. And I *would* go to him. I should have done it hours earlier. I didn't know what would come of it. He might refuse me. He might decide there was too much history, too many complications between us. If he wanted a good fuck he could easily find one for far less trouble than I was causing.

I heard Millie quietly talking in the living room and figured she must be speaking to Brayden. The two of them enjoyed a quiet ease with one another. It wouldn't be like that between me and Cord. There was a volatile electricity between us that fairly screamed for a pounding flesh resolution.

An erotic chill washed over me as I pulled the straps of my dress down, curling my bra over my shoulders. I stared at my body. I wasn't outrageously stacked or even much above average. My nipples hardened before my eyes as I pictured Cord's mouth covering them. I shuddered, closing my eyes and grabbing onto the edge of the sink. The time he'd taken my virginity on the floor of my father's garage, he'd only shown the smallest trace of conscience, although it was only later that I recognized it for what it was.

"You sure you want to do this?"

I was. Even though I was furious with him over the humiliation that followed, I couldn't deny how I had thrown away reason in favor of something far more raw and perilous. Perhaps that's what I was doing now.

Slowly I pulled the straps back up over my shoulders, smoothing out the soft cotton of my dress. After washing off my face and reapplying makeup that had dissolved over the course of the day and through a hearty crying jag, I was ready.

Millie was standing in the corner of the living room, her knee propped up on the couch arm, a faint smile on her face as she spoke quietly into her phone. She nodded at me.

"Bray wants a shout of reassurance that you're okay."

"Bray," I shouted from across the room, "It's Say! And I'm okay!"

Millie laughed and listened for a moment. "He's grumbling but says that's good enough." She grinned at me mischievously. "Good night, Saylor."

I feigned innocence. "I'll be back in a little while."

"No," she said with certainty. "You won't be."

It was Monday, not a party night, and aside from a few bursts of shrill laughter, the apartment complex was mostly silent. I walked slowly, trying to extract some enjoyment from the pleasant quiet and to quell the threatening nerves. By the time I reached his door my heart was thudding loud as a drum.

But it turned out I didn't need to be so anxious. After several minutes of knocking and a quick peek through the window which, ironically, reminded me of another dark night not too long ago, I realized that the Gentry brothers were not home. Perhaps they had ventured out in search of women or booze, or both. Or maybe they were busy with the danger that passed as their profession. A sudden mental image of Cord getting ferociously pummeled by a vicious, faceless opponent made me wince.

I gritted my teeth and settled cross legged right in front of their door. I sent two texts to Cord's phone but wasn't surprised when he didn't respond. It didn't matter where he was; he would need to come home at some point. It also didn't matter what he was doing or even if he rolled up here with some willing girl on his arm. I was going to tell him what I needed to tell him. An old folding chair was lying on its side in the shadows and I righted it, sitting down stubbornly and staring out at the stillness of the dark parking lot. Sooner or later everything was going to be laid out on the table.

All I needed to do was wait.

12

CORD

Of the three of us I had usually been the calm one, the brother who could call on a reservoir of cool strength when it was required. Of course being the steadiest one of the Gentry boys still wasn't an advertisement worth mentioning. Chase's foolishness was an intentional mask and half the time I couldn't tell what was going on in that head of his. And Creed, powerful Creed, battled an army of private demons. He kept a thick armor around himself that no softness could overcome.

I burst through the apartment door in bellowing fury, still smarting over the California fiasco. Chase was spotting Creed on the bench press we kept on the back patio. They didn't notice me right away and I paced for a moment, trying to get control of myself and failing miserably. A mason jar half full of loose change was sitting on the kitchen table and I picked it up, hurling it into the cabinets where it shattered into a thousand pieces.

Chase was first to the sliding glass door. He looked at me incredulously as I continued to stalk back and forth like a caged panther.

"What the hell, man?"

I started throwing empty punches at the wall. I imagined the satisfying feeling of inflicting damage at the end of each hook.

"Fuckin' shithead," I growled, lifting one of the crappy folding kitchen chairs above my head and knowing it simply had to be broken.

"Cord!"

Both my brothers were standing in the patio doorway now. They glanced at one another and then back at me as I held the rickety piece of furniture over my head.

"Don't," Chase said mildly. "Creed's fat ass already broke two of 'em. I won't be able to enjoy my Marshmallow Mates as much if I've got to stand." He smiled at me but it wasn't in mocking. I could see the concern in his eyes.

Creed wiped at the sweat running off his brow and watched me while I lowered the chair back to the ground and then sat in it. I still felt as if there was a hurricane churning underneath my skin.

"The fight tonight? I'm in it. I've got to get some of this shit out of my head."

Chase circled around and settled into one of the other chairs. "Looks like you already saw some action," he commented, pointing to my knuckles which were a little cut up.

"Just a little," I said with a straight face.

Creed downed a bottle of water and peered at me. "You get the better end of the deal?"

"What do you think?"

Chase laced his hands together on the tabletop. "What happened?"

"Dipshit made a grab for her so I got to him first." I sighed and leaned back in the chair. "Wasn't pretty, boys. I'm sure I broke a few more things on his expensive body."

"Good," Creed shrugged and opened another bottle of water but Chase looked troubled.

"There gonna be fallout from that?"

"Nah," I answered, though I was thinking uneasily of Saylor and the glance of disgust she'd given me after I offered to screw her on the freeway off ramp. "Not from him."

"And Say?" Chase asked, guessing where my mind was.

"Saylor believes the same thing she's always believed, that I'm a hellish thug. She might even be fucking right."

"She said that?"

"She didn't have to. I'm nothin' to her, I'm garbage."

Creed chortled lightly. "You know that ain't true."

I turned on him. "You trying to give me love advice? When's the last time you used a girl for more than exercise?"

He smiled thinly. "That what it is between you two? Love?"

I scoffed. "I barely know that damn girl."

Chase reached over and poked at me. "You know her," he teased.

"Enough of this shit. I don't want to talk about Saylor or that douche in Cali or anything else. I just want to go smash some poor fucker and maybe scavenge for something to meet my dick later. That all right with you boys?"

"Sure, man," Creed yawned. "I'm gonna go rinse off."

There were still several hours to kill before we needed to head out. I spent it eating three bowls of Chase's cereal and then playing Creed's apocalypse game with a stoic fury. My brothers kind of tiptoed around me the rest of the evening but I was of a single minded focus. If I thought about shit too much then I would have had to dwell on the small hope that there would be a knock on the door and she would be standing there.

When Creed bellowed that it was nearly time to get a move on, I looked down and realized I wore blood on my pants. The blood wasn't mine. Fuck it, I thought. Let whatever jittery gangbanger they threw in my direction see it and maybe get a little rattled. I taped up my hands just a little. Anything more would be cause for taunting and anyway I didn't need anything more. I headed out to the patio and pumped a few free weights to get my blood moving.

Chase was out there, already drinking. He appeared to be in an uncharacteristically somber mood as I grunted my way through a set.

"Send it to the dungeon, Cordero," he said. That was a thing between us brothers. Creed came up with it eons ago when daily battles were a matter of survival for us. He was always the most fearful that he wouldn't be able to control the madness. It had a simple meaning. Take whatever garbage threatened to overwhelm you and bury it in a place too deep to touch. It might mean lashing out first to take some of the edge off. But bury it just the same.

My brother was looking at me. "I don't mind taking the fight tonight," he said.

I shook my head curtly. "Let me do this. Then I'll send it the dungeon."

"You burying Saylor there too?"

"I should have left Saylor the fuck alone in the first place."

Chase grunted and took another drink. "You ever wonder," he mused, "whether someday there's gonna be payback for all the shit we've ever done? Like somewhere there's some great universal karma bank and one of these days we'll find ourselves overdrawn on our account?"

"No," I said flatly, standing up. "Because there's no such thing as justice. Or fairness. If there was then Benton Gentry wouldn't be free and breathing."

Chase's blue eyes went flat at the mention of our father. That was a forbidden subject. Creed told me once he couldn't dwell all those old nightmares. If he did then he might have to kill someone.

Speaking of Creed, he poked his head into the darkness. "Time to head out, boys." My brother was about to duck back inside when he decided to look at me more carefully. His eyebrows were raised with the silent question of whether I was really up for this.

I nodded and started to push past Creedence when Chase enveloped me in a sudden bear hug from behind. Chase did that sometimes though. The surprising part was when Creed grabbed us both and squeezed us in a tight embrace. Creed never did shit like that. He reached up and awkwardly patted my head because even though his own heart might be something only slightly softer than stone, he always knew when we were hurting and tried to right it. I closed my eyes for a moment and just felt grateful for the indestructible circle we made, my brothers and I.

Creed was the first one to break off. "Let's go," he said and held the door for us.

The place was a real shithole in South Phoenix. A former elementary school that had been shuttered for a good twenty years, it was the picture of urban blight. The parking lot was crowded with hordes of gleaming low riders and a smattering of high end vehicles that didn't really belong in this part of town but which no one would dare touch, not here. Especially not with some tatted up dude the size of Godzilla working security in the lot.

"You got business?" he barked as Creed eased the Chevy into one of the few empty spots.

"We do," my brother barked back. "Check with Gabe."

At the mention of Gabe's name, the tatted dude nodded and backed off.

We followed the noise out behind the school to the old athletic field. It was illuminated by a half dozen standing lights that had been brought in. With all the milling racket and turmoil I figured a fair amount of cash had to change hands with the cops who were unfortunate enough to work this neighborhood.

A fight was already underway. Some sucker in a cowboy hat was getting his face smashed by a fleet-footed wiry guy with a giant black cross tattooed on his bald head. The crowd was mostly jeering packs of men with their gang symbols and weapons on display in case anyone looked at them sideways. A group of them noted our entrance and laughed meanly, beginning to advance as they taunted us with obscenities in Spanish. Creed tensed and balled his muscles up but one look at those dudes and their hardware and you knew we would not come out ahead.

Gabe Hernandez interrupted, slicing through the crowd and impatiently waving the men off. One of them spat in the dirt and glared but retreated nonetheless.

"Gentry Boys," Gabe smiled. "Which one of you will do the honors?"

"That'd be me," I spoke up, pulling my shirt off.

Gabe seemed pleased. "Wait over on the sideline. I'll have your man out after this is done." He gestured to the bloody wreck of a cowboy lurching around in the spotlight. Gabe moved away to converse with a pack of cleanly dressed men who watched the action with quiet eagerness. I didn't have to be told who they were; the high rollers, the owners of those pricey engines outside, the ones who were entertained by blood and willing to pay top dollar for it.

Chase nudged me suddenly and I saw where he was pointing. At first I didn't remember where I had seen those guys before. I could only tell that, like us, they were a little out of place. But one of them nodded to us in recognition and it clicked that they were in the crowd of frat brothers whose buddy I had bested a few weeks back, the night I accidentally tackled Saylor McCann. A few of them watched us with a look of amusement as their hands groped the asses of some scarcely dressed females.

"You okay there, boy?" Creed asked and I realized I must have grimaced over the thought of Saylor.

"I'm in focus," I assured my brother and cracked my knuckles while we waited for the cowboy match to be called.

When the ref held up the hand of the winner and the beaten man crawled off to the sidelines, Gabe glanced over at us and nodded.

The ref was only about four foot eight but he had a voice like thunder. When he beckoned I strode calmly out to the center and waited.

"So we already got quite a few greens riding on the next battle! Not too late to toss your change in. On one side there's one of the Gentry Boys, some of the nastiest white boys west of Texas. He'll be taking on The Man, The Legend, *Emilioooo*." The announcer let the name drag and I figured it must mean something around here. Men shouted, women looked bored and money flashed as bets were finalized.

A roar rose from the far corner and a slight guy who appeared to be little more than a kid stepped forward. As he danced obnoxiously I noted that he looked all of about fifteen and I wasn't pleased to be charged with taking him down. It wasn't the kind of fight I was looking for.

But then the kid grinned at me and bleated a round of howling laughter before falling back into the shadows. What came out of there next was a few shades more challenging.

The dude was bigger than Creed. He was bald and the leathery cast to his bronze skin led me to guess he had seen quite a few more summers than I had. He took his time getting out, twitching his muscles and rolling his neck back and forth. His bare chest was a cornucopia of hard fought scars and faded ink. I was betting that if he hadn't seen the inside of the state facility in Emblem, he had done time somewhere.

Emilio smiled and the light glinted off the gold caps on his teeth. A few of his crowd shouted words in Spanish.

I kept my face passive but inside I was seething.

Easy win, they thought. Fuck, no.

Emilio thumped into the center of the clearing that passed for a fighting ring.

"Gentlemen," hollered the announcer, "I would tell you to keep it clean but what's the fucking point of that?" The crowd was in a riot for blood. I'd already seen the cowboy get carried off by his pals. I damn well wasn't going to be next.

"That's how I remembered you. Hit first."

It might not have been exactly what she'd said in a sad voice this afternoon but the memory pierced me in the final seconds before combat.

"That's right, sweetheart," I growled, putting my tight fists up.

"You talkin' to yourself there, trailer trash?" Emilio circled me, a gruesome smile on his face. "Or prayin' to your sorry bitch of a maker?"

I almost spat a creative suggestion for what he could do with his ugly comments. But I stopped myself. It was a distraction, and it was deliberate. I needed to keep my attention on his next move.

Emilio ran his meaty tongue over his lips and feinted, laughing when I flinched. So that was going to be his game. He was going to try to mess with my head until I got flustered enough to take a misstep. But up close I could tell that besides his scars, his arms weren't well cut and he carried an extra twenty pounds of pure flab around his gut. That meant something. It meant there were soft spots. All I had to do was reach them.

Emilio was grinning again. He believed I was like the frat boys, a privileged white kid who got off playing on the dirty side for a while. With a quick jab he got me in ribcage and I responded with a series of lightening blows to his upper chest. He had little choice but to hold in a defensive position as I rained a storm of pent up fury with jab after jab.

His corner quieted over that and Emilio backed up a few paces when I spent that burst. His face showed that he had changed his mind. He had recognized my ferocity and realized I might be more like him than like those quietly haughty college kids who were sitting on the sidelines.

Then his eyes dimmed and with a quickness I hadn't counted on, he got me square in the same spot he'd nailed the first time. It was a hard hit and I needed a moment to breathe it out. His friends hooted and shouted things in Spanish that I didn't catch. I still knew they were rooting for my destruction.

I thought he was moving in for another hit. I prepared to have a go at his upper body again but it was a trap. He caught me in a headlock and pummeled my ribs. He was strong as hell. I couldn't have twisted away if I tried. So I lowered my head into the middle of his chest and drove him back. I heard him grunting, felt his hot breath on my neck as his footing faltered. When he stumbled, his grip lessened enough for me to break loose. My right hook was ready to go and I unleashed it into his broad face.

I didn't get him as good as I'd liked, though it was enough to draw a trickle of blood out of the corner of his mouth. Other than spitting a stream of red saliva on the ground he seemed unfazed.

His next blow glanced off my right shoulder and I responded with another dive for his face. He was ready for me and before I was able to gather my arms into a defensive position he landed a jarring hit to the right side of my head. It wasn't enough to do real damage but it did ring the hell out of my ears and I shook my head, trying to clear my senses. I heard Creed, or maybe it was Chase, shouting my name, trying to bring me back. When Emilio managed to nail me right in the center of my chest I felt the wind leave my lungs in a sickening rush and I fell to my knees. The crowd howled as one voice and I saw Emilio's thick legs barreling my way to inflict some harm I wouldn't be rising from so easily. As I watched Emilio close in it seemed that every moment in my life, all the agonies and torments, had congealed into a featureless chaos to bring me here.

But then, you could assume the same about the next moment too.

"So Cordero Gentry is a philosopher now?"

"Cordero Gentry is a lot of things."

"Tell me."

The memory of her voice filled my lungs with air again.

Emilio drew back with a feral growl and aimed for my skull. He missed me by inches as I rolled backwards, feeling every scratch of the refuse littering the ground digging into my back while my body flipped. I was on my feet before Emilio even recovered from his errant punch. He only saw me coming at the last second and his face registered the shock of a man who was not used to losing games like this. I got him in the lower jaw and then belted a good round of hard hits to his chest until he was gasping, stumbling, teetering backwards. When he fell I recognized the distinct joyous howls of my brothers, Chase and Creed, the very legs I stood on.

There was a lot of shouting and a lot of money changing hands as bets were settled. Emilio even managed a rueful grin of respect before he was hustled away by his mob. A couple of the scowling frat boys caught my eye but I didn't give a shit about them. If they'd lost some of their beer money here tonight then so much the better.

After a few deep inhales I knew no ribs were broken. Bruised, yes, as the right side of my face was sure to be. The cheek was already puffing up and a small cut bled into my eye.

"Beautiful," Creed teased, tossing my shirt over. He went to collect our cash and we hurried out of that teeming hell.

It felt good to pull soft fabric over my sweaty skin. I settled into the backseat of the truck cab while Creed and Chase carried on in the front.

Chase swiveled around while Creed sped onto the Interstate towards the east valley.

"What do you say, man? Chippies and treats to cap off the night?"

"No," I shook my head. "Let's just go home."

"Home?" Chase spat. "What fuck you mean 'home'?"

Creed shushed him with a poke in the side. "That's fine, Cord. You look kind of wrecked."

Chase grumbled some more and I caught sight of my face in the rearview mirror. I'd been way more banged up than this for far less reward and it had never bothered me before. Except now all I could think about was the likely expression of horror on Saylor's face when she saw, once again, that I was no better than the rest of the alley cat Gentrys who skulked around the place we came from.

Grimly I watched the lights of the freeway whiz past. That girl couldn't cross my mind without thinking about how the folds of her dress hugged her hot little figure. But what really hammered me were the small glances of uncertain affection she gave me as I'd hoped that for once I had a right to something decent.

It was no good. Saylor wasn't going to be there waiting for me tonight. And even though it had been a while, I wasn't in the mood for a dirty fuck with some empty shell. I closed my eyes, wanting only the oblivion of rest.

Then we were slowing to a stop and Chase uttered, "Holy shit," in a tone of wonder that made me open my eyes.

She was bathed in the truck's headlights, squinting into the glare and looking so good my dick twitched.

Creed shut the engine off and both my brothers spun to see what I would do.

"Cord?" she called with a touch of uncertainty.

I opened the door and slid out, every muscle of my body even more tense than it had been in the seconds before the bout with Emilio.

Saylor bit her lip and approached me. I watched her face as she took in my ragged appearance. Instead of the shock I'd imagined though, she only seemed relieved. She stood before me and tilted her head back as she reached for my hand.

"I'm sorry," she whispered, moving hesitantly closer.

"I am too, Say. God dammit, I am too," I told her and laced my fingers through hers to show her it was true.

She exhaled with ragged emotion. "So now what?"

I ran my thumb over her palm. "Depends, baby. What do you want?"

She gave me a faint smile. "You already know."

The boys were at my back, holding off on saying a word for once. I was grateful. Chase unlocked the door to the apartment and he and Creed walked through it silently.

I nudged her. "Let's go inside."

She nodded and I snaked my arm around her shoulder as we crossed the threshold. Tonight would be the end of all uncertainty between us. I'd never wanted anything more.

13

SAYLOR

He was a mess. I saw that as soon as I laid eyes on him. I didn't know if he'd gotten the better end of the fight. It didn't matter. I didn't even want him to tell me about it. I just wanted *him*.

Chase and Creed were trying to stay in the background, which was fine with me. I saw them grab a couple of beers and head out through the sliding glass doors to the back patio. Cord ducked into the bathroom and examined his face in the mirror while I stood in the doorway, watching.

"You should put something on that," I said, pointing to the small gash above his right eye.

Cord squinted into the mirror and pulled off his shirt. Mixed in with his tattoos I could see the faint bruises on his chest but he scarcely seemed to notice, only smiling vaguely when he caught me staring.

"It's not as bad as it looks."

"I'm happy to hear that." I reached around him and turned on the sink, searching the medicine chest for something with antibacterial qualities.

Even though I had moved so close that my arm brushed against his, Cord didn't retreat an inch. The only thing I found to treat the cut was a brown bottle of hydrogen peroxide. I motioned for him to sit atop the closed toilet and soaked a wad of toilet paper.

I tilted his chin up, looking critically at the puffy area above his right cheek. "You should probably ice that."

He grinned. "Don't you think it gives me character?"

My mouth twitched. "I think you've got plenty of that already, Cord." I pressed the wad to his cut and he winced.

"Shit stings," he complained.

"You're a big boy. You can take it."

He raised an eyebrow and I figured he was about to say something smart but he only watched me patiently as I finished cleaning the cut.

"It's not bleeding anymore so it's not that deep," I told him, closing the cap on the bottle. "But you should take better care of that head." I leaned over to kiss his forehead, as he had done to mine when we'd sat side by side on the edge of the pool.

But Cord saw where I was going and jerked his head up so that our mouths met. I felt myself sinking, sinking fast, and when he opened his lips slightly I moaned, sliding my tongue inside his mouth. I could feel my body readying, opening, wanting to take him inside. I knew if he were to search with his hands he would find I was already wet as hell.

But Cord just drew back a little and gave me a grin full of sex and mischief. He looked down at himself and laughed lightly. "I could probably stand to shower."

I didn't know if that was an invitation. In any case, I had one of my own. I let my hand travel lightly over his, just grazing the fingertips. "Would you settle for a swim?"

Cord closed his hand around mine. "Yes," he answered, a gruff undercurrent in his voice that said he understood what I was really asking.

He grabbed a pair of towels from a hallway closet as an afterthought. I slipped my hand into his as we left the apartment and ventured into the hot night. There was a faint breath of humidity, telling the story of the approaching summer storm season. Far off in the east, flashes of light were breaking over unseen mountains.

"What are you looking at?" I wanted to know as he searched the sky.

"Moon's too bright," he finally said, holding my hand more firmly. "I've had this habit since I was a kid, of searching for the Three Kings."

"Orion's Belt," I nodded, knowing which constellation he meant. "Easier to see out in the desert. Three stars in a row."

"Three brothers," he said softly, confirming why he searched for the line of three which shone in the sky for all eternity. The Gentry boys were an entity unto themselves, the three necessary points of a triangle.

The pool was empty, as it usually was at this hour. Cord opened up the gate and shepherded me through it.

I pulled my dress off slowly, knowing he was watching as he unzipped his jeans.

"You went shopping," he observed.

"What?"

Cord gestured, a smile on his face. "Bra."

"Oh, yeah," I flushed, letting the dress fall to the ground.

Cord's smile disappeared as he watched me walk to the pool and climb down the steps in my black bra and panties. A moment later he joined me. This time he didn't bother to try and hide the hard arousal fairly bursting through his boxers. I couldn't wait to feel him inside me.

I wondered what he saw when he looked me over. Maybe he was thinking of the last time he'd undressed me, so long ago in a different place. Cord was looking pretty rough himself; bruised from the fight, wild eyed with lust.

"Does any of that hurt?" I asked him.

"No," he answered and jumped down the last step, going under completely before resurfacing and shaking the water from his short hair.

I glided over to the wall and he met me there, quickly pinning me in the corner with his strong arms on either side. The heat of his body was penetrating and his eyes were fixed on my face as if there was nothing else to see anywhere. He was waiting, I knew, waiting for me to move first.

My first kiss went to his chest. His skin was hot to touch, almost feverish. I licked at the edges of his sharply defined tattoos and let my lips travel along the hard contours of his muscles as he leaned his head back, breathing hard.

He seized me with a sudden, crude urgency. I welcomed it. One arm circled my waist and pulled me close while the other traveled up my back and higher, winding into my hair and forcing my mouth against his.

He let his tongue speak the language of desire while relentlessly exploring. Cord kissed the way he did most things, with intensity. We sank down into the water together, immersed to our shoulders. His knee pushed my legs apart and I felt the whole thick length of him demanding entry into my throbbing center.

"Cord," I moaned when he broke the kiss. I wrapped my arms around his shoulders and trembled as his hands traveled all over me. The feel of the water everywhere around us increased the erotic sensation and when he began to slide my panties over my hips I nearly climaxed right then and there.

"Feel that?" he whispered as he pushed against me. He knew exactly what he was doing. The blunt, rigid tip of his dick caressed between my legs, driving me mad.

"Oh hell, yeah," I breathed, moving in rhythm against him, straining to feel the rub against the sensitive nerves. "How could I not?"

His tongue ran down my neck. "You know what I want to do to you?"

I was going to go out of my mind in a minute. "I can guess."

He pushed partway inside of me and chuckled. "The hell you can, Saylor. There's things I want to do to you that you probably never even heard of." He pumped lightly, intentionally teasing me as I bit down on my lip and struggled to stand it as his hands rolled over my breasts. His fingers slid under the fabric of my bra and his voice was thick. "It'll be so good, honey, I swear. You'll love every second."

I was bucking against him, trying to push him in deeper. "I believe you. I want that so bad." The pressure he was exerting against me was sweet agony. Everything I felt was concentrated between my legs. I was so ready I could have screamed. Cord moved his hips, corkscrewing his way in a few centimeters deeper. He was teasing me, holding back.

"Not here," he whispered in my ear, suddenly pulling away and drawing my panties back up.

"Here," I whimpered, arching against him, just wanting him to not stop, to never stop. "Anywhere."

He shook his head and smiled. "No, 'cause it's not gonna be quick and it's not gonna be just once." He pulled at me. "Come on, baby. Let me show you."

I was weak-kneed when I climbed out. Cord wrapped me in a towel and pulled me against him, kissing me hard. My mind spiraled and I thought there was no power on earth stronger than the one between two people who were on the cusp of becoming lovers. He held me tightly to his side as we walked back to his apartment.

Creed was sitting outside, smoking a cigarette and softly strumming a guitar. He looked up when we approached but seemed unsurprised at the sight of us together and merely nodded as we passed.

Cord's bedroom was simple and neat. After switching on a table lamp he kicked the door closed, dropping his towel. Then, with a flick of his wrist, Cord impatiently dispensed with my towel and stared at me. I shivered, partly from my chilled skin, partly in anticipation over what he would do next.

"Saylor." The sound of his voice saying my name caused me to tremble harder. Cord pulled the straps of my bra down, running his thumbs over my nipples, stimulating them with purpose. But he never took his eyes from my face. "I'd never hurt you." When Cord said that he meant something more complicated than the way Devin had hurt me.

"I know," I whispered, moving closer to him. "I know that, Cord."

"Do you?" he tipped my chin up, looking at me critically. "Do you know that it isn't about a conquest this time?"

"Yes."

Cord pulled his shorts off, still holding my gaze. He was gorgeous; broad-shouldered, tanned and muscular with a classically chiseled face that still held a boyish vulnerability designed to melt hearts. A set of black tribal tattoos licked the sides of his torso, giving him a slightly dangerous appearance. He was also immense, rigid and erect. My insides convulsed with the desire to be battered by the hard pulse of him. Cord Gentry picked me up as if I weighed nothing and deposited me gently on the bed.

"Trust me, Say," he whispered, easing my panties down, prompting a brief memory that I quickly shushed. What was happening between us now was far different. Cord kissed me again then pulled back. "I'm gonna fuck you good as you deserve and this'll be one hell of a night. Just trust me." He ran his hands down my thighs, lightly grazing the throbbing place between my legs which was wet and ready. "I've been wanting to be inside you so much. It's been fucking killing me."

I twisted underneath him, wanting more and wanting it now. No guy had ever spoken to me so frankly yet so gently during intimacy. It had its own kind of raw power. "I trust you," I said, whimpering a little and struggling not to shriek my demand. I knew his desire was as strong, maybe stronger. He was savoring the moment. I needed to let him.

With sudden brusqueness he spread my legs wide. And when I felt his broad thumbs opening me up, I cried out a little from the insanity of it. He wouldn't be able to hold back much longer. But he wanted to hear something from me first.

"Be sure, Saylor, be sure. Because you know this?" He fingered me more deeply, searching for and finding the place that controlled me as I quivered. "I know how to own the hell out of it."

His words were doing as much to push me to the brink as his hands were. "I'm sure! God, I need you, Cord, please!" I didn't care if

Chase and Creed heard me begging. Even if they were standing right there in the room I wouldn't have had the will to stop this.

"Shit, honey, you've made me crazy," he swore and then eased himself inside of me.

Cord was done holding back. There was so much to him that for a split second I felt a slight pain as my body stretched to take him all in. I pulled my knees back, widening my legs as far as they would go while Cord withdrew a little and then pushed the whole of his powerful body in without mercy.

I didn't want mercy though. I urged him to go harder, not caring about the noise I was making. It was reckless, wild, just like Cord himself. There were no rules here, nothing but the frenzied pounding he gave me. This was a wild abandon I had never known and I closed my eyes to it, raising my hands above my head and then gasping when he gripped my wrists hard on either side and used that leverage to increase his rhythm.

"Cord," I moaned, "I'm close. I'm so close."

He nipped at my neck. "I know you're close, baby. Aw, fuck. Never felt nothing so wet as you or so fucking incredible."

I channeled every bit of my concentration into the rising wave. I knew even before it hit me that it wasn't going to be some quick burst that lasted a few seconds and then disappeared. No, Cord was bringing me somewhere that consumed and shattered.

He didn't let up as I shook underneath him, every ounce of my focus directed to that inner chaotic ecstasy. I moaned and shouted, calling out foul things I'd never uttered before. He kept at me, pumping deep and hard, waiting until I'd gone over the crest before he lost himself in his own conclusion.

I pulled his large hands over my breasts and he kneaded the flesh as he came, shuddering and pushing himself even deeper. I wrapped my legs around him more tightly, wanting to keep him inside of me as long as possible while he moaned and cursed and finally spent everything he had.

"Say," he panted, finally rolling off. "Fuck, that was good."

I took his hand and pressed it to my lips as Cord opened an eye and grinned at me.

"Real thing proved way better than my hand," he said mildly.

I slapped at him. "Does that mean you've jerked off with me in mind?"

Cord propped himself up on an elbow and ran a casual finger over my hip. "Yup. More than once."

"Me too," I admitted.

He was interested. "Show me."

I kissed him lightly along his jawline. "I will. Remember, you promised it wouldn't be just once."

Cord seized me, pulling my body atop his. "It won't be once," he said, reaching down and massaging between my legs as the muscles there continued to tremble with delicious ecstasy. "It won't be twice. It won't ten goddamn times. I don't think I'll ever get enough of you, beautiful girl."

I ran my tongue over his lips. "So you just want me for my body?"

Cord shrugged. "I want you because I want you. I mean really, I could snap my fingers and take my pick of fleeting fucks." I couldn't stop my face from falling and he grew instantly serious. He pushed my hair back from my face and tipped my chin up. "I didn't mean that the way it came out, Saylor. You're not just a way to pass the time. You're the first girl I've wanted to wake up with, to hold in my arms afterwards instead of hurdling out of bed to get to the next episode. I meant what I said before I pushed into you and I don't say shit like that." He held me more tightly. "And as a rule I don't *feel* shit like that either." His kiss was so gentle. I let him wrap me in his arms as our mouths played with one another.

All of a sudden Cord broke off and stared at me critically. "I don't know what it is about you, baby. Maybe it started with things that happened a long time ago. Maybe it's because you always seem to have an answer for me or because you're the first decent thing I've ever touched. But believe it, Saylor; you matter to me in a way no other girl ever has. I think about you all the time and there's nothing more I want than to be good for you."

Love.

I couldn't say it out loud. I only listened to the word in my head and settled on his chest as he covered us with the same quilt he'd lent me weeks earlier. I dozed off to the feel of his hand sifting through my hair.

And when he was ready again, he let me know it.

14

CORD

She was fucking exquisite. My morning wood jumped up a notch when I gently uncovered her naked body. Her long brown hair fell across her sweet face as she sighed lightly in her sleep. The softness of her skin called to me as I remembered the taste of it.

I needed to taste it again.

Saylor stirred as I worked my way over her, taking each rose-tipped breast lightly in my mouth before letting my tongue move over her belly. She said my name in a soft breath that spoke straight to my dick.

"Spread 'em, baby," I whispered, lifting her hips to meet my thrust.

It was so warm in there. I slid in and out of her, marveling over how wet she got in only seconds. I'd filled her so many different ways over the course of the night she'd never known what hit her. It was the first time in my life I'd ever been so far gone about anyone that I didn't give a shit about rubbers. It was stupid, I knew it. But it was so fucking good that way and I didn't want anything getting between us. I grinned as her legs tightened around me while she squirmed impatiently to the rhythm, clenching tightly. It was what she did when she was getting close to coming.

"Not yet," I told her, withdrawing as she whimpered, her green eyes opening and fixing me with a look of frustration.

But before she could say a thing I flipped her over and pulled her towards me. She opened herself, figuring I just wanted to do her from behind, but I slid my hands under her body and forced her to rise so that she straddled me with her back flush against my chest.

"Cord," she grumbled, searching for me, eager to satisfy the demanding throb that was about to push her over the edge.

As I crushed her against my chest I reached around and put my hands on her tits because she seemed to love having her tits grabbed and because I loved grabbing them. As she guided me inside, a small gasp left her throat and I immediately went to working her hard. The feel of her hair brushing over my skin was so sexy I almost exploded.

"Now kiss me, Say," I ordered her and she twisted her head around to find my mouth waiting for her. She broke the kiss as she came, writhing in my hands and atop my dick. It was a power that called to the animal in me but I waited until she'd gotten all of hers before I bent her over and took that soft body again.

Saylor wilted into the sheet, her face flushed. "Shit," she breathed.

"Hell of a way to start the day," I agreed, playfully sucking on her shoulder.

She pulled the bed sheet over herself in a sweetly modest gesture that made me want to wreck her resolve all over again.

Saylor was watching me intently and I got the feeling again, as I had several times last night, that she wanted to say something. I'd tried to tell her what she'd done to me, what she meant to me, but it had sounded better in my head. She'd never really answered with an explanation of her own, though the fact that she'd waited for me for hours in the darkness might be all the explanation I needed.

"You hungry?" I asked her.

She smirked. "For real food or for your food? And don't tell me it's got protein," she warned, tossing her hair.

I pulled on a pair of shorts, enjoying the way her eyes skated over my body. I'd promised her she would love every second of our time together and as a blush crossed her face I knew she had.

Only the beginning, sweetheart.

Jesus, I couldn't say that to her. It sounded corny as hell.

Saylor plucked a shirt off the floor and pulled it on. "Okay if I wear this for now?"

I shrugged. "Wear whatever you want. Or, preferably, don't want."

She pulled the collar of the shirt over her face. "I like this," she said in dreamy tone. "It smells like you." And then she gifted me with such a smile of utter fucking brilliance I almost threw myself at her feet and begged her to wear my ring.

"Okay," I said hoarsely, not having an answer for her, or to her. It wasn't just sex, but then I'd known that even before last night.

As Saylor walked over to the window, cracking the blinds open and squinting into the sun, I pressed at the sore spots on my torso where Emilio had landed his best shots.

"Cord?" she said, still facing away.

"Yeah?"

She didn't look at me. "Last night was incredible."

"Told you it would be."

"You did," she said softly, crossing her arms and resting her head against the window frame.

"Hey." I went to her, wrapping my arms around her waist and kissing her neck. "We can do that all the time, you know. In fact, I'm counting on it."

She laughed lightly. "Well at some point we'll have to sleep. Or we'll just stumble around in a sex-drained delirium."

"Sex-drained delirium," I mused. "Sounds like a heavy metal band."

Saylor ran her fingers over my arm and leaned back. She exhaled shakily. "I care about you, Cord. So much."

I closed my eyes and tightened my hold on her. "Me too," I muttered, knowing it was inadequate. She deserved a guy who would tell her all the pretty things she wanted to hear.

"You scared me yesterday."

I had a brief flash of the look on her face as I beat the shit out of her ex. I should explain things to her. I should let her know it wasn't even him I was fighting. It was all the rage of old fears and the reason I couldn't return to our hometown.

But all I said was, "I'm sorry, Say."

"No," she faced me. "I didn't mean the mess with Devin. When I came here looking for you and there was no one home I thought things might be hopelessly screwed up between us. I didn't know if you would even want to hear me out anymore."

I swallowed. "Well now you know otherwise."

Saylor smiled faintly. "You told me once that Cord Gentry was a lot of things."

"I did. And he still is."

She pursed her lips for a moment and her next words emerged slowly. "Is he a boyfriend?"

"Boyfriend?" I laughed at the word. It sounded childish, frivolous. But then I saw the way her eyes clouded as she pulled away slightly. "No, hey, come here. You may as well hear it. I've never been that kind of guy before." I cupped her face in my hands. "But I want to be with you. I want to fuck you senseless every night and wake up with you every morning. If that's what a boyfriend does then I'm all over it."

She circled her arms around my waist and rested her cheek against my shoulder. "Good enough," she said, and then swatted my ass. "So what's for breakfast?"

Chase was already in the kitchen. He gave us a huge shit-eating grin as we walked in holding hands.

"When's the wedding?" he laughed.

"Knock it off," I told him. "Big C still hibernating?"

"Nah, he's out for a run. I'm gonna issue fair warning; the beast is pretty grumpy today on account of not getting any sleep." He raised his eyebrows meaningfully.

Saylor fell for it. "Why didn't he get any sleep?"

"Well, girl," Chase laughed. "You're awful fucking loud."

I thought Saylor would shrink from embarrassment but instead she only smiled. "Only when the fucking's good," she said cheerfully and Chase spit his juice all over the counter.

I was rifling through the cabinets. "Don't we have anything besides this Marshmallow Mates crap?"

"Sure we do. We have potato chips. And don't call my cereal crap. It's got calcium and folic acid in it."

Saylor sat in the nearest chair and crossed her long legs. "What does folic acid do, anyway?"

"It's a key nutrient which prevents birth defects during the course of fetal development," Chase answered as I threw a towel at him.

"Clean up your mess. And how the hell do you know that?"

"Because," Chase answered jubilantly, "I am the smart one, remember?" He tapped his head. "There's all kinds of useless junk storing itself up here."

"I remember," Saylor spoke up. "You got moved to my honors classes for about ten days in middle school." She giggled. "You were an absolute menace."

Chase grabbed me around the neck. "Didn't anyone tell you, love? Every Gentry is a menace."

"So I've heard," Saylor said, looking at me.

I put a bowl of cereal and a glass of juice in front of her. "You got to work today?"

"Yeah." She popped a spoonful of cereal in her mouth and looked around in exasperation. "What's the deal? You guys don't have a clock?"

I stretched, yawning. "Don't need one. My inner timekeeper assures me it's somewhere between eight am and noon."

"It's nine fifty seven," Chase said, peering at his phone.

Saylor nodded. "I've got to be in at noon. Get off at nine tonight."

I reached under the table and ran my hand up her leg. "Want to do something after?"

She squeezed my hand between her knees. "I could do something after," she said in a low, sexy voice.

Chase groaned. "You fools are making me nauseous. And hard. I'd be curious to see which urge would win that battle. Fuck it. I'm heading out to the gym."

"What gym?" I asked. "Didn't we buy all that crap sitting out back so you could lift out there?"

Chase shrugged. "I have to have nice things with tits to look at while I lift. Gives me motivation. I got a membership to Western Fitness, up by campus. I'm gonna get as bulky as Creed so that asshole can't screw with me no more."

"Well," I laughed, "don't hurt yourself."

Chase stopped joking and stared at us earnestly. "This is good," he nodded. "The two of you are all kinds of cute together. I mean that." He whistled on his way out the door and Saylor smiled at me.

"I like seeing you this way."

I looked down. "Bruised and bed-headed?"

"Yes. But I meant I like seeing you with your brothers." She paused. "Back in the day I never really thought about what it must have been like for you guys, growing up in Emblem the way you did with the odds stacked against you."

I stirred the milk at the bottom of my bowl. I didn't want to dredge that crap up right now. "Everyone has their challenges," I muttered.

Saylor took my hand. "You beat yours though, Cordero. '*He conquers.*'"

"Did I?" I said rather flatly and she blinked, taking her hand away. "Hey," I snapped. "Just don't go pitying me, okay?"

Saylor bristled a little. "I don't feel pity for you, Cord. I admire you. If you think that sounds patronizing then I don't really care. I think you're amazing."

Well that wasn't something I'd ever heard from a girl before. Or anyone else for that matter. I sat motionless, expressionless, as Saylor sighed and continued.

"I get that your life has been one long series of battles. But not everything is a fight." She pressed my hand urgently against her soft left breast, over her heart.

"This," she said with intensity, "this is already yours."

I started massaging and she arched into my hand, her heartbeat accelerating. I pushed back from the table, rougher than I'd meant to, and Saylor's green eyes narrowed. She didn't back off though, nor did she protest when I pulled her into my arms.

But when I set her down in the middle of the living room and pushed the tee shirt up over her naked hips, she struggled to rise. "Your brothers-" she sputtered.

"Aren't here," I answered curtly, withdrawing my rigid dick. I ran my hands over her, pausing between her legs. She trembled a little and reached for me but I held her off.

"So this is mine?" I asked, fingering her harder. I'd already learned which spot I needed to hit.

"Yes," she squirmed.

I teased her with a swirling motion and pushed another finger inside. "All of it?"

"Yes! Okay, Cord?"

"Show me, Saylor."

I thought she would just spread her legs open and pull me in. I underestimated her. Saylor's eyes flashed with gritty determination and she pushed on my chest with all of her strength. That girl had me straddled and mounted before I could blink.

It was a wild ride and we climaxed together in a slick, clutching fury. She had to leave me a short time later, needing to shower and change before work. We kissed for a tender eternity before I released her.

Saylor touched my face and whispered, "See you later, Cord Gentry."

I tried to bury the sudden impulse to snatch her back to my side as she pushed her hair behind her ears and gave me one last happy grin.

I hated letting her go. Partly because I knew it wouldn't be long before I wanted to pound her again. Then partly because I was fearful that the magic of these hours was fleeting, that the ugly realities I knew of the world would conspire against us.

And that it was a battle we would eventually lose.

15

SAYLOR

Brayden was watching for me. He flung open the apartment door when I was still twenty feet away. He stood in the doorway scratching his neck with a smile that said he knew damn well what I'd been doing.

I paused, shrugging. He laughed before wrapping me in a brief hug. I thought about what a blessing it was to have even one person in the world who knew something of your mind without any words passing between you.

My best friend poured me a cup of coffee, sat down at the kitchen table and waited.

"Where's Millie?"

"She had to go to work. Not everyone can while away the hours waiting for the prodigal cousin to show up." Brayden removed his glasses and wiped the lenses on his polo shirt.

"So that's what you were doing. I suppose you want to hear all the rough and dirty details?"

He wagged a finger. "Don't be gross, Say. We're still blood."

"Tough shit. I'm going to torture you anyway. It was phenomenal, Bray. Awesome. Jesus, I didn't know there were so many places a guy could put that thing."

Bray made a show of falling out of his chair and pretending to have acute appendicitis.

"Quit it." I tapped him lightly with my foot.

He grinned at me from the floor. "I knew you were into him."

"Right, as always," I grumbled.

Bray rolled over and got to his feet, settling back in the chair. "Tell me one thing, Saylor. Is he good to you?"

Quick as a flash of lightning my mind's eye saw every moment I'd been with Cord these past weeks, from the tender to the sour and finally to the passionate.

"He's good to me," I said softly. "He is."

Brayden nodded thoughtfully. "Well that's the crux of the equation isn't it?"

"You're the master engineer. You tell me."

"What I can tell you is that if the foundation's not solid there's no point in fixing anything above it."

I caught his eye. "You and Millie have a solid foundation."

He cocked his head curiously. "She told me you'd talked."

"We did," I nodded. "We talked. She's fantastic, Brayden. You don't need me to say so."

"No," he agreed. "I don't need it. But it's still nice to hear. And Say? You could do a hell of a lot worse than Cord. I know he's still got a few rough edges he's trying to iron out but I see him with you and he's trying. Trying to be one of the good guys, you know?"

"I do," I sighed, checking out the kitchen clock. "Look, thanks for waiting around for me. I've got to be at work in an hour so I should get in the shower."

Brayden wrinkled his nose. "Yes," he said with disdain, "please shower. I'm sure you really need to after last night."

"Pig," I shoved him.

"Hey," he called after me before I closed the door to the bathroom, "you were the one bragging about your man's creative penile functions."

I laughed as I stepped under the shower. I felt like I'd just run ten miles after spending a month in bed. It was a good feeling though.

By the time I dressed and coaxed the Civic the mile to Cluck This, I was beginning to sense the tedium of the long hours that stretched between now and the time I would see Cord again. Customers streamed through steadily, as they always did, and I found myself looking to the door with hope every time it opened, thinking Cord might casually drop by.

Another waitress, a girl named Truly, poked me in the side as I stumbled lazily through my shift.

"Look lively, new girl," she teased, shaking her head. Her hair was jet black and partially shaved on one side. "You get laid or something last night? That why you're ambling along in this dreamy fugue?"

I made a face. "I guess I'm more transparent than I thought."

"Nah," she shrugged. "I'm just more perceptive than everyone else." Her dark eyes looked me over merrily. "So he was good, huh? I guess that's why you're all walkin' funny and shit." I must have appeared a little shocked because she was quick to laugh. "Don't worry, no one else will be able to tell, sugar. I warned you I'm awful observant."

I laughed and tried to energetically proceed with my job but checking the time every ninety seconds kept interfering. Around five o'clock I realized I was starving so I took a break and grabbed a chicken sandwich from Martin, the chef, before settling into the staff table in the rear. When my phone buzzed in my back pocket I smiled, hoping it was Cord. No such luck.

"Hey, Mom."

My mother's voice was raspy and irritable, just the way I remembered. "Saylor. How come I had to find out from your asshole father that you're back in the state?"

I didn't feel like apologizing. "Yeah," I said coolly, "I am. I left you a voicemail two weeks ago. You never called me back."

"Well," she huffed. "You didn't say it was important. What happened? John said you took off on your boyfriend or something."

"Or something," I said flatly. I didn't want to talk about Devin.

She sighed on the other end. I tried to picture her; skinny, crabby and with a perpetually showing bra strap. My father had been her high school boyfriend. She'd had a scholarship to ASU that went to waste when she got pregnant and stayed in Emblem instead. Amy McCann was one of those mothers who seemed befuddled by the role. When I was younger it used to hurt that even getting her attention was such a chore.

The only honest conversation we'd ever had was when I was thirteen. She'd been drinking all afternoon in the kitchen and when I rolled through the door after school, she looked at me clearly and asked if I wanted to be like her. I'd stared at my mother, taking in her over processed hair, garish fingernails and the remnants of the prison guard uniform she had halfway removed. And I told her no. No, I did not. My mother nodded as if she approved and told me to work my ass off to make sure things went differently.

I had hoped that maybe when she exited her miserable marriage and I left home, we'd find our way to some sort of mutual affection. So far that hadn't really happened.

"I don't have any money to give you," she said huffily and I heard the click of a lighter.

"Oh. Well, don't worry. Streetwalking pays pretty well."

"What?"

"Nothing. So how are you, Ma?"

Her mood immediately brightened. "Oh, baby. Everything is fantastic. I'm sorry we haven't had a chance to talk about it. I'm getting married, Say!"

"Huh?"

"Saturday, at Rooster's Roast."

"Wait, what?"

"Ceremony is at 4pm. You think you could pick me up a floral bouquet? Something with gerbera daisies?"

"MOM!"

She paused. "What's wrong?"

I rubbed my temples and stared down at my chicken sandwich. "Let's start at the beginning. Who the hell are you marrying?"

"Gary Chavez. You've got to remember Gary."

I blinked in disbelief. "Gary the Gnome?" Gary Chavez was the mayor of Emblem when I was a teenager. He earned his nickname for obvious reasons. I tried to picture The Gnome with his hands on my mother. Then I tried to picture him as my stepfather. Both attempts were miserable fails.

"That's nice," I managed to say. "But you're getting married this Saturday to Gary Chavez at the Rooster's Roast and you're only telling me now?"

I heard my mother blow smoke out of her mouth in a hiss. "I just said so, didn't I?"

It was pointless to argue. "Yes, you did. Gerbera daisies? I think I can handle that. Is it okay if I wear black?"

She was confused. "All right. You'll be hot though. The ceremony is going to be out on the back patio."

"Okay. I'll show up naked then. With my boyfriend."

"Boyfriend. What boyfriend? You don't have a boyfriend anymore. That's what John said."

"Dad doesn't know. I just found about it myself. His name is Cord."

"Cord," she repeated, but I could tell she was losing interest. "Terrific. Well, I'm actually up to my eyeballs in wedding prep so I need to skate here. But I can't wait to see you on Saturday."

"Me too. Hey, congratulations to you and Gary."

"Saylor? Did you say your boyfriend's name is Cord?"

"Yes," I answered sweetly. "Cord Gentry."

"Cord *GENTRY*?" she howled as if I'd just admitting to screwing Count Dracula.

"Bye, Mom." I ended the call, smiling as she sputtered.

I remembered I was famished and that it would be hours before I could eat again so I gulped down my chicken sandwich. Yesterday, the abrupt news of my mother's impending nuptials to Gary the Gnome would have upset me. But now I only found it vaguely amusing. It was amazing, I thought, how different the world looked when you could see the love in it. My mind wandered for the last few minutes of my break, recalling the ecstasy of strong hands and a stronger dick. Nothing had ever been as good as it was with Cord last night. The blood rushed to my face and I felt a surge of warm longing between my legs.

Truly floated by, wagging a finger. "You're doing it again."

I flushed with embarrassment and took my plate back to the kitchen, returning to work. The crowd grew heavier as the dinner hour wore on. I was rushing around behind the bar and didn't see Cord until he was two feet away, staring at me.

"Hey," I breathed, coming around the side and throwing my arms around his broad shoulders. He smelled of heat and aftershave. I shoved my hips against his, and not giving a shit if Ed, the pious manager of Cluck This, got bent out of shape.

He answered me with a crashing kiss that fired every nerve in my body. Cord's hands circled my waist, his thumbs insistently massaging the flesh beneath the waistband of my skirt.

"Missed you," he whispered, backing me into a far wall next to the rest rooms as he pressed into me.

I licked at his left earlobe. "I thought you just came here for the chicken."

"I'll come for you," he answered, grinning with lewd meaning.

We were out of sight of most of the patrons, but just barely. Cordero Gentry drove me wild, calling on uninhibited senses I didn't even know I had. That's the only way I can explain what drove me to reach between his legs and cup the stiff swelling there, rolling my fingers over it before grasping the length scarcely being held at bay by his pants.

He groaned and arched into me with a penetrating look in his blue eyes that said he was willing to let this go as far as I was. But when a sweet, blue-haired old woman stumbled out of the Ladies Room I lost my nerve, dropping my hand.

"Later," I pleaded with him as he held me fast.

"Coward," he smiled.

I kneed him lightly. "I'll make you pay for that insult."

He lifted me a few inches. "Make me pay," he growled. "Make me pay hard."

"It's a promise." I edged around him and heard a low whistle at my back. Creed and Chase were sitting at a nearby table, evidently enjoying the show. I smirked. "Chicken baskets for all?"

"Indeed," Cord nodded, stretching and adopting a casual expression as he returned to his brothers.

I was useless for the rest of the evening as the Gentry boys opted to linger long after their food was done. The knowledge that Cord's eyes watched my every step drove away whatever competence I had. I'd meant it completely today when I told him I was his. The words that had passed between us might not be the stuff of flowers and poetry. No. They were more. They were lust and possession blended with the strongest yearnings of the heart.

"I want to fuck you senseless every night and wake up with you every morning."

Finally, after breaking six glasses and spilling a plate of cheese fries in the lap of a hulking biker, it was nine and I was finished for the evening. Cord held his arm out when he saw me headed to their table and I happily allowed him to pull me into his lap.

Chase busted up across the table as he finished his third beer. "You're the crappiest waitress I ever saw."

I smiled at him as Cord nuzzled my neck. "Find any tits at the gym?"

"Some," Chase said vaguely, "but they couldn't seem to find me."

"Well that sucks."

"No shit."

Creed was slumped in his chair, scowling at the floor. Of the three Gentry brothers he was the most mercurial. I'd never heard him talk much, not even when we were kids, but there seemed to be a hell of a lot of chaos behind the scenes.

Cord gripped me around the waist and inhaled. "You smell pretty."

I raised my eyebrows. "I smell deep fried."

"So? I like my meat greasy."

I elbowed him with false irritation, then swiveled around to see his face. "You're still looking a little rough there, cowboy," I said running my hands over his faintly bruised cheek.

"Cocksucking bastard," Creed slurred, kicking out at the table with a loud crash. A few people gasped and I saw Ed glaring at us.

Chase glanced uneasily at Cord. "Told you we should have cut him off before he had those last two shots."

Cord pushed me gently off his lap and grabbed his brother's arm. "Big C," he said softly. Creed regarded him with a murderous glare. Cord moved in slowly and whispered something in Creed's ear. I glanced at Chase with my eyebrows raised but he just stared across the table, looking sad and uncertain. Whatever this was existed only between the brothers.

After a moment Creed nodded and allowed Cord to pull him to his feet. Once he was standing, Creed blinked and appeared to regain some of his senses. Still, Cord kept a firm hand on him as they made their way to the door. Chase rose and nudged me, motioning that I ought to follow.

Once we reached the parking lot, Creed tore off his shirt and leaned heavily against the hood of the old Chevy truck. I noticed the words scripted in Latin across the front of his chest in the same place Cord's were. I couldn't make out what they said in the dim light but they didn't appear to be the same words as Cord's tattoo. I'd already seen that Chase had ink of his own as well.

Creed took a couple of deep breaths while his brothers stood quietly nearby. He raised his head and noticed me standing there, then broke into a slightly sheepish grin. "Guess you've witnessed my weakness, Saylor."

I tried to return the smile. "No big deal, Creed. You've had the privilege of observing a few of my flaws, too."

Cord stepped over to me and wrapped an arm around my shoulders. I reached up and squeezed his hand.

"Hey," Chase yawned, fishing a set of keys out of his pocket. "I'll get the big fella home. You guys can take off if you want."

Cord rubbed my shoulder absently as Chase hustled Creed into the truck. "You sure?" he asked.

"Yeah," Chase shrugged. "He'll be all right. Just give him an hour or two for the shadows to fade."

"I'm all right," Creed confirmed, already in the passenger seat with his eyes closed.

Cord stared at Chase for a few silent seconds. Chase gave him a barely perceptible nod and then climbed behind the wheel.

"We'll be home soon," Cord called and held up an arm in farewell. He watched the tail lights of the truck disappear around the corner and then pulled me to him.

I rubbed his back. "Cord? What was that about?"

He sighed. "Creed drinks too much and he gets a little lost, thinks we're still at the mercy of the old man, fighting for our lives. Most of the time he's fine but when he's had a few, shit starts to run together in his mind, that's all."

"Oh," I said meekly. "You ever feel that way? Lost?"

His gaze was far away. "Not lately." Suddenly he looked down at me. "Listen Saylor, don't mention this to him later, okay?"

I nodded, squeezing him lightly around the middle. "I understand. It's kind of excruciating to let the world see your scars, you know?"

He put his hands gently around my face and tipped his head forward to meet mine. "Yeah," he said in a hoarse voice. "I know."

16

CORD

I didn't want to follow my brothers right away. Saylor gave me the keys and I raised my eyebrows as the engine in her crappy car shuddered to life.

"Two hundred and ten thousand miles, huh?"

"And still ticking," she smiled.

"Ha! Barely."

When Saylor pulled her seatbelt on, her skirt rode up a little. My hand went straight to her thigh, holding on firmly.

Her big green eyes blinked at me. "Where are we going?"

I massaged her leg, smiling at the rush of heat as my fingers dared to venture a little higher. She squirmed a little but didn't scold me. "There's a place I want to show you. It's on campus. I go running down there sometimes."

Saylor ran her fingers up and down my arm. "Okay," she said softly.

I drove with one hand on the wheel and the other on her. She didn't object. All day I'd thought about what she'd said. How she was mine, both in heart and body. Christ, I couldn't even begin to describe what that did to me. Me, the guy who could never zip himself up and hop out of bed quick enough, was gutted just like that.

We had to park about a block away, closer to Mill Ave. I jumped out of the car and over to the other side before she even got the door open. When I grabbed Saylor underneath her arms and lifted her, she wrapped her limbs around me and breathed a little sigh.

I held her like that for a few minutes, just enjoying the feel of her body covering mine. Eventually she slid her legs down and stood.

"It's a nice parking lot," she said sarcastically, looking around.

"Quiet," I told her, pulling her along and pointing. "We're going to see that."

"It looks like a building."

"It is a building. It's the university art museum. See those stairs there? They lead up to the roof."

I pushed her in front of me, mostly so I could watch her cute ass jog up the stairs as I followed.

"Hey," I prodded her teasingly, "can't you go any faster? We ought to do something to get you in shape."

"Screw you," she answered, turning slightly, but I could tell she was smiling.

"You have," I reminded her smoothly. "You will again, honey. Real soon."

"Maybe," she said, giving a little hop to the top step that ended in a wide stone platform.

"*Maybe?*" I snarled, seizing her and then backing off when she flinched a little. I saw red for a second, remembering the face of that shithead in California and knowing this was his fault.

"Sorry," she muttered, crossing her arms and looking down.

"Hey," I tilted her chin up, "nothin' to be sorry for, babe. Just know that when I touch you, *every* goddamn time I touch you, it'll never end badly."

Her expression was soft. "I know." She kissed me and wrapped her arms around my neck and I cursed all the time I'd wasted on nameless fucks that meant nothing when I could have had this. I breathed her in, stroking her gently and then lowering her to the ground. I rolled to my back beside her and we spent a few minutes quietly looking at the sky. It reminded me of the night she came back into my life, when I'd lazed on the roof of Brayden's apartment with my knuckles still singed from the latest fight, thinking about the shitty years my brothers and I had somehow managed to endure.

"You still draw?" she asked suddenly.

"Sometimes." I pointed to my arm. "Sketched this out for my cousin who also happens to be an occasional tattoo artist."

She pushed herself up on one elbow and stared at me, her soft hair falling over my shoulder. She examined the centaur on my arm. "Beastly warrior of legend, immortalized. You're good," she said seriously. "You were even when we were kids. I remember."

I grimaced a little, thinking of how once I'd sketched her portrait as a way to get between her legs. But Saylor didn't seem to be focusing on that. She was thoughtful.

"There must be a reason why you hang out on the roof of an art museum. You ever consider doing anything with your talent?"

I shrugged, shifting a little. "My mom was an artist. Did you know that?"

Her voice was gentle. "No, I didn't. She's not one anymore?"

I gave a short laugh. "She's not much of anything anymore. But yeah, she had boxes full of old paintings she'd done before drugs and Benton Gentry destroyed her."

Saylor took my hand and kissed it, saying nothing.

I sighed, remembering. "She had a stack of old art books, too. Well, she did until Benton got pissed for nothing and shoved them into the backyard fire pit. There was one I always used to look at. One picture in particular. I could never get enough of staring at that thing. It had these three clocks melting somewhere in a barren wasteland. I don't know, it just always got to me."

"*The Persistence of Memory*," Saylor said. "Salvador Dali."

I was surprised. "That's it."

She smiled. "I took an art history class sophomore year. Want to hear something funny? I used to have a print of that painting on my dorm room wall."

"Hmm," I shrugged. "That's some coincidence."

"You ever think about taking art classes?"

"No. Who the hell takes classes for art?"

"Don't be obtuse, Cord. You damn well know people take classes for art."

"Doesn't seem like a wise thing to spend money on."

She moved closer and pushed her hand underneath my shirt. "I could argue with you."

"Go ahead. You won't win that fight."

"You think so? I can fight too."

I flexed my arms. "Listen, little girl, I've never lost one."

"Never?"

"Never. Never even suffered a draw."

She moved her hand lower, unzipping my pants. "Would you be willing to suffer a draw now?"

I started to move my hips. She understood what I wanted and pulled my hard dick out, squeezing it as her small hand moved from the base to the tip.

"I might," I grunted, having trouble talking. She grinned and bent low, taking me in her mouth.

It was fucking heaven, watching her juicy lips close around me. She kept her eyes closed and rolled her tongue down the length. I groaned and grabbed her hair when she found the sweet spot. I loved that she didn't even glance around, didn't seem to give a damn that technically anyone could come waltzing up those stairs at any time.

"Take it off," I barked. She dropped my dick and propped herself up, staring at me with raised eyebrows. I tugged at the buttons of her blouse. "Your shirt, baby. Take it off. I want to come all over your tits."

"Jesus, Cord," she snorted but I could tell she was into the idea. I watched as she kneeled and slowly unbuttoned her shirt.

"Quit staring at me," she warned and I could see her blush even in the dark.

"No," I said sternly, rising and pushing her lightly onto her back. I straddled her chest and rolled my balls over her rapidly hardening nipples. "Now I want to hear you say it again, all that stuff you said this morning."

"What?" she whispered. The wind was kicking up all around us and the air smelled like dirt. In the distance a clap of thunder sounded. Saylor squirmed underneath me. I knew how eager she was getting.

"Yeah, honey," I told her, enjoying her smooth skin. "I know you're wet and aching for it. Don't worry, I'm gonna take care of you." I let my hands wander everywhere. "I just want to hear you say it again. This is all mine."

"It is," Saylor moaned, "you know it's yours."

"I know, Say. I still want to hear the words come out of your sweet little mouth."

"It's all yours, Cord. My heart, my body. I want you with everything I am. It might even be love. No, I *know* it is. And I don't give a shit if anyone thinks it's too soon or impossible. It is."

The thunder grew closer and I pushed her tits together, trapping my dick between them. Her eyes glittered in the dark as she watched me get off. She continued to twist underneath me and I knew how badly she wanted me inside her.

"Soon, Say," I promised, squeezing her tits around my dick as I let it rule me, finally coming in a mighty spurt all over her chest.

"Oh fuck, baby. Fuck, that's good." I shuddered and let it all spill out in a slippery pool. She giggled a little as I rubbed my own semen over her chest.

"Think that's funny?" I grumbled as I pulled her skirt down over her hips. I ran my tongue over her belly and started to go lower but she shied away.

"Cord, wait."

I bent my head and darted my tongue out, teasing her clit. She was wet as water. I smiled and teased again, enjoying her little gasp.

"What?" I asked innocently, sliding her skirt down further.

Saylor was up on her elbows. "It's just…I'm laying here on the roof of a university building completely freaking naked-oh shit! Holy shit Cord, that feels amazing!"

As soon as she uttered the word 'naked' I buried my face between her legs and shoved my tongue straight into her hot center. She let out a small moan and kicked her skirt and panties the rest of the way off so she could throw her legs open. I grasped underneath her bare ass and lifted her a little so that I could reach deeper. I pulled back a bit and teased her, darting my tongue in and out so that I was putting the faintest playful pressure on her most sensitive spot.

Saylor cursed incoherently and gripped my shoulders. I raised my head.

"You want me to stop?"

"No," she whined.

I pushed a finger inside. Damn this girl was sexy. She fairly dripped at the snap of my fingers and came quick as lightning.

"What do you want?" I asked quietly. "Tell me, Say. Tell me your every insane fantasy and I'll do it all."

She grabbed my head with both hands and pushed my face between her legs. "Just finish me, Cord. Please, or I'll fucking scream."

"Yes, ma'am," I grinned and then got her done with my tongue while she bucked and trembled.

She moaned my full name once and then was quiet, just lying there and keeping her head turned away. I stroked her hair.

"You okay?"

"Yes," she whispered and then rolled over, burying her face in my chest.

"You want to go home?"

"With you?"

"Of course. Night is just getting started."

Saylor started pulling on her clothes. She seemed a little off balance but I let it go, giving her a few inches of space.

"Cord?" She'd gotten her skirt back on and her shirt buttoned. Her voice sounded a little sad, almost uncertain.

"Saylor," I answered, zipping up my pants and waiting.

She hugged me fiercely, surprising me with her strength. Then she let out a little sigh and rested her head on my shoulder.

"My girl," I whispered, kissing her and tightening my arms around her body.

"I am," she said with a note of stubbornness.

Before there was Saylor I never found myself wishing I knew what was going on inside a girl's head. I always figured it would involve all kinds of syrupy shit with unicorns and wedding dresses. But Say might be a little more complex than most girls. I wanted to hear about everything. Until I remembered that she'd already told me everything important.

"It is for me too," I blurted.

She moved back a few inches and peered up at me curiously.

"It is," I insisted and pushed her thick brown hair out of her face.

She didn't ask what I meant. She only closed her eyes for a few seconds and breathed deeply with a small smile on her face. I pulled her up to her feet.

"Let's go."

"If I can walk," she laughed, actually stumbling around a little unsteadily.

"You don't need to. Get on my back."

She was easy to carry. We were beside her car inside of a minute. She stretched and rubbed her belly as she climbed inside. "I'm hungry."

"Not me," I grinned, starting the car. "I just ate."

Saylor crossed her arms and blushed. "You're wicked."

I squeezed her knee. "But you knew that already."

She stared at me closely. "I know *you*."

"And?"

"You're incredible, Cordero."

God, she killed me. I didn't even have an answer for that which wasn't full of cheese and bullshit so I didn't say anything. We went to a Taco Bell drive thru and Saylor ordered a quesadilla and a soda. She raised her eyebrows when I ordered a dozen tacos.

"You planning on eating all that tonight?"

"Nah, I'll have a couple. The boys will eat the rest."

She smiled. "I love that."

"Tacos?"

"Not really. I love how you guys do everything in consideration of each other."

"That we do," I said soberly.

Creed was passed out on the floor next to the sofa. It was better than having him stare blackly into the darkness, mooning over shit that couldn't be helped now. Saylor stood over him, peering down curiously before she disappeared for a moment. When she returned she was carrying a blanket. I felt a strange tightening in my chest as she kindly covered my troubled brother.

Chase finished gulping down a couple of tacos and poked me in the arm. "That's a keeper," he said without a hint of mockery.

"Damn straight," I said, tossing the rest of the tacos in the fridge. Whenever Creed's haze wore off he was bound to be hungry as a bear.

"Guess who I saw today?" Chase spoke up as Saylor joined us, sucking on her soda.

"Who?" I asked, staring at her lips around that straw and remembering what they'd looked like around my dick. She saw me staring and flicked her tongue out.

Chase belched. "Our fine frat brother friends from the ring."

"Huh?" I tore my attention away from dirty things. "Where'd you come across those assholes?"

He shrugged. "At the gym. Two of them stood on either side of my bench and said if I showed up on their turf again they would fuck me up." He cracked up. "They actually said that. 'Turf'. Like this is West Side Fucking Story or some shit. Well, I stood up and flexed a few, letting 'em know I was not a man easily daunted by a pair of suntanned pussies. They snarled like beaten dogs and took off." He grinned confidently. "They won't be back, not unless they want some organs reconfigured."

I frowned. I didn't like this. Chase failed to realize guys like that weren't keen on being fair.

"Just watch out, okay?" I said carefully.

He scowled, pointing at Saylor. "Tell your man not to get all mother hen on me. I get enough of that from Big C."

"No," Saylor objected, hugging me. "I like his sweet side."

Chase gagged a little but then laughed. "Don't keep me up tonight, kids."

"We'll be quiet," Saylor soothed at the same time I snapped, "Get some fucking earplugs."

Chase sat down to play Xbox while Creed snored away on the floor. I stared at them. My brothers. More than that, the parts that made me whole. I'd long assumed that was all there'd ever be in the way of family, the three of us. No one else.

"Hey," Saylor waved a hand in front of my face. "Where are you? You're far away."

"No," I held her. "I'm right here, babe. With you."

Saylor unbuttoned my shirt and traced the words tattooed on my chest. "I should stop by Bray's. Let him know where I'm at and grab a few things." She bit her lip. "That is, if you still want me to stay."

"Course I want you to stay." I remembered something. "I got you a present while you were at work today. It's a surprise."

She looked stunned. "What kind of surprise?"

"Later. Let's go take care of your little errand and then I'll show you everything."

She gave me the eye. "I think I've already seen everything."

I was getting hard. Again. "Believe me, Say McCann," I told her, "you haven't."

17

SAYLOR

Cord wanted to come with me to Bray's place. Holding hands with him on the walk over there made me feel young and shy, as if we were on our first date or something.

"You're blushing," he observed. "You thinking about me?"

I held his hand more tightly. "I have to. You're my boyfriend."

"Hmm. What else does custom dictate you must do for me?"

"It means I am obliged to drag you to my mother's wedding this Saturday."

Cord stopped and stared at me. "What?"

"I know, right? She calls me this afternoon and drops the bomb that she's marrying Gary the Gnome at Rooster's Roast. It's on Saturday. I'm supposed to provide the floral arrangements. She likes daisies. The big kind of daisies." I was babbling. "I'll need to do some fast talking to get Ed to give me the night off but I'm sure Truly will cover for me."

Cord continued to peer at me in the most disconcerting fashion. "Rooster's Roast," he said slowly. "That dive off Main? Think it's run by an old Greek couple now?"

"Yeah," I shrugged. "Should be classy as hell, knowing my mom. I mean that with the most virulent element of sarcasm, by the way."

He seemed to be digesting everything. "It's in Emblem."

"Of course."

Cord cleared his throat. "Saylor, I don't exactly hang out in Emblem."

"Neither do I, Cord. Forget it, it's fine. My mom just wanted to meet you is all," I lied.

He snorted. "I think she's already met me. I'm pretty sure she showed up at my house and screamed that I was a worthless little dipshit after that business between us got around town."

I was surprised. "She did?"

"Sure" he nodded. "Then she offered to castrate me with some hedge clippers."

"Wow, I didn't know she cared. It kind of makes me feel warm and fuzzy. Did she scare the shit out of you? Please tell me yes."

Cord shrugged, smiling. "It was all right. My Uncle Chrome was around. He talked her down."

"Oh. How?"

He raised his eyebrows. "How do you think?"

My mouth fell open. "Are you telling me your uncle screwed my mother?"

Cord shrugged. "Pretty sure. After he disarmed her they disappeared into an old trailer. We could see the thing rocking from a block away."

"Gross. I am completely repulsed now. I am going to expectorate my undigested quesadilla all over that poor gecko on the sidewalk."

Cord laughed.

I shoved him. "You're bullshitting me. Tell me you're bullshitting me."

"Nah," he grinned. "I'm not that creative."

"Okay. Well now that we've gone to a place no one should ever visit again, what do you say? About Saturday?"

Cord sucked in a breath and looked skyward. "Is this important to you?"

"I don't know. No. Maybe." I was struggling. "Maybe I just wanted to walk in with some eye candy on my arm."

"Really?" he grinned.

"I don't particularly want to go back to Emblem. The very concept makes me so exhausted I want to curl up and take a six day nap. But going with you just makes the prospect a little less awful. When I'm with you, I feel...better."

Cord had to think I sounded like an idiot. I did sound like an idiot.

He stopped walking and turned to me, pulling my face to him and running his lips over mine. "What'll you give me?" he asked in a husky voice.

"What do you want?"

He ran his fingertip across my collarbone. I shivered.

"I want a lot of things," he responded glibly.

"Name a few."

He started rattling off on his fingers. "Your pussy, your ass, your tits."

I sighed. "Be serious, jackass. I'm talking about something deeper here."

Cord nodded eagerly. "Yeah, I feel pretty seriously and deeply about those things."

I squeezed my thighs together as his hand went underneath my shirt. "Damn, Cord. You're getting to me right now. You know that? Of course you know that."

He laughed. "Good. Need you to be wet and ready when we get home." He took my hand and pulled me along. "I'll go with you, Say. If it means something to you."

I stopped him. "Cord?"

"What?"

"Kiss me."

He did. He spread his hands across my lower back and pressed me firmly against him as his tongue invaded. It was the kind of kiss that electrified, inflamed and made me fervently believe every man on the planet ought to take lessons from Cord Gentry.

"Oh, stop it already!" Brayden's irritated voice pulled me away from Cord's lips.

He was leaning over his apartment patio with an irked frown. "Glad I didn't run over to hold the front door for you guys," he complained. "I'd have been standing there for a while."

I rolled my eyes at him and opened the apartment door as Cord followed closely. Millie was curled up in an overstuffed chair next to the television. Her eyelids fluttered but she merely sighed in her sleep. Brayden appeared and put a finger to his lips, as if we were too clueless to know that it was a good idea to keep quiet when someone was asleep in the same room.

The boxes we'd retrieved on that dreadful trip to Cali were stacked neatly by the front door. I rifled through them briefly, finding a few articles of clothing which I stuffed into my purse. After grabbing my toothbrush from the bathroom I was ready to go.

Bray was standing barefoot in the living room, appraising Cord with a stern look as if he was assuming the role of disapproving father. He shot a quick glance to his sweetly sleeping girlfriend and then followed us outside.

"You going to the wedding?" I asked as soon as he'd shut the door.

Bray blinked. "Yours? Am I the maid of honor?"

"Nooo," I poked him while Cord chuckled. "My mom is getting married on Saturday. To Gary the Gnome."

Brayden seemed impressed. "No shit. My invite must have gotten lost in the mail."

"Maybe your folks will be there."

"Well, my dad refers to your mom as 'that rancid bitch who fucked my brother over' so probably not."

"Right," I muttered. "Sometimes I forget who hates who."

My cousin looked from me to Cord and then back again. He seemed amused. "So do I!"

Brayden's eyes got wide behind his glasses when I threw him a rather irritated glare. He held his hands up. "Kidding. Totally kidding." He nodded to Cord. "Anyhow, what's the plan? You guys living together already? If I was the conventional type I might argue it's too soon."

I glared at him. "If I was the sensitive type I might argue that I can figure it out for myself."

Cord piped up. "And if I was the manly type I might argue that I actually have an opinion about all this."

"You do?" Bray gasped in mock surprise. "And what is it? Tell me, Cordero Gentry, what exactly are your intentions towards my dear cousin? Leave nothing out please." He crossed his arms as if he was settling in for a long explanation.

Cord wasn't daunted. He circled a firm arm around my shoulders and looked Brayden square in the eye. "I know how much Saylor means to you," he said quietly. "I know she's your family the way my brothers are mine. And even though you've seen the worst of me you shook my hand once anyway and offered friendship." Cord coughed and stepped up. "I won't fuck her over, Bray. I'll swear on whatever you want me to swear on."

Brayden blinked rapidly. He removed his glasses and pretended to swipe at imaginary tears. "That was beautiful. Really. Wow. I'm aghast."

"Bray!" I hissed but Cord laughed.

Brayden grinned at him. "I'll shake your hand again, buddy. If you're willing. In friendship."

I watched as the two men who meant the most to me abandoned old memories in favor of new ones. As they completed their little male ritual of affectionate back slapping, Millie opened the door. Her lovely face was still flushed from sleep.

"You guys are loud," she complained.

"Sorry, babe," Brayden called as she went to him, hugging him around the waist.

Cord stood behind me and rested his hands on my shoulders, massaging lightly. Millie noticed and winked at me.

"You ready?" Cord asked.

I was. I really wanted to be alone with Cord. I could feel how much he wanted to be alone with me.

"Sure. 'Night cuz. 'Night Mill." They started to turn back to their apartment when I called Brayden's name. "Hey, did you know that my mom and Cord's uncle had some kind of clandestine screw fest out in the desert?"

Brayden grinned. "Of course I knew that. I thought everyone knew that."

"Well," I grumbled, "*now* everyone does."

Cord practically pushed me back to his apartment. He had quick hands. They wandered over my ass repeatedly as he propelled me forward.

"What's your hurry?" I teased, though I was pretty damn eager too. As fantastic as our little rooftop exploits had been, there was just no other substitute for having all of him buried inside me. My underwear was soaked and I couldn't wait to get out of it.

"No hurry," he insisted, unlocking the door.

I could hear Creed snoring from the living room. Chase's light was on but his door was closed. As soon as we reached his bedroom Cord pulled his shirt off and I automatically licked my lips, staring at the muscular sculpture that was his chest.

"Oh yeah," he said suddenly, pulling a bag from underneath his bed.

I dropped my purse on the floor. "What's that?"

"Your surprise. Did you forget?"

"Yes," I sank down on the bed.

Cord wore the look of a shy little boy as he placed the bag in my hands. I discerned its flat shape and knew what it was immediately.

"I know it's not a real high end machine," he was explaining as I removed the box from the bag. "I would have just given you mine if it was any better. This way you can start writing again. Say? You all right? You hate it?"

"No," I whispered in disbelief, fingering the HP label on the box. "No, I don't hate it Cord."

"I had a little bit of money saved," he said a bit bashfully. I looked at the bruises on his body and understood what it cost him to bring any money in. A basic laptop like this ran about four hundred dollars these days. I knew that to most people it wasn't a fortune. To Devin it would have been pocket change. But to Cord it was a whole lot. And to me it was everything.

"Are you crying?" he asked, sounding baffled. "Shit, I get that your writing's a supremely personal thing. I'm not trying to push you or nothing-"

I silenced his words with my mouth. I kissed him hard and long, trying to let him know with my body what I couldn't quite express with words.

"Thank you," I finally managed when we broke for air. I knew Cord couldn't really afford this. But I also knew it would hurt him if I didn't accept his gift.

"You're welcome, babe," he said, smiling in a way that tore me in half just a little.

Gently I slid the box to the floor. I stood in front of him and traced his lips with my finger as he wrapped his arms around my waist. My forehead touched his.

"Make love to me, Cord."

He made a strange sound in the back of his throat and then reached underneath my skirt, pulling my wet panties away from my skin. "I will, baby. Over and over."

I took my own shirt off as he leaned back a little, watching. When I unhooked my bra and let it fall to the floor Cord took his dick out, holding the stiff entirety in his hand.

"So gorgeous," he groaned, staring hungrily at my naked body as I slid my skirt down. "Hotter than shit. Always were, Saylor, but more now than ever."

I kissed his shoulders, his chest. I bent down and took him my mouth, tasting the little drop of salt at the tip. Cord didn't want that though. He very gently pushed me away and then onto the bed, immediately lying on top of me.

"Too heavy?" he asked, settling firmly on my chest as his iron length throbbed on my belly.

"Just right," I answered. I pulled my knees up on either side of him and ran my hands over the smooth, muscled skin of his back.

He rocked back and forth on me a few times, just outside where I wanted him. Then he leaned over and started rifling around his bedside drawer. He found what he was looking for and ripped open the package with his teeth.

"Let me." I took it from him. He pushed himself up with his palms so I could roll the condom over his dick. I watched as he reached down and checked to make sure it was all the way on.

"What's wrong?" he asked when I moaned a little.

"I was just remembering how much I loved it last night, feeling you come inside me."

Cord was breathing hard. "We keep going like that and you'll wind up with a little Gentry growing in your belly."

"Maybe I *want* a little Gentry growing in my belly," I joked.

"Christ, Saylor," he groaned, burying his face in my neck. "You have no idea what a fucking turn on that is."

I kept it up, scarcely able to believe the words coming out of my mouth but liking what they did to him. It was just a game, but it got both of us even hotter. "Maybe one of these days I'll let you get me knocked up."

He slipped inside of me. "Maybe I already have."

"Could be." I bit my lip as he began to push harder. "You know, I felt you spilling out of me for hours last night. Fucking hours, Cord."

He was moving faster, harder, hitting the spot which would make me explode pretty soon.

"Keep talking, Say."

"I love the hot feel of you." I was beginning to pant as the wave started to carry me along, rising ever higher before it would crash mightily and take me with it. "One of these days, Cord, I want to feel part of you growing inside me. I love you that goddamn much."

"I will, honey. Shit, not tonight. But I will. I'm gonna fuck that tight little pussy until I make a set of triplets inside you. How would you like that?"

I was close, so damn close. "I like it. I want it. I'm coming, Cord. Go harder! Fuck, go harder!"

In the back of my mind I realize we were once again making a ton of noise. But other than dimly hoping Chase had found some earplugs, I didn't care a whit. Cord grimaced and let out a roar as he came. When he collapsed into my chest I kissed his sweaty head.

"Are triplets hereditary?" I laughed.

"Probably," he answered, absently kissing my right breast. "We're the only set I know of in the family, but my grandfather was a twin. There's a few more pairs of those scattered on the ragged branches of the Gentry family tree." He pulled the condom off and tossed it on a nearby trash can. He shook his head. "You keep it up, Saylor, and you really might wind up with a whole litter of Gentrys kicking around inside you."

I tried to imagine what it would be like, to marry Cord and have his children. I'd never thought about such things before, not with anyone. Witnessing the sad demise of my own parents' marriage and their rather lackluster take on parenthood had left me a little soured on that version of 'Happily Ever After'.

"You have a weird look on your face," Cord noticed, relaxing back on the bed, splendidly naked.

"Do I?"

He nodded, then reached over and tapped my head. "There's a lot going on there. Makes me wish I had, what-do-you-call-it? ESP."

I settled against him, enjoying the combination of our flushed, sweaty skin. "You don't need Extra Sensory Perception. You can just ask."

"Okay. I'm asking."

I sat up on one elbow. I cleared my throat. I touched the letters on his chest.

He conquers who conquers himself.

"Come on, Say. Spit it out."

"All right. The only relationship I've ever had was Devin and that was…"

"A big fat fucking shit show," Cord finished with a frown.

"Yeah," I muttered. "You remember me in school, Cord. I guess I never really broke out of that shell. I was kind of a loner, didn't have too many friends."

"Neither did I."

I laughed. "Bullshit. Everyone in our class either feared you or wanted to fuck you. All three of you."

"I know," he yawned. "It was so lonely."

"Look, you wanted me to be serious."

"I know, baby. I'm listening."

I fidgeted. "The things I say to you, that's not just passion talking, Cord. That's me."

He didn't say anything. He just stared at the ceiling. It was excruciating. When he finally did speak, the words came gradually. They were difficult to hear.

"When I was pretty little, maybe six or so, I drank some bad water. It was summer, the morning after a thunderstorm, and there was some rainwater that had accumulated in a rusty old drum out back with the other garbage. Town had shut off our supply again, likely because the old man didn't pay the bill. We were so goddamn thirsty and all we could find was warm beer. Creed and Chase, they balked at that brown water, warned me not to touch it. But I was so desperate I didn't care. The taste was fucking awful. Wasn't long before I started vomiting. Must have been some nasty bacteria in there 'cause I didn't stop for days. I sweated it out on the floor of the trailer while my brothers sat beside me and cried. Christ only knows where the old man was. My mother, she didn't even know where *she* was half the time. But as I thrashed on the dirty, stinking floor, feeling like a tribe of rattlers were warring in my gut, she found me. She told my cousin, Declan, to get some bottled water. Then she held me all night, forcing me to drink a few sips at a time. Saylor, that was the only time I recall feeling anything like love come from either of my parents. And other than Creed and Chase, I'd never felt it much from anyone else. Until now."

I clutched at him, crying softly. Cord, however, was dry-eyed. He curled his strong arms around my body and kissed me tenderly.

"Go to sleep now, my beautiful girl. You've found my heart. This is real. It'll still be here in the morning."

I wrapped my arms around his broad chest. "Sweet dreams," I murmured.

Cord laughed lightly in the dark. "I don't dream, honey. Too much ugly shit mixed in. It can defeat you. Now get some rest while you can. Remember, I promised to screw you over and over again."

18

CORD

You can't do a thing about the places your subconscious takes you.

As Saylor sighed in her sleep with a sweet smile on her face I let myself sink into the luxury of oblivion. It dragged me back to Emblem.

The desert isn't like the woods. The ground is flat and the brush is sparse. There are only so many places to hide. It's even more difficult if there are three of you running together, frantically searching for someplace where the monster can't reach you. You can hear him howling, closing in, with your mother's blood already on his hands and his raging thirst to draw some of yours.

One of your brothers hesitates in the dark, among the scratchy creosote. He is desperate. You are all desperate. Your brother thinks maybe if you run in separate directions the beast at your heels will be confused. He will wear himself out as he always does, eventually. And then you might have the luxury of another sunrise.

All you need to do is wait it out.

Alone.

But you shake your head.

No. NONONO!

As one you are weak. As three you are strong. You need to stay together. But your other brother sighs and agrees that you should scatter. You listen to them scrabble towards opposite corners of the night. The monster still closes in, knowing the lay of the land even better than you do. He is older, stronger, and he has always been here. He shrieks your name and it is an awful sound. But you hesitate to move, wanting him to follow you instead of your brothers. You have already learned something important; as terrible as it is when his cruelty seizes you, it is pure agony when he hurts them.

He will not touch them.

You will not let him.

As he crashes your way, you veer off into the darkness at the last possible second. All the harsh things on the floor of the desert claw at your bare legs as you run but this doesn't stop you. This pain is nothing. However, the sudden shriek of anguish you hear is everything. He has found one of them.

With blind terror you stumble towards the sound of your brother's torment. Suddenly you remember some of the things your uncle taught you. A large rock nearly trips you but you are glad because you pick it up. The terrible sounds grow closer. Your voice begins to rise in a growl as you feel the nearing heat of him, the evil creature who gave you life. But tonight he will be surprised because you have something to show him.

You know how to be a monster too.

It is in your blood as well.

I awoke at the foot of the bed, my hand aching. I'd punched the floor in my sleep, my dreams forcing me to believe it was something else, someone else. Gingerly I flexed my fingers and determined nothing was broken.

My body was covered in sweat even though I could feel the air conditioner on full blast. The bed springs creaked and I looked over to see Saylor lying naked atop the covers, sleeping as soundly as she had been while I held her before drifting off myself. I pulled a cover gently over her body, glad that she didn't open her eyes. I couldn't touch her just now. I just fucking couldn't.

I yanked my boxers on and headed out the bedroom door. Except for the roar of the aging air conditioner and the faint disturbance of

Creed's snoring, the apartment was silent. I bent over the bathroom sink and ran the water. It was warm but I splashed it on my face anyway. I gripped the sides of the sink, feeling weak and trying to breathe through it. Nothing worked. I needed to be sick.

Saylor found me with my head in the toilet. "Cord?" I'd left the door open and she peered around the corner, a blanket covering her body. "You okay?"

I flushed the toilet and grabbed a bottle of mouthwash. "Fine. I'm fine, baby. Fuck."

She came softly into the room and knelt beside me. I spit the mouthwash into the sink and fell back against the wall. Saylor touched me.

"You're sweating. Food poisoning?"

I shook my head. "Hey, can you turn that light off?"

She sent the room into darkness, then pulled my head into her breast. She stroked my neck. "What is it?"

"Dreams," I whispered, pushing my face into the cool comfort of her skin.

Saylor knew when there shouldn't be any words. She merely held me for a long time, until the demons receded and I felt strong enough to carry her to bed.

I entered her gently and after she trembled her climax I released myself inside of her, just how she liked. As I held her in my arms I drifted away again.

This time there were no dreams. There was nothing sweet blackness until Creed crashed into something in the living room and screamed like a tortured banshee. I opened my eyes and cursed the stark rays of the summer sun that peeked between blinds.

Saylor had already slipped a yellow sundress on. She grinned at me with perky cheer.

"Good morning!"

I yawned wide, feeling my jaw crack. "Morning, beautiful."

Creed had slammed his ankle on an end table. He limped around, cursing the entire time. Chase was already shoveling that awful cereal down his throat. He held the spoon in the air, mocking.

"For a big guy you sure have a low pain threshold."

Creed glared. "Screw you, pretty boy."

Chase grinned broadly. "We're all pretty." He noticed Saylor. "Hey, can you cook, sweetheart?"

I grabbed two coffee mugs and handed one to Saylor.

"No," she answered pleasantly, "can you?"

Chase grumbled into his cereal bowl. Creed bumped me out of the way, trying to get to the coffee pot.

"Last thing I remember I was eating chicken and wondering which of the fine ladies sitting at the bar would invite me inside first. Woke up with my face in the carpet, and not the nice kind of carpet."

He looked at Saylor and frowned slightly.

"We have a talk last night?"

She blinked at him innocently. "No. I don't remember even seeing you."

"Good," he nodded, looking relieved.

Creed disappeared into the shower a few minutes later and Chase grudgingly offered us bowls of his marshmallow garbage.

I enjoyed watching Saylor as she stirred copious amounts of sugar into her coffee and gave Chase a hard time. At one point he looked pensively at the two of us and pointed his dripping spoon in our direction.

"I should get one of these."

Saylor looked down at herself and then raised her eyebrows. "A dress?"

"No, wiseass. A girlfriend."

Saylor laughed. "Are you the boyfriend type?"

Chase kicked me. "Is he?"

I threw a spoon at his head and glared.

"He's doing a pretty good job so far," Saylor glanced at me, blushing.

My brother thought that was freaking hilarious. "He's doing good jobs all over you, huh? So," he leaned in, "you guys really go at it bareback?"

"Jesus," I sputtered. "You were listening?"

Chase stood and belched. "Well I'm not fucking deaf. What's the big deal?" He grinned nastily at Saylor. "And yes, multiple births are hereditary. So I hope you've got a whole lot of room in that there cavern, doll face."

I got angrily to my feet, knocking over my chair. Saylor, however, was simply giggling. She tugged at my arm.

"It's okay, Cord."

"Dipshit should keep his ears to himself," I muttered.

Chase scowled. "Now that doesn't even make an ounce of coherent sense, Cordero. You're getting pretty humorless in your old age. Do something with him, would you, Saylor? I'm going to the gym."

As Chase shoved a baseball cap on his head I remembered something.

"Not so sure that's a good idea. You know, you going to the gym alone after the trouble you had yesterday."

My brother waved a hand. "Because I always let a few momma's boy punks with chin pubes dictate my movements, right? I'll be back by lunch, unless my pussy hunt proves successful. Then I'll be back by dinner. You working tonight, Say? I'm in the mood for chicken again."

"Yeah, Chase. See you later."

I shook my head as he whistled and jogged out the front door.

Saylor wanted to head back to Bray's and spend some time sorting through her boxes before work. She swung my hand as we walked in the shade towards her cousin's apartment.

"After all," she sighed. "I can't just leave all my crap sitting in their foyer. They only have a one bedroom apartment."

"We can haul it over to my place," I shrugged.

Saylor glanced up at me, blushing. "Oh, I wasn't hinting around that you ought to be the depository for me and my meager collection of garbage."

"Why not?" I made a grab for her ass and she squealed.

"It's broad daylight!"

I grabbed her anyway. "So what? You like it."

"A little. Okay, a lot."

"Anyway," I continued, thinking aloud, "you really deserve a place to sleep that's a little more permanent than Brayden's couch."

Saylor laughed. "Maybe I can crash with my mom and The Gnome."

"Or with me."

She stopped in her tracks. "What?"

I slid my hands over her. "If all this is really mine, I should be able to have it whenever I want, right?"

She blushed, shuffling a little. "What are you asking me, Cord?"

I pulled her to me and ran a finger over her lips. She closed her eyes briefly and shivered.

"I want to be with you, Say," I told her, reaching into the back of her dress and letting my hands travel down further over her silky skin, over the small of her back and into her panties. "I want to be with you all the time. Do you want to stay with me?"

"Yes," she whispered, pressing firmly against my body. "I want to stay with you."

I kissed the tip of her nose, then the corners of her mouth. "Good." I thought of my brothers for a second. Long term girls had never come up before. But if I knew anything about them they'd recognize Saylor was different. Somehow I'd known it all along. She was fucking permanent.

Saylor needed to get ready for work. I told her we could use the truck to haul all her stuff back to my place after she was done tonight. Before we kissed goodbye she looked at me a little incredulously.

"Cord Gentry," she shook her head, "where the hell did you come from?"

"Someplace ugly," I admitted, stroking her soft hair, "but it's all looking a lot nicer now."

As I walked back to the apartment alone I thought about what I was going to say to the boys about Saylor moving in. I was sure Chase wouldn't give a shit but Creed might take a step back. I caught him as he was coming out of the shower and blurted it out. He looked at me and raised his eyebrows sky high.

"For good?"

"I sure as hell hope so."

"All right, then," he nodded, looking wistful. "All right, she's welcome here if you're sure she's what you want."

"She is," I answered.

"Damn," my brother shook his head with a grin. "Must be nice."

I had a lot of energy and nothing constructive to do with it. I lifted a little out on the patio but the heat was fucking ridiculous. Ten minutes out there and I was soaked with sweat so I jumped in the shower.

When I got back to my bedroom I looked around. I didn't have much. I might never have much in the way of money and shiny stuff. I knew Say wasn't real keen on the idea of me fighting and suddenly it seemed like a crappy way to earn a little green. Last night when we'd climbed to the top of the university art museum, she'd said some things that got me to thinking. I wasn't at all convinced that I belonged in a classroom like Saylor suggested. But once upon a time, drawing used to give me a fair amount of peace when I needed it. It was something like how I imagined Saylor's writing was to her. My cousin, Declan, bounced around doing ink for a living. He was the one who'd gotten the three of us done a few years back when he'd dropped in out of nowhere and stayed with us a while. He'd been impressed by my centaur sketch and suggested that I give him a call if I ever wanted to take up the trade, saying he would show me the ropes. I might do that now. I just might. I'd heard he was somewhere around the way of Emblem. Maybe when I headed down there this weekend with Saylor I ought to look him up.

I felt a little sick over the sudden memory of my hometown. My mind's eye saw the high fences of the prison, the desolation of the outlying desert where I'd once scrounged out a childhood. I hated going back there. But I didn't have it in me to turn Saylor down, especially not after she'd looked at me with such earnest shyness and said what it meant to have me by her side. It was time to put away the past and maybe in an odd way that meant revisiting it. I could handle it.

With nothing else to do at the moment I started cleaning the hell out of the apartment. Dirt was a thing with me. Chase liked to tell me I was 'OCD on a stick' and that might be true, but I couldn't handle filth, mostly because for so many years that was all I saw when I looked around.

After a few hours of solid elbow grease I was pretty pleased with the results. I'd heard Creed wander out some time earlier, mumbling about going downtown for some sheet music. If any one of us had real talent for anything, it was Creed. I hadn't been bullshitting when I told Saylor he could be famous with that voice of his, if only he'd scrape the rusty paint off his heart and let people hear a thing or two.

My stomach growled and I realized it had been a while since I'd eaten. I grabbed a banana from the kitchen and felt myself smiling as I unpeeled it, thinking of Saylor's mouth on my dick. It was a nice thought. As I chewed I considered heading down to Cluck This and coaxing Say into a few stolen moments somewhere quiet. I knew she would. Saylor might act a little shy sometimes but there was a whole lot of dirty in that girl. It made me love her even more.

Love.

Now there was a word that hadn't crossed my mind a whole lot over the past twenty two years. Of course I loved my brothers. But we didn't exactly run around squawking about it all the time.

Creed banged his way through the front door as I was scrubbing the kitchen floor.

"What the hell are you doing?" he bellowed.

"Using your toothbrush to clean dirt out of the grout," I answered with glee.

Creed dropped the bag he was carrying and made like he was going to knock me on my back. I rolled out of the way, laughing.

"I'm just screwing with you."

He glared at me and opened the fridge. "So that's not my toothbrush?"

"No," I smiled. "It's Chase's."

Creed didn't find anything worth scavenging in the fridge. He closed the door. "I guess he hasn't noticed yet."

"He hasn't been home."

Creed glanced at his phone. "It's almost six. Wasn't he supposed to be back by now?"

I was on the verge of issuing some flippant remark about our brother's unending quest for pussy when a wave of disquiet washed over me. Creed was looking at me curiously.

"What?"

"Nothin'. He tell you about those shitheads giving him a hard time at the gym yesterday?"

"I heard you guys talking about it. He would have called if he ran into trouble." Creed was beginning to sound uneasy though. There were scientists out there who have devoted a lot of energy trying to prove there was some sort of sensory connection between siblings who began life together. Once, when Creed busted his wrist falling through the rotted floor of an old barn, I swear I felt a flash of pain in that instant even though I was three blocks away and knew nothing about what happened for a good hour.

Creed was already calling Chase's phone. He seemed unsurprised when it went straight to voicemail. My brother looked at me for a long, silent moment.

"Yeah," I nodded, already heading out the door. "Let's go."

19

SAYLOR

If I had any friends they might have said I was crazy. It wasn't too long ago I'd crawled over the state line bruised and violated by a man who'd said he loved me. Those friends I didn't actually have might have argued that it was too soon, that I hadn't really dealt with the trauma I'd experienced, or that I was mistaking sex for love. Finally, these imaginary friends might have thrown up their pretend hands and scolded me for choosing to overlook a damaging afternoon that ended in a dirty garage six years ago.

But I didn't have friends. I only had Brayden, my pseudo brother who seemed to understand that Cord wasn't perfect but he was far from a villain. Most importantly, Cordero Gentry was more than what I wanted. He was what I needed

Bray was home earlier when I'd rolled in fresh out of Cord's arms and practically singing. He'd just stopped by to grab something he'd forgotten. Millie was already gone, which I was sorry for. I suddenly wanted to gush all about love and sex to someone who didn't have the same eyes as me. It was too much like looking into a mirror.

"What's up, Say?" Bray asked and his tone implied he already guessed.

I smiled. "Everything."

Brayden went cross eyed. "Are you giggling? Nah, Saylor McCann isn't a giggler. She's an astute observer of life's foibles and circumstances."

"She's a giggler when she's happy."

My cousin sighed and looked at me, shaking his head a little. "This is a big deal, isn't it?"

I was honest. "I think so. Yeah, it is."

He smiled. "Good."

Brayden merely nodded when I briefed him on my conversation with Cord. I was glad. Glad he didn't press me all the ways my fantasy audience would have. My cousin kissed me on the cheek and set off on his day while I got ready for work.

Truly was in a state when I got there. Ed had been giving her crap about her looks, telling her she needed to comb over her hair so the shaved part of her head didn't show.

"Bastard's wound so tight he likely shits out diamonds," she hissed as she swiped a table with a clean rag. Her deep southern drawl made everything she said slightly more hilarious.

"Not diamonds," I said, filling the salt shakers. "Quartz maybe."

"Cubic fucking zirconia," she laughed.

I figured now was as good a time as any to ask her for a favor. She listened with a bemused expression. Truly was really quite beautiful, a slightly smudged fairy tale princess come to life with big breasts and a whole lot of *y'all*'s swinging around.

"Don't blame you one bit, sugar," she grinned, propping a knee up on the table as she sorted a stack of menus. "He's a mighty fine slice of manhood."

"Can't argue with that," I grinned, feeling a rush of heat surge between my legs as I indulged in a brief memory of the ways Cord had acquainted me with the aforementioned manhood.

The crowds were typical but they made the hours pass quickly. I remembered Chase's comment about dropping by for dinner and by five I was scanning the door pretty faithfully for any hint of the Gentry brothers.

Finally, when I looked up as a shadow fell across the door, I saw

Cord scanning the crowd impatiently. A few of the girls sitting by the front noticed him and sat up a little straighter. I was getting used to the flush of pure pleasure that rolled through me at the sight of him. I waved him over with a smile.

Cord cut through the crowd in a few quick strides. I collided with him, feeling the shock of his hard muscles against my body. But when I moved to collect a kiss I saw he was glancing around in a troubled manner.

"What's wrong?"

He shrugged. "Probably nothing. Just can't get a hold of Chase. He hasn't been in contact since he took off for the gym." Cord gestured out the window to the austere gray exterior of the Western Fitness Gym, which was across the street. "He walked over, didn't take the truck. We checked the gym but he wasn't around. Creed's taking a closer look. He hasn't been by here, has he?"

"No," I shook my head.

Cord looked disappointed. He absently rubbed my arms and looked around as if his brother could possibly materialize among the greasy chins. I tipped his chin up, meeting the tense look in his clear blue eyes.

"Hey," I said gently, "I'm sure he's fine. Maybe he found some action, just like he's always hoping."

"Yeah," Cord coughed. "Maybe. Look at me, chasing after my grown brother. It's just..." Cord sighed and ran a hand through his hair, "For a smart guy, Chase is missing a few kernels of wisdom. The fight or flight sense that's gotten me out of trouble more than once? He doesn't have it. He needs some looking after, you know?"

I tried to soothe him, holding him close and kissing his neck. Cord threaded his hands through my hair, sought my mouth and kissed me firmly. "Can't wait to have you again," he whispered in my ear as I pressed my hips into his. He was so hard. I felt him against my stomach.

He kissed me one more time and backed away with reluctance. "Let me go haul that jackass out of whatever warm hole he's crawled into," he laughed, abruptly grabbing me, lifting me in his arms, his breath hot in my ear. "Then later I'm gonna crawl into you."

Cord stole a quick feel of my breasts and then retreated. I hadn't realized what a spectacle we'd created until I saw how many heads were raised, eyes wide. Truly flashed me the thumbs up sign from where she watched behind the bar. I bit my lip and she chuckled.

As I grabbed a broom to sweep away a litter of French fries, I thought about how deeply in tune the Gentry brothers were with one another. It wasn't something you saw often among grown siblings, particularly men. But then I remembered the awful story of the pool and how there were likely a hundred others I hadn't yet heard. The brothers were bound by blood and by tribulation. It was a near certainty that their efforts to protect one another had gotten them out of Emblem alive.

I put the broom down, feeling suddenly uneasy about Cord's worry. He'd been raised with everyday danger. As a result he'd grown an instinct for it. Without even meeting Devin he'd known what a poor idea it was for me to confront him, no matter what kind of peace had been promised.

If Cord was anxious about his brother's lack of contact there might be something to that concern. Ed appeared and snapped his fingers as a warning against idling around. I returned to work, briefly forgetting everything else but the immediate demands of the dinner crowd. As the sky darkened and I stood before a family of eight, dutifully taking their complicated order, I heard sirens in the background. The sirens seemed irrelevant to me until they came closer. They arrived screaming in my ear and with garish flashing lights that seemed to come from all directions. They parked in front of Western Fitness Gym and were joined by others.

As I went to the window, a knot of incoherent fear rising in my belly, a pair of lanky guys spilled through the door. I saw them gesturing to the commotion across the street and approached them.

"Do you know what happened?"

They weren't the sort of guys used to being approached. They were eager to talk to me. "Some poor dude got laid out in the alley behind the gym."

"Who?" I whispered.

They looked at me curiously. "Well, I don't know *who*," one of them said.

The other one piped up. "The way he looked, I doubt his own mother would recognize him."

I heard Truly calling to me as I dropped my apron on the floor and darted outside. The traffic light took forever to change. I ran across the street, knowing there was no real reason why my heart had painfully lodged in my throat. A crowd of gawkers were clotted together on the sidewalk. Officers half-heartedly tried to keep them back for the sake of the poor guy who was being loaded onto the stretcher.

A tall man with a ratty beard held his phone up over everyone's heads, obviously recording to his sick voyeuristic heart's content, as if the human tragedy in front of us was staged for his entertainment. When I shoved him and knocked his arm down in a fit of anger he gazed at me in disbelief.

"Bitch," he swore as his phone clattered to the concrete.

By muscling my way through the throngs and ducking under the arm of a weary cop I managed to get within a few feet of the scene. The stretcher held the shape of a man. A muscled arm rose to touch the bloodied face it was attached to. Those boys who had rolled into Cluck This might have been right. His own mother might not have recognized him. But I did. He looked so very much like someone I loved.

A middle aged woman in a paramedic jacket blocked me from moving forward.

"I know him," I gasped as the stretcher was lifted into the ambulance. "Chase!"

I saw him roll slightly at the sound of my voice but one of the paramedics gently righted his body before climbing into the ambulance after him.

The female paramedic was gesturing to one of the police officers.

"This girl says she knows him." She patted me on the shoulder. "He didn't have any identification," she explained.

The young officer, who looked like he might have been on the job for all of about ten days, stood there and waited for me to speak.

"His name is Chase Gentry. Please, is he going to be okay?"

The officer didn't acknowledge my question. "You family?"

"No, I – I'm a friend. Oh my god, I need to call his brothers."

The officer was already speaking into his radio, repeating the name 'Chase Gentry'.

The paramedic, who seemed the motherly sort, began ushering me away. "Your friend was apparently jumped in the alley behind the gym. He has some head injuries and possibly some internal bleeding."

"Where are they taking him?" I asked as the doors to the ambulance closed.

"St. Luke's," she answered, squeezing my hand. "If you know how to contact his family, please do so immediately." Then she left me among the murmuring crowd and climbed into the front seat of the ambulance.

I stared as the vehicle began screaming and pulling away. Part of my mind kept insisting this wasn't real, that the bloody man I'd seen on the stretcher couldn't be the strong, wisecracking Chasyn Gentry.

Except he was. He absolutely was.

My legs felt as if they wouldn't support me so I sank down onto the curb, pulling my phone out so I could say the most difficult words I'd ever had to speak.

"How bad?" Cord asked in a flat voice.

"I don't know," I whispered. "They've taken him to St. Luke's."

I heard Cord repeat the news to Creed. I heard Creed's cry of anguish.

"I'm going to meet you there," I said, rising and preparing to cross the street. "Cord, I'm sorry. I love you."

He had already hung up.

When Ed told me I had no business leaving in the middle of the dinner rush I told him to go fuck himself. I watched dispassionately as his jaw dropped and then pushed past him so I could grab my purse from the lockers. I figured I probably didn't have a job anymore but I didn't give a damn. Truly held a comforting hand out to me and I squeezed it briefly before leaving.

"Let me know if you need anything," she said, and I knew enough about her to realize she didn't offer such things lightly.

My mind was a roaring tornado on the short drive to the hospital. I worried for Chase. I'd begun to see Chase and Creed as more than Cord's brothers. They were my friends and I cared for them. My fears weren't just limited to Chase's injuries though. When Cord came barreling through Devin's door and went straight for the bastard's throat, I saw how he'd lost the struggle in that moment to contain the rage that threatened them all. What would the pain his brother had suffered do to him? More importantly, what would he and Creed do in retaliation?

When I reached the hospital, Chase had already been whisked somewhere into its antiseptic depths. Since I wasn't family, the woman at the front desk merely gave me a sympathetic smile and told me to have a seat. I couldn't. I stood in front of the building, knowing Cord would come roaring up there any moment.

The old Chevy shuddered with a painful screech as Cord braked to a halt. Creed spilled out first, his rugged face on the verge of collapsing into tears.

"You know anything?" he asked me.

I shook my head.

A young guy in a beige polo with the name of the hospital emblazoned on the front ran up to Cord and started yelling about he couldn't park there.

Cord glared at him, then threw the keys over. "Do whatever the fuck you like with it," he growled.

I tried to hold him but he seemed made of wood. He was looking grimly at the building.

"Did you see him, Saylor?"

"Only for a second," I said, touching his cheek. "He was on the stretcher. He looked pretty bad." Cord's blue eyes closed as if they were trying to blot out terrible things.

Creed had already headed inside. I put my hand on Cord's back and moved him towards the door.

"It'll be okay," I told him, trying to pull him close. He gave me a look of sharp incredulity.

"How the hell do you know that?"

I couldn't answer because I really didn't know. It was just something you were supposed to say when things looked awful.

Creed was already beside the triage station, talking to a doctor. A few police officers stood nearby. I hung back a little when Cord went to them. Whatever soft words the doctor uttered made his shoulders slump in a heartbreaking way. The doctor placed a comforting hand on Cord's shoulder. Cord didn't seem to feel it.

Creed stood a few feet apart. He was looking down a long corridor as the doctor continued to speak to Cord. There was a loud scuffle at my back as a little girl was brought in with a bandage around her leg. Her mother was shouting that the child had been bitten by a neighborhood dog. The little girl, who was only about five, looked up at me with grieved, perplexed eyes. I wanted to reach out to her. I wanted to tell her it was going to be okay. But Cord was right; how the hell did I know it would be?

I waited until the doctor headed down a long corridor, followed by the police officers. The Gentry brothers stood there in bleak silence. Cord didn't seem to notice the feel of my arms around him. An aging nurse approached us and ask if we would be more comfortable waiting in the more private area, for those whose loved ones were in surgery.

It was a slow, silent walk down a series of long hallways. Creed kept apart from us, his eyes on the ground. I glanced up at Cord a few times. He looked lost.

"Surgery?" I finally asked in a gentle voice when we reached a room filled with comfortable chairs and a scattered collection of grim-faced people.

Cord nodded stiffly and sat down. "Yeah, they think there's been some kind of internal rupture so they hustled him in there. His head's also messed up, a bad concussion. I don't know what else yet." He swallowed painfully. "I don't know, Say."

Creed let out a cough and held his head in his big hands. "Who?" he moaned.

I didn't miss the way Cord's jaw set. "Later, Creedence," he said in a voice that frightened me. It spoke of blood and revenge.

Cord leaned over and exhaled raggedly. I rubbed his back helplessly. He came to life all of a sudden and wrapped his arms around me tightly, burying his head in my breast. Creed watched us with bleak, hooded eyes. I gathered Cord's powerful body in my arms as best I could and ignored the attention we were beginning to attract.

I kissed him and said things with the word 'love' repeatedly, hoping it made some small difference as he cried softly.

20

CORD

I was unaware of time as we sat in that waiting room. Creed sat across from me doing nothing, saying nothing. Every so often our eyes would meet and I saw the mirror of my own wrath. The furious Gentry blood that I'd long struggled to control was boiling over. When I thought of the men who had nearly killed my brother I thought of murder. Creed did too. I was sure of it.

Saylor squirmed in my lap and held me together as best she could. Every so often she would grab me tightly, as if on some level she was aware of the conflict in my soul. It would all have to wait though.

Police officers came and went. Chase hadn't been real aware when they'd questioned him upon arriving at the hospital. He knew he'd been attacked. He didn't know who had attacked him. Haltingly, I told the officers of the threats by the fraternity boys.

"Do you know them?" frowned one of the officers; a thin, dark-skinned man whose sharp eyes were a contrast to his weary, overweight partner.

"Seen 'em around," I grumbled, eliciting a harsh glare from Creed. If we started doing some talking about the fighting rings then Chase wouldn't be the only one laid up in the hospital.

"I see," said the officer with a flat expression that told me he understood that I wasn't going to say much.

Doctors also came. We were told Chase had a concussion, most likely from being kicked in the head. His injuries indicated the likelihood of multiple assailants, which I had already figured since my brother was no slouch in a fight. It had to have been an ambush.

The surgeon, Dr. Nguyen, didn't pull any punches. Chase's internal injuries had required the removal of his spleen.

"Spleen?" Creed asked. "So that's no big deal, right? Don't people get that shit removed all the time?"

Dr. Nguyen spoke softly, kindly. "You are likely thinking of the appendix. The spleen is more significant. Although it is completely possible to live a normal life, its absence may make it more difficult for the body to fight off certain infections."

"Oh," Creed slumped. He looked away, blinking rapidly. Saylor reached over and took his hand but if he noticed he gave no sign.

I swallowed. "Can we see him?"

"Soon," the doctor nodded. "He is in recovery now and from there he will be moved to a room where we would like to keep him through the weekend." He paused. I thought about what a crappy job this must be, to inform people about terrible things that had happened to the ones they loved. "He is really quite fortunate," he continued. "The severity of the beating he took could easily have resulted in far worse injuries."

I guessed what he was hinting at; Chase was lucky to be alive. Saylor thanked the doctor and asked if we could be informed immediately when Chase was ready for visitors. Creed still stared blankly at the wall and I sank back into my chair, pulling Say down with me.

As Saylor's soft arms surrounded me again, I tried to focus on the feel of her. It was safer to do that than to stay with the seething rise of violence in my heart. Creed had already gone the other way. I could see it in his face. One word from me and he would charge the castle with everything he had. I held on to Saylor, trying to push the vicious shadows away. I wasn't ready to follow Creedence yet.

Saylor retreated at some point to call Brayden and let him know what had happened. Creed leaned forward and spoke my name.

"Think I'll give Gabe a call," he said and I knew why. Creed had already made up his mind that those college boys were the culprits. He had already decided what needed to be done. Gabe Hernandez, the sleazy point man in the world of underground gambling brawls, knew everyone. He would know where to find them.

"Wait," I answered, watching for Saylor. "Let's get him whole and get him home and then we can deal with whatever needs to happen next."

Creed shook his head. With his jaw clenched and his eyes icy he reminded me of someone far more frightening. How many times had I seen that same expression on my father just before he tipped over the side and into the madness? Benton was worse though; he liked going in that direction. It was what served him and kept him animated. Whenever I fought in the ring I struggled to control the satisfaction of the hit, the draw of blood. There was always a fear that I never really named but was still aware of. It was the fear that if I liked it too much then it would put me in the hole with generations of Gentrys. And then I wouldn't be able to climb out again.

"I'm not waiting long, Cordero," growled Creed. He meant he would go without me.

"We don't even know for damn sure who did it," I reminded him.

Creed glared at me and balled his fists. "I know," he answered. "And you fucking know so don't pull that shit with me."

Saylor walked quietly back into the room and I straightened, choosing not to answer Creed for the moment. Say took my hand and sat down.

"Bray and Millie want to know if there's anything they can do. I told them I didn't think so but they want you guys to know they're available for whatever you need."

"I only need one thing," Creed said quietly, his eyes still squarely on me.

Saylor glanced at him uneasily. She seemed on the verge of saying something but then a nurse came into the room and called for the family of Chasyn Gentry.

Creed walked ahead of us and I could read the coiled rage in every step he took. He kept a stony expression in the elevator and didn't say a word. Say hung back a little when we reached the room. She thought it would be a better idea if I went in without her. Creed was already inside.

Saylor ran her hand over my cheek. "I'll be right here."

I'd spent so many hours expecting the dreaded worst that anything short of catastrophe would have been a relief. Chase had a nasty lump on his head and his right cheek had suffered a bad slice that must have bled a lot and was being held together by stitches and tape. His nose was obviously broken and an ugly collection of bruises showed on his face. Creed was kneeling beneath the IV drip and I could tell from his ragged breathing that he was struggling mightily to control himself.

"Hey, little brother," I said softly as I pulled a metal chair over to his bedside.

Chase opened a blue eye and blinked, trying to focus on me. "Don't start that shit," he warned, his voice dry and raspy. "I already get enough from Big C." He struggled to sit upright and pulled at his hospital gown. "Someone get this fucking handkerchief off me."

"Well," I joked, "it must not be too serious if you're already fretting over your wardrobe."

Chase flopped back into the pillows with a low moan. He tried to pull the gown off anyway and then noticed the IV attached to his arm. "How fucked up am I?"

"You've looked prettier," I admitted.

He looked down at his bandaged abdomen, the site of the surgery. "This sucks," he said with a scowl.

Creed spoke up, his voice low and toxic. "What do you remember?"

Chase grimaced slightly and tried to get comfortable. "Cops already asked me that. I lifted, I swam laps, showered and exited out the back. Then something like a train hit me and next thing I know there's lights everywhere and people taking fucking pictures."

Creed's eyes had narrowed to icy blue slits. "Did you see them?"

Chase shook his head and then made a face as if the small movement hurt. "Naw, I didn't see shit. Nobody gave me any crap at the gym. The hit just came out of nowhere."

Creed bent his head and Chase tried to reach over and touch him. "Hey," he said gently. "Creedence, it's all right. Doc says I might even live a few more days."

I felt helpless as my brothers grasped hands like two little kids. Chase was doing his best to be valiant but I could read his pain and I couldn't do a damn thing about it. Once, when Benton was spinning out of control in a drunken fury, he'd turned squarely on Chase. Chase had faced him down, spitting, which brought a roar from the crazy bastard. Chase knew he'd gone too far and shrank back against the far wall as our mother watched, glassy eyed, from a chair in the kitchen. Knowing that Chase was about to face the brunt of that wrath, I stepped between him and our father, taking the blow myself. It was a kick to the stomach and it knocked me flat. Benton might have killed us both if Creed hadn't circled from behind and hit him across the back with a tequila bottle. It was just one battle of many although it was one of the last, as our father began to realize that the boys he'd created wouldn't be boys for much longer.

Chase tried to keep up a stream of chatter but quickly became visibly pained and exhausted. Eventually a nurse dropped in to take his vitals and administer pain meds. I gently tucked my brother in as he rolled to his side and closed his eyes.

I saw Creed settling into a chair. He flipped on the television and turned the volume low. "Look, I'm gonna hang out and keep an eye on him. That cool with you?"

"Course it's cool. Why don't we take shifts? They've got visiting hours and shit that we can't do anything about but at least we can be here as much as possible."

Chase snorted from the bed. "I can hear you guys," he complained. "And I'm not a fucking infant. This is no big deal."

But I looked at the bandages and noted his wince of pain. No, we weren't going to leave him alone with it. Creed looked me in the eye and nodded, silently telling me he was putting vengeance under wraps for now. Only for now.

I found Saylor waiting patiently on a chair in the hall. She gave me a relieved smile and held up my keys. Last time I'd seen them was when I'd thrown them in the direction of some dipshit who ordered me to move my truck. While I was in with Chase, Say had gone downstairs and learned the hospital valet service had parked the truck in one of the outer lots. She lifted the keys when they weren't looking.

"Thanks, babe," I said, oddly touched that it had even occurred to her. I was going to toss the keys in to Creed but thought better of it. I wasn't real sure where his head was at and didn't want to risk him going off on some fool's mission to avenge our brother.

"You hungry?" Say asked me, drawing an arm around my waist.

"Yeah, I could eat," I admitted. "What time is it?"

"Noon. We've been here at the hospital about sixteen hours."

"Jeez, Say. You know, you didn't have to hang out here the whole time."

She looked hurt. "Of course I did. Anyway, come on. I'll buy you a plate of wretched cafeteria food."

We grabbed a couple of quick sandwiches and brought some food up to Creed. As Chase slept softly, Saylor crept over and put a gentle hand on his head. Creed had his mind made up that he was going to hang around all afternoon. He didn't see a reason why we both needed to be there. We compromised that he would stay on until five. Then I'd return and stick around until visiting hours were over. It went without saying that we weren't calling anyone back in Emblem.

I hovered over Chase's bed for a moment and felt something sharp twist in my guts. It was a bad feeling, similar to the way I'd felt a second before barreling through that apartment door in California.

"Send it to the dungeon," I muttered aloud, partly to Creed and partly to myself. Creed only gave me a flat look while Saylor's face was curious.

I drove back to the apartment in Say's car with one hand tightly around the wheel and the other hand on my girl. She leaned her head into the seat and watched me with tired eyes.

The apartment was quiet in a terrible way. It was suddenly an awful thing to be there even for a few minutes without my brothers. Saylor closed the door behind her and wrapped me in a hug while I allowed myself the luxury of touching her everywhere. She ran her hands over my back and kissed me tenderly. I let out a shaky sigh and wandered into the kitchen to get a glass of water. As I stood there in front of the sink, rapidly swallowing warm water from the tap, I was all right. I was in control. I would damn well stay that way.

Then I saw a box sitting on the table. It was stupid. It had cartoonish pictures of multicolored marshmallows with absurd faces. But the sight of Chase's box of cereal sitting there all forlorn cracked me the fuck open. I threw my glass against the wall and drove a furious fist into the center of the kitchen table. Saylor gasped as the cheap piece of shit furniture broke right down the center.

"Cord!"

I kicked at the pieces savagely, my hand throbbing from the force of punching the table.

"No!" She had launched herself into my arms. "Stop it!" The force of her body was enough to propel me backwards slightly and I wound up with my back against the fridge. Then, before I could fend her off, Saylor did something unbelievable. She got to her knees and wildly tore at the snap of my jeans as her hands yanked the fabric down. My dick was hard as steel before she even got her mouth all the way around it. I wound my hands all through her hair as she licked my balls, cupping each one in her mouth. I used her hair to cover my dick and wanted to come in the middle of that thick brown curtain but I knew that wouldn't be enough so I lifted her.

Saylor's jaw was set, her face obstinate. She knew I was battling and she was determined to pull me back to her side.

"I love you," she said stubbornly.

"Then love me," I answered, pushing her arms over her head and lifting her shirt. I went wild at the sight of her creamy body. I needed to use every fucking inch of it.

"Yes," she whispered as my mouth went to her breasts, my hands pushing inside her shorts. She strained against me, already wet. I got rid of it all; her shorts, her panties, the lacy black bra I'd ripped off her before. She kicked everything off into a corner and pulled my shirt over my head. Saylor pressed her palm against the words on my chest and pushed me back a little.

"This what you want?" I asked, lifting her onto the tiled counter as I spread her legs wide apart. "You want me to conquer you, baby?"

"Yes, it's what I want," she answered firmly and then sucked on my neck. She went at it hard, in a way that I knew would leave a mark, as if we were teens who needed to advertise our sexuality. It drove me berserk. I grabbed her ass, pulling her towards me, and her legs went tightly around my waist. When I carried her to the living room I was inside her, just barely, as she sucked the skin raw on my neck.

I fell back to the couch, Saylor straddling me. The fall of her weight pushed me in so deep I didn't think I'd ever find a way out, which was just fine. She let out a cry and her forehead bumped my shoulder.

"Ride me, Say. Ride me damn hard."

"Cord," she moaned as her body began to glisten with sweat. I licked the salty skin between her breasts as she pushed herself to a frenetic rhythm. A few times I was on the verge of shattering but I shoved it away. I shoved everything away; the fear and the rage of the past day, the certainty that more terrible things lay ahead. All the blackness that lapped at the edges of my heart and threatened to knock me down was gone when that girl screamed my name as her body shuddered on top of me.

"That's right," I clutched her, grabbing handfuls of her sweaty hair. "Who's fucking you, baby?"

"Oh god, you are!"

"No, honey. My name, Saylor. The whole fucking thing."

"CORDERO GENTRY!" she yelled and tightened around me so

hard I couldn't do a thing but yield, coming inside of her with furious gasps as she trembled and uttered a near painful cry.

Say collapsed a little, her head sinking to my chest. I gathered her in my arms and nipped at her neck in the gentlest way. She raised her head, pushing her hair back, her green eyes regarding me sorrowfully.

"Is it enough, Cord?"

I pretended not to know what she meant. "What, Say?"

"Me," she whispered. "Us. Is it enough for you?"

I kissed her lips briefly. "I don't want a damn thing to do with other girls since you came along."

She smiled vaguely. "That's nice. But it's not what I was asking."

I picked her up and headed for the bedroom. "Come on, let's get some rest for now."

The room was cool and dark. Saylor sighed but settled into my bed, rolling towards me. I held her and marveled at how we fit together, like lock and key. In that moment there was only the two of us and that's how I wanted it. She ran her fingers up and down my arm until I felt a small chill. I captured her mouth with mine and kissed her hungrily before pulling back.

"You need to shave," she observed.

I touched the thickening stubble on my chin. "You're right," I shrugged. "You love me anyway?" It was a flippant question but she took it seriously.

"So much, Cord."

"Good, then we're even."

"Are we?" she smiled. "Are you settling for a draw again?"

"Hush," I said, pulling her to my chest and yawning. "I need a few hours of shut eye here or else I'm gonna start hallucinating."

Saylor fell into an easy sleep. I watched her for a while as her long eyelashes fluttered on her cheeks. She looked so angelic it made my gut hurt. I planted a kiss on her forehead.

"I do, Say," I whispered. "So much too."

I figured she wouldn't hear me, but either she wasn't quite asleep or my voice seeped into her subconscious. A small smile broke out on her face and she tightened her hold on me.

Sleep should have come easily for me too. I needed it badly. The thought of doing anything more taxing than laying here next to Saylor almost made me groan aloud. Creed's grim face kept intruding. There was something else, too. I wanted to make them suffer, whoever hurt Chase. My fists clenched as I struggled with the itch to make someone bleed for the cowardly attack on my brother. I knew it would feel good to put the hurt out, the same way it had felt good to pound on Devin for what he'd done to Saylor. But I also knew what a thorny road that was. I'd seen too many of my kind walk it before. I didn't want to go. I wanted to stay here, in the arms of the girl I loved.

"It's enough," I whispered in her ear although I wasn't at all sure. She must have descended more deeply into her dreams because she didn't seem to hear me this time.

21

SAYLOR

I awoke to a buzzing noise and realized it was my phone. Cord was sound asleep next to me. I pulled a blanket around my naked body and padded into the living room, finding my purse on the floor where I'd dropped it hours earlier.

"Brayden," I sighed into the phone.

"Say. How is he? I called the hospital looking for information but they kindly said 'Tough shit, you're not family'."

Briefly I told Bray about Chase's injuries. I left out the increasing agitation I was sensing between the other two Gentry brothers. If Cord and Creed thought they knew who had attacked Chase, what would they do about it?

Bray repeated his offer. He said he was available in any way Chase or the boys needed. I told him I would get the message to them. The sound of my voice must have awakened Cord because he wandered into the living room, yawning and naked. He searched around the floor for a few seconds and then started pulling on his boxers.

I looked out the window, surprised to find bright daylight. The last twenty four hours had been so hectic and draining I'd lost all sense of time.

"It's five o'clock," I told Cord. He nodded, finding his phone and calling Creed as he walked back to the bedroom while talking quietly. By the time I followed him, he was done with the call.

"He was in a lot of pain," Cord said, coughing once and peering at me sadly. "They had to give him a higher dosage of meds to deal with it. And he also started running a fever. Could be nothing, but could be a sign of infection."

"I'm sorry." I held him. "Let's get you back there."

Cord wanted to know if I would mind driving Creed back. The truck was still at the hospital and he wanted to just keep it there until it was time for him to leave tonight when visiting hours ended. I also got the feeling he was trying to keep Creed as contained as possible.

"Besides," he grinned a little and grabbed me, running his hands down my legs, "I need you to come back here and keep my bed warm."

"I can do that," I answered, kissing him. I wasn't relishing the idea of spending time alone with sullen Creed but I brushed off the feeling.

Back at the hospital, Chase was flushed but sleeping soundly. Creed merely nodded when Cord asked him to return with me to the apartment. I paused over the prone form of the rowdy, sharply intelligent Chasyn Gentry and felt a surge of emotion as strong as if he were my own injured brother. This was immediately followed by a twitch of rage toward whoever was responsible for hurting him. I tried to imagine that feeling magnified a hundred times in the hearts of Cord and Creed. The notion made me shudder.

"You ready?" Creed asked me, a little sharply.

Cord bent down and kissed me. "Later, honey." He gave me a brief swat on my rear end. "Think about me."

"Couldn't stop if I tried," I told him. He stared down into my eyes for a long moment before Creed cleared his throat irritably.

It was already awkward as we walked down the corridor together and took the elevator to the ground floor. Creed stayed several feet away from me at all times and kept his head down while I struggled for words. Chase was easy; he was a goofier version of Cord. But Creed gave intensity a new meaning. I was sure there was a lot going on in his head. And I suspected I didn't want to know about it all.

"You hungry?" I finally asked brightly when we reached the parking lot.

He just gave me a mute blue-eyed stare.

I cleared my throat. "It's the dinner hour. You know, a time of day when people usually require some sort of sustenance. I thought-"

"Not hungry, Saylor," he cut me off, scowling as he tried to open the passenger door to my car and found it locked.

"Well, all right then, sunshine," I grumbled, unlocking the doors and starting the engine.

I searched the radio but there seemed to be a conspiracy of commercials on every station. I sighed and glanced over at my passenger. He took up a lot of room, even more than Cord. In fact he was an intimidating mountain of prickly muscle, all packaged in stony silence. It wasn't hostility, not exactly. But it wasn't pleasant either.

As I navigated the streets of Tempe I decided to overcome Creed's aloofness by being annoyingly perky. A commercial ended and Lorde's *'Royals'* came on the radio. Despite the fact that I couldn't carry a tune with a gun to my head I began belting out the words. Creed looked a little startled but I didn't let that dissuade me. I turned up the radio and raised my voice as I tipped my head out the window and serenaded all of Tempe.

"Man," Creed chuckled when I paused for breath, "you suck."

"Holy shit, so you can smile! God, I wondered. Wait, are you okay? Does your face hurt?"

He rolled his eyes. "Quit it, you're starting to sound like the boys. Can't have you ganging up on me too."

"Well," I said, relieved that he actually *did* know how to complete several sentences in a row, "I heard you don't suck. At singing, I mean."

"I've heard that too. You know what? Pull into that Burger King drive thru. I want a Big Mac."

"Big Macs are only at McDonald's," I told him, gladly pulling up anyway. "But I'll treat you to a Whopper."

As we drove away with a couple of greasy bags, Creed seemed to warm up a little.

"You care if I eat in your car?"

"Well," I sighed, gesturing to the frayed seats and warped dashboard, "I was trying to keep it looking new but I'll stand down this once."

Creed passed me a bag of fries, which I accepted happily, shoving a handful in my mouth. He devoured his hamburger in about three bites and stared broodingly out the window as we pulled up to the apartment building.

I'd forgotten all about the table Cord had broken in a fit of sudden anger. Creed raised his eyebrows and kicked over one of the pieces.

"What the hell happened here?"

"Nothing. I did that," I told him as I retrieved Chase's half full box of cereal from the floor.

"Bullshit," Creed snorted.

"Seriously," I flexed my arms. "I'm stronger than I look."

Creed stared down at the fractured table and frowned. "It doesn't get away from him very often, you know."

"Cord?"

He nodded. "Yeah. He and Chase both, they can bottle it back up better than I can."

"Oh."

Creed gave me a hard look. "He told you stuff, didn't he? Hell, he probably didn't have to. I'm sure you remember a few things about what we came from."

I cleared my throat. "I'm sorry."

Creed picked up the two pieces of the table, tried to fit them back together, then gave up and let them fall. "What are you sorry for? Anyway, that shit was a long time ago. That's what I'm always telling the boys. That's what I told Cord a few weeks back, the night he brought you home and he was all keyed up, thinking how you surely hated him."

"I don't hate him," I said quietly. "I love him."

That made the most inscrutable of the Gentry brothers take a step back. "Good," he said, nodding, "I thought maybe that was it." He walked over to the television and switched on the Xbox. Within seconds he was shooting animated figures.

"Hey," I called.

Creed didn't take his eyes from the television. "What?"

"You okay with me sticking around and waiting for Cord?"

"Why wouldn't I be?"

"Just thought you might be tired or-"

"I'm not tired," he interrupted. "I dozed off at the hospital."

"Okay," I said slowly, not really sure if he'd given me an answer. I turned and started to head towards Cord's bedroom, figuring Creed ought to be left alone with his fictitious killing quest.

The knock at the door brought Creed immediately to his feet. He pushed me behind him before he looked through the peephole, then breathed a sigh of relief.

"It's your cousin."

Brayden and Millie were waiting on the other side of the door looking like a set of worried parents. Creed opened the door and motioned for them to come inside.

"We happened to be walking by," Brayden explained, following us to the living room "and saw that the light was on..."

"He's lying," Millie said cheerfully, "we've been stalking this place for an hour." Her eyes landed on Creed and she turned serious. "How is he?"

"Pretty fucked up," Creed admitted, sinking back into his chair in front of the television.

"Doctor wants to keep him a few more days," I told them, "on account of the surgery and the concussion. Cord's staying at the hospital until visiting hours are over."

Bray's glance flicked over to Creed. "The cops catch the sons of bitches?"

"No," Creed scowled. He tensely drummed his fingers on his leg.

"Somebody had to see something," I said. "It was broad daylight after all. The cops might still-"

"They won't," Creed said firmly. "Any justice that gets meted out will have to find another way."

I didn't like the sound of that. I didn't like it at all. I looked helplessly at Bray and Millie. Brayden stared sadly back at me but Millie took a stroll around the living room.

"This yours?" she asked, picking up a weathered guitar that had been leaning on the far side of the couch. It was the same one I'd seen Creed playing the other night when he was sitting out front. I remembered how Cord had spoken repeatedly of Creed's musical talents.

He paused the controller and peered at the guitar in Millie's hand. "Yeah," he admitted. "It's mine."

Millie smiled sweetly and brought it to him. "Play something? Please? Music heals the soul you know."

I waited, figuring Creed would grunt some noncommittal response and go back to his video game. But surprisingly he stared into Millie's sweet face for a moment and then took the guitar, nodding slowly.

As Creed carefully tuned the instrument, Millie dragged Brayden over to the couch and then waved me over. I settled next to them on the arm and watched Creed as he finished tuning. He cleared his throat.

"Not used to playing for an audience," he grumbled.

"We're not an audience," I told him, "we're just us."

Creed stared at the three of us for a second and then bowed his head as the guitar came alive in his hands. I thought the opening bars sounded vaguely familiar. And when Creed began singing I was immediately caught by the deep, soulful resonance of his voice. Everything about him changed when he sang. The hard lines of his posture softened and his face relaxed. All the emotion contained by his stoic exterior came through in his singing. At the moment I could not think of another voice on the radio that could top Creed Gentry's. When he got to the chorus I realized the song was very familiar. My father was a vintage record hoarder with special affection for albums of the late sixties, early seventies. Creed was singing a hauntingly beautiful song I remembered well.

When he came to a stop he looked at us bashfully. Bray and Millie broke into loud applause and I smiled at him.

"No wonder why you complained about my singing," I laughed. Creed shrugged, setting the guitar down.

"Man, you're good," Brayden gushed. "You ever think about trying to get some gigs at the clubs in town? They're always on the lookout for talent."

Creed shook his head. "Nah. Can't picture myself playing for a bunch of drunk bastards and party girls."

"'*Danny's Song*'," I said, remembering the name.

Creed nodded, looking surprised. "That's right. I have a tendency to gravitate towards the oldies. Don't know why."

"Kenny Loggins wrote it for his brother, you know. Danny is his brother's name."

"No," murmured Creed, "I didn't know that." He was looking troubled again, likely thinking of his own brother lying in a hospital bed several miles away, perhaps wishing he could write a song that would make a small difference.

"What's that say?" Millie asked, pointing. "Your tattoo."

Creed glanced down. The first few buttons of his shirt were undone and a few letters of black script were visible on his chest, the same place as Cord's tattoo. Creed loosened a few more buttons so we could see the Latin words.

Millie stepped forward and read the words. "*Concedo nulli.*"

"'Yield to no one'," Brayden translated and Creed nodded.

"Damn right."

Millie and Bray chatted with Creed a little while longer before heading home. I walked them to the door and hugged them both, grateful for the warmth of family.

"I'll call you tomorrow," Brayden promised, squeezing my elbow on the way out before wrapping an arm firmly around Millie and heading into the twilight.

Creed hadn't returned to his game. He was sitting with his head lowered, deep in thought.

"You want to watch a movie or something?" I offered.

He shook his head. "Not especially."

I paused, waiting to see if he would say anything else. Creed wasn't a talker though. He chose his few words carefully then moved on.

"Well," I finally said, "think I'll go hang out in Cord's room until he gets home."

Creed didn't answer so I shrugged and began walking down the hall.

"Saylor?"

I turned around to find him staring after me.

"You're all right," he said. "Really. This thing between you and Cord, I'm glad for you guys."

I blushed, pleased. I figured that was likely the closest Creedence Gentry came to an endorsement.

Creed rose and went to the back patio, perhaps to use the set of weights the boys kept out there. I retreated to Cord's room.

The first thing I saw when I turned on the light was the computer, still in its box. I'd forgotten about it. As I sat on the edge of the bed and withdrew it from the packaging I was overcome once again by the level of sweet caring that led Cord to make the purchase.

I hadn't really written much of anything since returning to Arizona. Every few days I would sit in front of Millie's blank laptop screen and tap out a few lackluster sentences of the story I began to think would never be finished. I had told Cord I didn't know how it ended because I didn't know how to write about love.

But as I set up the computer I thought about Cord; the crashing passion as his body invaded mine, his cool humor, his tender eagerness to please me. The hot rush that coursed through me wasn't just lust. I missed him. Suddenly I couldn't wait to start typing and breathe words into the complex nature of the heart.

"When I looked at him I saw a man. I saw something else, too. He was wild and fierce. The fears my people had long whispered might have been

justified. But he'd saved me more than once and the refuge I found in his arms was incomparable. I'd struggled to suppress the rising tide of emotion but he wouldn't allow it. We were born on opposite sides of an invisible line and had been told our kind would never find peace with one another. But when he touched me none of that mattered. This was a battle that could have no winners. The best outcome was a draw. And in the end there was only us."

"Saylor. Say."

He'd crept into the room without me even hearing. Cord grinned at me as he sat on the edge of the bed. I reached for him, shutting the lid of the computer.

"You were lost," he said, stroking my hair with some amusement.

"Not lost," I objected, climbing into his lap. "Just inspired." I glanced at my watch. It was half past ten. "Visiting hours over, I take it?"

Cord nodded tiredly. "Yeah. Hospital said they'd call if there was any change. They're giving him some antibiotics to fend off possible infection."

"How's he feeling?"

"Ah, you know Chase. He'll laugh his way into a pine box." Cord grimaced. "He's hurting. His pride might be as battered as his body."

"He was jumped for crying out loud. Not exactly a fair fight."

Cord's eyes narrowed. "No," he said gravely, "it wasn't."

The way his face fell to brooding reminded me of Creed. I recalled Creed's cryptic comment about dispensing justice but I didn't want to talk about that now. I just wanted to be in Cord's arms.

He watched me as I unbuttoned his shirt and slipped it from his bronze shoulders. I touched the mark on his neck and laughed, remembering our frenzied coupling in the living room hours earlier.

"First time I've ever given a hickey."

Cord grinned. "Yeah, I got some looks back at the hospital. Chase blustered a little about satisfying my horny needs while he was laid up." He ran his hands over my breasts. "Speaking of which..."

It didn't matter how many times we were together or how recent it had been. I always wanted him. I couldn't imagine that would ever change. I shifted as he slipped his hand under my shirt and touched my bare skin.

"Aren't you going to close the door?" I breathed, uncertain as to Creed's whereabouts and not really wishing to be on display.

Cord enjoyed getting me worked up. He unhooked my bra and pulled my shirt over my head, touching everywhere.

"And if I don't close the door?" One hand dove boldly between my legs and the other circled around the back of my neck, massaging.

"Then I'll almost certainly let you fuck me anyway," I told him honestly.

Cord laughed and leaned into the middle of the room, slamming the door closed. He had his pants down and my legs open before I could blink.

"I missed you today," I told him, arching and moaning a little as I felt him graze my moist core.

"I'm right here," he answered, looking closely into my eyes.

"Then stay here," I whispered.

Cord's answer was a furious thrust.

22

CORD

I envied how Saylor could fall into a peaceful asleep so effortlessly. After yet another long, satisfying climb all over each another, she fell back with a sigh and was breathing evenly inside of five minutes. I stared into the dark without blinking.

The noise of the sliding glass door being pushed open got me away from her side. I needed to talk to Creed and I didn't want Saylor to hear me. As I pulled on a pair of jeans I covered her with a blanket and slowly opened the door.

Chase had gazed at me balefully from his hospital bed and asked what I was planning next. I'd tried to shrug it off, playing dumb, but he knew better.

"Don't, Cord," he had warned, as he tried to focus amid the dulling effect of the meds. "Just don't."

When I got to the living room I found Creed, sweaty and naked from the waist up. He must have stayed out there quite a while, pumping iron to push back against the unanswered wrath. He pointed to the ruined kitchen table.

"Nice going. Maybe we can glue it back together."

"You think so?"

"Nope."

"You make any calls tonight, Creedence?"

He hesitated. "Nope."

I sat on the couch, relaxing slightly. Creed eyed me as he chugged a glass of water. I took him at his word. If he said he didn't call Gabe to root out a short list of suspects, then he was telling the truth.

I patted the couch next to me. "Sit down, man."

Creed pulled a shirt on and sat unhappily at my side. He drummed his fingers on his thigh. It had always been a habit of his. Maybe it was the music inside his head trying to break out.

My brother sighed. "He talk to you much?"

"A little. He was kind of out of it. Cops came by again too. No witnesses apparently and the exterior camera only watches the street. There's nothing in the alley."

"It was them," Creed said flatly and I watched his hands clench.

"What do you aim to do about it, Creed?"

He threw me a disgusted look. "What the hell do you think? Those sons of bitches nearly killed our brother. Tonight they're probably all sitting around doing shots and sucking pussy while Chasyn lies in a hospital bed with his guts rearranged."

"I know that," I snapped. "You think it means less to me than it does to you? He's my fucking brother too. I would kill for either one of you, C."

Creed's eyes bored into me. "Is that so?"

I stood, challenging him. "Is that what you're asking here? You need someone to die in order to move on?"

"I don't know. Maybe."

I exhaled raggedly, unsure whether he was serious. "Jesus, you're crazy. Crazy, man. I don't want to spend the rest of my life in a cage. Neither do you. This isn't a matter of just trying to make some cash or hack our way past Benton. This is a turn down a bad path with no way out."

He was disgusted. "Fuck you, Cord. What happened? Now you found yourself a situation and you just want to play house and cater to your dick?"

I wasn't going to talk about Saylor. "She ain't got nothing to do with this. We go your way and best case scenario is we'll end up just like the old man, maybe even worse."

My brother's eyes were cold. Slowly, he rose and stood inches away. Creed was bigger, stronger. Always had been. But I was the more adept fighter, if it came to it. I hoped to god it wouldn't.

As my brother and I stood toe to toe he blinked and I saw what the last twenty four hours had cost him. He was hurting bad. I knew how he felt. I was hurting too. I cleared my throat and pointed to the pieces of kitchen table that sat sadly on the floor.

"You see that? That was me teetering on the edge. I want blood too. There's been moments when it's all I think about. But we got to let it lie tonight."

He looked at me evenly. "And tomorrow?"

I ran a hand through my hair, suddenly feeling the weight of the tough day and the late hour. "Tomorrow is tomorrow. Tonight let's-"

"Send it to the dungeon," Creed nodded. Suddenly he winced and crossed his arms, talking quietly. "Earlier, Chase was drifting in and out between the fever and the meds. He asked for Mom once. Only once."

"No," I froze. "We're not fucking calling them. It was just the pain talking. He wouldn't want that if he was in his clear mind."

Creed sighed wearily. "You ever wonder, Cord, how she could let it all happen? I mean, aside from being a bruised junkie, she was our mother. How does a mother sit there and watch her flesh and blood get tortured by a madman?"

I didn't want to think about that. Not tonight, not ever.

"Go to sleep, C. I'll keep my phone by my ear in case the hospital calls."

Creed gave a short laugh. "You gonna be quiet for the rest of the night so that I *can* sleep?"

I rolled my eyes. "Yeah, I get it. We fuck too loud. We'll work on it, okay?"

He closed his eyes briefly. "Okay. Listen, you wake me up if there's any word."

"Of course. And take another shower, man. You stink."

Creed pushed me back into the couch and started to stalk off to the bathroom. When he reached the threshold of the hallway he turned around and gave me a hard look.

"Tomorrow, Cordero," he said, letting me know he still expected to revisit the topic of avenging Chase whether Chase wanted to be avenged or not.

"Tomorrow," I agreed.

I sat down on the couch and dialed the hospital. A sprightly nurse named Anna told me Chase was sleeping peacefully and that his fever, for the moment, had subsided. She promised to phone immediately if anything changed for the worse.

The sound of the shower echoed through the apartment. When Creed was finished he went straight to his room and closed his bedroom door softly. I checked the time. It was after midnight. We needed to be back at the hospital at eight when visiting hours resumed.

Saylor was sitting up in bed when I returned to my room. Her long hair hung over her bare shoulders as she gathered the sheet to her breasts.

"Hey," I said, surprised. "What are you doing awake?"

"Heard you shouting," she answered with her head down.

"Were we?" I frowned. "That was nothing, Say. Just me and Creed butting heads."

"Cord. What are you going to do?"

"About what, Saylor?"

She glared at me. "Cut it out. You know damn well what."

"Look there's some things I'm just not gonna talk to you about, okay? Any shit that goes down between me and my brothers is off limits. Hey now, don't pout about it. I can tell when you're getting ornery."

She smiled a little. "Ornery, huh? Is that what I am?"

I yawned. "It's good. I like that you have a little bite to you."

Saylor peeled the covers back. "Come to bed. You're tired."

I slipped between the cool sheets and took her in my arms. "Were you writing earlier when I walked in here?"

She smiled vaguely. "Yes."

"You figure out an ending to your story?"

"Almost. I think they have to be happy, my characters. For a long time I thought there was no way they could be. Now I don't think it can possibly be otherwise."

"Good." I yawned again. "It's good to be happy."

"Are you?"

"Right now? Here with you? Yes."

Saylor lightly traced the words on my chest. "You think it would be all right with Chase if I visited at the hospital tomorrow?"

"Yeah," I said, telling the truth. "I do."

She sat up suddenly. "Guess what? I heard Creed sing tonight."

"No kidding. How the hell did you wrangle that?"

"I didn't. Millie did. He should sing more often though." Her voice was a little awed. "Music, it breathes life into him. You already knew it, huh? I never saw him like that before."

I decided to tease her. "Hey, don't go crushing on my brother. It's gross."

"Come on," she shoved me. "Don't be a sicko. I just wanted to let you know that I care about them, both of them."

I couldn't help but be touched. I knew she meant it and to hear it out loud made my heart a little sore. How could I think about doing anything to jeopardize what I'd found in her?

"Go to sleep, Say," I said, my voice a little hoarse, and kissed her gently.

She did it again, where she fell into unconsciousness within five minutes. Before she did though, she hugged me hard and murmured, "Don't dream."

I didn't dream. But when I woke up my head was pounding as if I'd spent the night banging it against the wall. I swallowed a handful of Advil before heading over to the hospital.

Creed was never a morning person and he seemed to be in a special kind of funk when he wandered out for a cup of coffee. I jingled the keys to the truck. "You gonna be ready soon?"

He shrugged. "Soon as I can get my legs under me and wipe the shit out of my eyes." Creed stared at me a moment as the coffee pot finished sputtering. "Just give me ten minutes. And then later, we can talk again."

"Great," I muttered, holding my aching head.

As I got behind the wheel I chased the pills with a sizeable portion of caffeine. By the time we got up to Chase's room I was starting to feel normal again. Creed saw the doctor over by the nurses' station and went to go have a few words with him.

Chase had gained a roommate during the night; an old man who thought there were cats all over his bed and kept shouting about it.

My brother threw me an irked look as I walked in the room. "I don't like this hotel," he complained.

When I called the hospital first thing this morning I'd been told Chase's fever had returned again. I could see it in his face; his eyes were too bright and his face was flushed underneath the bruises and swelling. They had upped his dose of antibiotics in the hopes that would do the trick.

I patted him lightly on the shoulder, just feeling glad to be in the same room with him. "How are you feeling?"

Chase's right eye was still swelled nearly shut. He closed the other one and leaned back into the pillows. "I don't want to answer that. I've been asked that question seventy five hundred times in the last twenty four hours. I just want to get the fuck out of here."

"Soon," I sighed, although I really had no idea.

He opened his eye and glared. "How soon? Can you slip the doc a twenty to speed up the discharge? Hey look, there's a pretty girl hanging around behind the curtain. Saylor! Get the hell in here so I can have something nice to look at."

Saylor peered around the corner, smiling shyly. "Hi, Chase."

He held a hand out to her. "Come here, baby. I'm all worn out at the moment so my usual gallantry is falling by the wayside. God, you look hot."

Saylor grabbed his hand and giggled a little. "I brought you a present."

"Good. Can I stick my dick in it?"

"Jesus, Chase," I laughed. "What have they got you doped up on?"

"At the moment, nothing. But lying in a hospital bed treats you to all kinds of tolerance. I asked a hot nurse to sponge bathe me and show me her boobs. She'll be back in an hour so you guys will need to leave before that comes up."

"Whatever," I rolled my eyes. "You're full of shit."

Saylor fished around in her purse and withdrew a large plastic bag. "Here," she tossed it to him. "That's your present. I wouldn't recommend sticking your dick in it. You'll ruin the marshmallows."

"Aw," he smiled, grabbing a handful of his cereal. "Thanks, princess. I knew you cared."

I looked at the IV still attached to his arm and the bandages on his abdomen. "Are you supposed to be eating that?"

"Probably not, but I'm starving. Cord, can you be a real brother and run down to the cafeteria for a steak?"

"It's eight am," I argued. "They're not likely serving steak right now."

"Whatever. Eggs then. Get me eggs. Or a bagel."

I shook my head and glanced at Saylor. "You want to come?"

"No," Chase objected, pulling Saylor down on the bed. "She's gonna stay here and spoon feed me."

"Hey," I growled, "just because you're flat on your back doesn't give you license to feel up my girl."

"Sure it does. Take your time, Cordero."

I left with a smile, although it disappeared when I left the room, thinking about the bandage surrounding Chase's abdominal incision. What I wanted more than anything was to take my brother home. I'd happily absorb his wisecracks all goddamn day if he could only come home. Sons of bitches, the ones who did this to him.

The tension in my muscles was nearly unbearable. If I hadn't been walking through a public place I would have given in and punched the nearest wall.

23

SAYLOR

Chase dropped the act as soon as Cord was out of sight. He stopped smiling and pointed to the chair next to the bed. "Sit."

"Stop *scratching* me! Stop *looking* at me! Little lions everywhere. Fucking *every*where!"

Chase rolled his eyes and shouted over the curtain. "It's okay, Larry. They're all filing past on their way to the litter box. They'll be gone at least ten minutes. Take a breather, buddy."

I heard the old man grumble but he quieted down.

Chase's expression was sober. "What's going on, Say?"

"You mean with Cord?"

He sat up a little. I saw sweat beading on his forehead from the effort. "Yeah, with Cord. And Creed. What the hell are they up to?"

"You think they check with me before they make plans?"

Chase sighed. "So they *are* making plans?"

I felt my heart sinking. "I believe they are."

"Goddammit," he swore, balling his fist. "What good do they think it will do, going off on some bullshit blood mission?"

My heart began to beat faster. Hearing Chase say the things I only suspected brought it home. I'd seen Cord's wild wrath yesterday. The monster in him was subdued, for now. It might not stay that way for long.

Chase shook his head miserably. "Stop him, Saylor. Creed doesn't hear much of anybody but Cord will listen to you."

"You think so?"

He leaned forward eagerly and grabbed my hand. "Yes. He's head over heels for you, sweetheart. If anyone can bring him around it's you."

I felt a lone tear escape and travel down my left cheek. "I kind of like him at this point too."

Chase's wiseass grin returned. "Aw, you love him. You want to make cute little babies with him and shit."

I blushed, not answering. I could scarcely articulate the crazy roller coaster of emotion Cord Gentry had taken me on.

"Hey." Chase poked my knee.

"What?"

He cleared his throat, looking a little uncomfortable. "There's something you should know. That mess back in Emblem with you and Cord?"

I waved him off. "We've been over that. It's over. It doesn't matter now."

"Well, I've got to tell you something anyway. It was all my idea, Saylor. I was the one who brought it up, who thought you'd be easy to get to." He paused, looking sadly down at the bed sheet. "And I'm the one who made sure it was news. I told everyone who had ears. I mean, Cord did what he did, obviously. Can't excuse that. But he wasn't the one who spread the gossip around everywhere. He wouldn't have. That was all me." Chase cleared his throat painfully. "I'm sorry."

I was quiet for a moment. If I tried, I could summon the hurt and humiliation of those long ago days, but what for? It was a long time ago, in another place. Back then I didn't really know the three of them any more than they knew me. But I knew them now. Chase and Creed were my friends. And Cord was my heart.

Chase was waiting for me to say something. Maybe to tell him to go to hell or to sigh and say I'd already forgiven him.

"What's yours mean?" I suddenly asked.

He was confused. "What?"

I pointed to the tattoo on his upper chest which was visible around the neckline of the hospital gown. "Cord said you're the one who has a thing about Latin. So what's yours mean, Chase?"

He looked down at himself and pulled the hospital gown away with a slow smile. "Read it."

"*Vivo pro hodie.*" I shrugged. "Something about living."

"Loosely translated it's 'Live for today' although there is some academic disagreement as to the English to Latin formatting."

"Hmm. Live for today. Very prescient."

Chase gently prodded his bandages. "Seems so, doesn't it?"

"I'll try," I whispered. "To keep him from doing something stupid."

"Try hard, Saylor."

"Hard as I can."

"And if verbal persuasion doesn't work, feel free to use your tits. By the way, being as how I've suffered so much, may I see them just for a quick moment?"

"Asshole," I laughed. "No."

I heard my phone buzzing in my purse and glanced at it. "Shit, it's my mother. I'm sure she's wanting to remind me about her wedding tomorrow. Oh well, that's what voicemail was invented for. Did you know my mother is marrying Gary Chavez?"

Chase cocked his head. "The Gnome?"

"The one and only."

"Speaking of hot McCann chicks, your mom can certainly compete. I remember this one time she and my uncle-"

"Stop," I begged, shuddering. "Just stop. Some memories ought to be buried in the molten crust of the earth's core and never revived."

"Okay. Will you still spoon feed me my cereal?"

"Better than that. I'll let you eat straight from my palm."

Creed happened to walk into the room at the tail end of that conversation. He gave us a perplexed look and then jumped a foot in the air when Larry from beyond the neighboring curtain began shrieking about invisible cats once again.

Chase yelled back. "It's cool, Larry! Animal Control was just here and took all the animals away."

"What the fuck?" said Creed, wrinkling his nose.

Cord showed up with a Styrofoam tray loaded with scrambled eggs and bagels. Chase sniffed and pushed it away. "I'm not hungry anymore. Give it to King Kong."

"I am hungry," Creed acknowledged and prepared to dig in.

It was nice being with the three of them. It was like being part of a family. Bray and Millie stopped by around noon with some flowers and balloons. Chase asked Millie if she would like to give him a sponge bath. She smiled and politely declined.

Truly called and I was glad to hear from her. She said she convinced Ed, the sour manager of Cluck This, that I suffered from extreme premenstrual paranoia and was being medically treated.

She issued a throaty laugh. "He says you can come back to work whenever your hormonal imbalance is corrected."

"You're a peach," I told her, smiling and glad to have found another friend.

I listened to my mother's barking voicemail. She went on for a seeming eternity about daisies and issued a slew of reminders about how I needed to be at the restaurant by three pm tomorrow. I just shook my head, deciding not to call her back for the moment and marveling over how quickly I went from being scarcely thought of to an integral ingredient of her wedding festivities.

She wasn't going to take it well when I told her I wasn't coming. After all, I couldn't expect Cord to leave his brother's bedside for a day trip to Emblem. I didn't want him to. I didn't even want to go myself. It seemed more important to be here, for Cord and his brothers.

Cord found me sitting in the hospital lobby, absently staring into my phone.

"Hey, pretty," he grinned and my stomach did a little somersault.

I jumped up and went straight into his arms. He smelled so good. He felt so good. I wanted to stay there forever. I didn't want to revisit the tense conversation I'd had with Chase upstairs and the fears over what the coming days would bring. I just wanted to be with Cord and tell all the cruelties in the world to go fuck themselves.

"Hey," he rubbed my back. "What's wrong?"

"Nothing." I breathed him in, reveling in the mix of soap and aftershave, getting a little hot between my legs in the process.

Cord knew. He always knew. He held me closer so I could feel him hardening. "You want to get out of here for a little while?"

I kissed him. "Always."

"Come on," he pulled at me. "Let's just go up real quick and see if the boys need anything before we go."

I loved having his arm around me as we made our way back to Chase's room. I hugged him around the waist and closed my eyes, thinking about the intoxicating feel of his broad, naked chest against mine.

Cord tensed suddenly, and then swore loudly. I opened my eyes and saw a flurry of medical staff rushing in and out of Chase's room.

"Maybe something happened to the old man," I said but the sinking feeling in my gut intensified when I noticed Creed standing outside the door with a sick expression.

Cord rushed over to him with me right behind. "What the hell happened?"

Creed could hardly talk. "Fever spiked and I heard one of the nurses comment that his heart rate is erratic."

"Damn," Cord moaned and tried to see into the room.

There were several doctors bent over Chase. One peeled back the bandages on his abdomen and they talked in low voices.

Larry of the Cats noticed us in the doorway and wagged a finger. "Told you all to get rid of the little lions," he said sadly.

Cord collared a nurse as she exited Chase's room. "Can you tell me what the hell's going on with my brother?"

She gave him a sympathetic smile. She was likely used to being grabbed by agitated people all day long. "The doctor will be out in a few moments to brief you on Mr. Gentry's condition."

Creed slouched miserably against the wall while Cord stared silently at the floor. I couldn't do a thing but watch helplessly.

Before long, Chase was being wheeled out of the room. He was lying flat with his eyes closed and his hand over his face. Cord started to go to him.

"Chasyn!" he called. Chase raised a hand and waved limply.

The news was grim. Chase was exhibiting signs of serious infection. The incision had broken and there was evidence of renewed internal bleeding.

The doctor hurried away amid promises to update us with any news. Then something happened that broke my heart. Cordero and Creedence Gentry sank to the floor together and cried.

24

CORD

Another day with another endless wait and the rage had returned. Underneath that was the skulking fear that had been with me since I was a kid. It wasn't the dread of what kind of hurt might befall me. It was worse. It was the speechless terror of losing my brothers.

Saylor tried to keep me with her. She held me. She said things that meant to ease the pain. She reached out to Creed but he ignored her. I couldn't explain to her that when Chase had been wheeled away he wasn't a man. He was a terrified boy who was the mirror of my own self. For the first time Creed and I hadn't been there when he really needed us. We'd failed him. We'd failed each other and the unbreakable bond that had ruled us since we knew our names. It wasn't logical, but that's how it seemed anyway.

Eventually the doctor returned and advised Chase was stable. The bleeding had been stopped and he was beginning to respond to the antibiotics. He would be returned to his room shortly and then we could go see him.

Saylor sighed. "God, that's a relief." She laced her fingers through mine. "You want me to get you anything?"

"No," I said, a little sharply.

Say just nodded and kissed my cheek. "I've just got to use the restroom and then call Brayden. I'll be right back."

"Fine."

Creed was drumming his fingers on his thigh and staring at me. I stared back, silently giving him an answer to last night's conversation. He was right. This shit couldn't stand. It just couldn't.

Saylor brought us sodas from the vending machine. I cracked one open and drank but didn't taste a thing. I was numb. I wondered if that would change when I inflicted some pain on someone else, someone who had torn my brother up. My hands fairly ached to ball into fists and crush bone. It would mean so much more than fighting a stranger in order to earn rent money. It would be personal.

The evening was well underway by the time we were called back up to see Chase in his room. Larry and his unseen cats were gone, replaced by a middle aged guy who'd gotten nailed in the backside with birdshot while he was hunting up north with his buddies. His florid-faced wife yelled at him in one continuous stretch of obscenities.

Chase was no longer flushed. He was pale and visibly weak, although he tried again to hide it with bravado.

"They serve beer down in that cafeteria?" he asked with a watery grin.

"No," I answered, trying to smile back. "Behave and I'll sneak you in a wine cooler or two."

"I'm trying," he grumbled, then noticed Saylor. "So *now* can I see your tits?"

She was incredulous. "You call that behaving? I don't even know how to answer you. You've got a one track mind."

"Hey," I nudged Creed. "I'm gonna run Saylor home and then I'll come back for you."

He gave me a long, penetrating look. "All right, Cord. I'll be waiting."

I reached over and tapped Chase's shoulder. He looked as if he were struggling to stay awake. "I'll be back, man."

Chase didn't answer me. I thought he might be dozing off but he reached over and grabbed the hem of Saylor's shirt, forcing her to turn around.

"Talk to him!" he snarled and then fell back, sweating.

Saylor looked as if she might cry. I led her out of the room and to the elevator. We didn't speak until we reached the parking lot.

"What was that about?" I asked casually, unlocking the truck.

She got in and waited for me to get behind the wheel before answering.

"Chase thinks you guys are on the verge of doing something foolish."

I started the engine. "Oh yeah?"

"So, are you?"

"Am I what?"

"Don't bullshit me, Cord. I know you've got some suspicions about who attacked Chase. Why don't you tell the police everything you know?"

"Won't make a damn bit of difference. Even if the police arrest them, their folks will have them out of the pen inside of a day. They'll never do time."

Saylor hissed through her teeth and looked out the window. "But *you* will. You'll be on the other side of the razor wire in Emblem with all the other lost fucks who lose years just like that." She snapped her fingers.

I scowled. "You don't know what the hell you're talking about."

"*He* knows," she said quietly.

"Who?"

"'*Who?*'" she mocked me. "Chasyn. He knows you're up to something, you and Creed. He begged me to talk you out of it." She grabbed my arm. "What do you think it will do to him when the two of you get hauled off in handcuffs? You think that will help him recover? What do you think it will do to me?" She was breathing heavily as tears began to fall. "For god's sake, I love you."

I closed my eyes. The agony in her voice would bury me if I let it. "Calm down, Saylor. Nobody is going to prison."

"Can you promise me that? You know, I heard you guys talking last night. Can you promise that you're not going to jump with Creed off the fucking deep end and do something violent that will destroy the lives of everyone who loves you?"

"Well," I laughed shortly. "At least that would be a short list."

"Cord," she cried and I couldn't take it anymore. I shut off the truck and pulled her to me.

"I'm right here, baby," I whispered, even though it wasn't true. I wouldn't really be there again until I was finished with what needed to be done.

Saylor calmed down and relented although she still watched me anxiously. I drove slowly through the streets of Tempe. Suddenly she gave a small sigh.

"I never called my mom back."

"Oh yeah. I forgot about the big day tomorrow. What time are you going?"

She raised her eyebrows. "I'm not. You think I'm going waltzing down to Emblem in the middle of all this shit?"

"It's your mother's wedding. You should really go, Say."

She glanced at our surroundings and sighed unhappily. "You're dropping me at Brayden's?"

"Yeah," I said casually. "Is that okay? I mean, most of your stuff is still there for now. Anyway, I'll be back late tonight and you probably want to get some rest for tomorrow."

Her bright green eyes fixed on me sadly. "That's not it, not really. You just want me out of the way so you and Creed can descend into the pits of hell together."

There was no humor in my chuckle. "Just like a typical fucking Gentry, right?"

She looked away. She was struggling not to cry. Christ, I couldn't handle her crying again.

"I'll be there to see Chase in the morning," she said quietly. "Before I go."

"Okay," I shrugged. "I'll be there too." I touched her cheek. "This isn't 'goodbye'. It's just 'good night'. Now come here and kiss me, baby."

There was a desperate quality to the way she climbed over the seat and wrapped her legs around me. We got sweaty together, kissing for a long time. I wanted more. I wanted it all. I wanted to lose myself in her sweet body again and banish the demons of retribution. But I came from a long line of violent people who knew such shadows aren't easily pushed aside. Saylor might be right. I just might be headed to hell.

Finally, reluctantly, she pulled away. "Good night, Cordero," she whispered and walked slowly over to her cousin's apartment.

I love you too, Say.

But it was the wrong time to tell her. I returned to the hospital without glancing back. Creed was waiting for me.

Chase was doped up again, sleeping soundly. The man who'd been shot in the ass was watching television as his wife complained about everything but the color of the sky. He noticed me watching and sighed, pointing in the direction of his unhappy significant other as she prattled on.

"Thank the good lord that visiting hours end soon, eh?"

Creed pulled me out of the room and into the hallway. His eyes were bloodshot. I wondered if he'd slept at all since Chase's attack.

"I put in a call," he said. "Haven't heard back."

"Did you tell him what's up?"

He scoffed. "In a voice mail? Fuck no."

We ate garbage from the vending machine and hung out at Chase's side until hospital staff told us we needed to get out. I stopped at the nurses' station and asked again if they would give me a buzz if anything changed during the night.

Creed looked around when we got back to the apartment. "Where's Say?"

"Brayden's. I can't let her get mixed up in whatever happens next."

Creed's hands went to his hips and he looked down with a sad expression. "And after that?"

"Don't know. It's up to her I guess."

My brother nodded. "Fair enough."

He tensed at the sound of his ringtone. "It's Gabe."

Creed put the phone on speaker. "Hey, man. Thanks for calling back."

"Naturally. How can I help you, Mr. Gentry?"

Creed glanced at me. "You may have heard something about my brother, Chase, getting jumped behind a gym in Tempe."

Gabe waited a long time before answering. "I may have heard that," he said warily.

"Chase had run into some trouble down there, a certain pack of college boys who don't take kindly to losing."

"Yes, few people do. Especially over privileged brats who believe the odds should always be stacked in their favor."

"Do you know them?" I asked. It was a formality of a question. Gabe Hernandez had set up fights with them on at least several occasions. Of course he knew them.

"Are we foregoing trial by jury?"

"Fuck that. They'll never see the inside of a courtroom and you know it."

"I know that you boys are asking me to be an accessory to whatever flavor of revenge you feel like dispensing."

Creed's breath came out in a low hiss. "What do you want, Gabe? As compensation for ah, accessorizing yourself?"

A jingling sound came through the phone, as if Gabe was twirling a set of keys around while he considered. "I've been growing tired of these pocket change brawls. Been looking to step up the game and join the big leagues. We're talking huge payout, boys. But I need a fighter who isn't afraid to bleed."

He was talking about more than blood. Creed had told me a little about the high stakes battles. They were brutal. A man could get his spine cracked, or worse. I hadn't been willing to go that route if it was just money. But for this, for the opportunity to right a gruesome wrong on behalf of my brother, then yeah. I would. I opened my mouth to say so but wasn't in time.

"Done," Creed spoke up. "I'll fucking do it."

"Hell yes, the big fellow with a chip on his shoulder. You got yourself a partner, man. It might take me time to get some action set up which is worthy of you but rest assured it'll happen."

Creed rolled his eyes. "Beautiful. Whatever. Now tell us what we need to hear."

"I will. Of course if I flat out gave you names that might be misconstrued." He was quiet a moment. "Let me see here. You got a Facebook profile? Oh, look at that. There's Cordero. I'm going to send you some friend suggestions. Do with that information as you please."

Creed practically snarled. "Believe me, we will."

"I'll be in touch, Creedence."

Creed tossed the phone on the couch. "Don't fucking look at me like that, Cord."

"I'd have done it," I said quietly. "I should be the one."

My brother stared at me a minute, breathing heavily. "It doesn't always have to be you."

"What the hell is that supposed to mean?"

"It doesn't mean a damn thing other than you don't need to take the brunt this time. Now sign in to your account. See if Gabe sent you the info yet. When Gabe says he's gonna do something he might mean in three minutes or he might mean in three days. But eventually it'll come."

"You know he sure as shit won't be forgetting about your agreement. He'll be back to collect at some point."

Creed looked away. "I know."

I checked my phone. "Nothing yet."

"Well then I guess we wait. We got anymore beer in the fridge?"

"Yeah, I think so. None for me though."

I sat down on the couch with a taste of sawdust in my mouth. What the hell were we doing? I had one brother in the hospital and the other who had just made a deal with the devil. I was wishing for Saylor with all my heart even as I knew it was impossible to go to her right now. This was dirty shit and Say was nothing but clean. I had to keep her out of it and if I lost her along the way, then that would be my punishment for sinking into the abyss.

I can't fucking lose her. Please don't let me lose her.

Creed joined me on the couch. He had a beer in his hand but he didn't drink it. He didn't talk either. I didn't know what populated his personal purgatory but we were each in our own misery as we eventually fell asleep side by side.

When I woke up, the first ribbons of sunrise were lighting up the sky. I checked my phone. Gabe had fulfilled his end of the bargain. There were two 'friend' suggestions. I looked at each one in turn. I recognized the faces. All reason fled. There was only hate and the roar of blood between my ears.

25

SAYLOR

Bray and Millie were kind enough to tread lightly, not asking me many questions beyond the superficial. I was grateful. Restlessness consumed me as I lay on the couch and stared at the dark ceiling. My phone was right next to my ear but I didn't expect he would call.

There was nothing simple about Cord. There never had been. And now there was a tremendous battle waging inside of him that I could do nothing about. I'd given him everything of me that I could. If he still turned away and chose something ugly then there was no point in fighting anymore.

For a moment I felt a flash of anger towards Cord Gentry. He'd crept into my heart and nothing would ever be the same again. I couldn't imagine finding that connection with anyone else. It was almost terrible, to really love someone.

The night was restless and in the morning I wasn't in the mood to talk much. I had no desire at all to return to Emblem and a less than zero yearning to attend my mother's wedding. Still, it seemed even less appealing to moon around waiting to see if the man I loved would be hurt or imprisoned.

"You can borrow a dress," Millie said delicately.

"No thanks," I grumbled, smoothing out the simple black maxi. It was the only dress I had that didn't require dry cleaning. With a jolt I realized it was what I was wearing the day I went to California. It was the one I was still wearing the night Cord and I made love for the first time.

Millie's voice was gentle. "Say? You want to talk?"

I shook my head, packing up my purse for the day. I hadn't bought my mother a wedding gift but the hell with it. With a flash of brilliance I dug into the recesses of my bag and unearthed the Target gift card she had sent me for graduation. Perfect.

"I'm out of here," I sighed.

Brayden peered at me from behind his glasses. "You going to the hospital first?"

"Yes."

"Okay," Bray said, exchanging a look with Millie. "Say hi to Emblem for me."

"Sure thing. I'll cut a length of razor wire from one of the perimeter fences as a souvenir."

He shrugged. "Might be an interesting day to make a homecoming. There's an execution tonight and I hear it's brought out a gaggle of protesters."

"Awesome. Can't wait. Love you guys." I started to head out.

"Saylor?" Brayden called.

I turned around impatiently. "Yeah?"

Bray gave me a goofy smile. "Love you too, cuz."

I took a turn past the boys' apartment but the pickup truck wasn't out front. Of course, visiting hours at the hospital had started an hour ago. I hoped that's where they were. I would have prayed about it if I had anyone to pray to.

"Thank you," I breathed with relief when I saw the familiar outline of the crappy Chevy pickup in the parking lot of the hospital.

Creed was standing outside Chase's room drinking a cup of coffee.

"Hi," I waved.

He didn't smile at me. "Hey."

"So how's he doing?"

Creed let out a relieved sigh. "Better. Fever broke last night and infection is subsiding. We may be able to take him home in a day or two."

"Good." I stared at the floor. "Cord in the room?"

"No. He went down to the cafeteria. Chase decided he might be hungry again."

"So what did you guys do last night?"

"Nothing." Creed looked away. "Played video games and took a nap."

"Right." I couldn't keep the sarcasm out of my voice. "See you, Creed."

Chase's roommate, the man who'd been shot in a hunting accident, was in the process of being discharged. His loving wife unleashed a rainbow of colorfully affectionate vulgarities as he shuffled around, trying to pack up. He looked as if he would much rather stay where he was.

Chase had his eyes closed. I pulled the curtain around his bed and sat in the nearby chair.

"Hi Saylor," he said without opening his eyes.

I squeezed his arm briefly. "You scared us yesterday, tough guy."

The swelling had gone down in his face but the skin was still mottled with severe bruising and the cut on his cheek was looking pretty raw.

"Do me favor?" he asked. "Hand me that bedpan over there."

I made a face. "Are you serious?"

He opened his eyes. "No."

"Good, because there are limits to the terms of my friendship."

He studied me. "You look nice."

"I've got to put in an appearance at my mom's wedding."

"Black is a good look for a wedding. Taking Cord with you?"

"I wish," I said softly. "I tried, Chase. I tried to talk to him. Fact is I don't know which way he's going."

The saddest look in the world crossed Chase Gentry's face. "I know. Neither do I."

Beyond the curtain the irritable couple were arguing about who was responsible for breaking an heirloom ceramic plate last Easter. At one point it sounded as if the lady was beating her husband over the head with a shopping bag.

Cord walked in carrying a tray of food. He paused when he saw me and then broke into a grin that made me curse him all the more for holding my heart so desperately captive. His arms went around me and our mouths met.

"Missed you last night," he whispered in my ear and I thought how if I could only keep him safe and whole then I would never need to make another wish again.

Chase cleared his throat obnoxiously and after a minute Cord pulled back. He looked me over. "You leaving soon?"

I took his hands and stared into his eyes with as much pleading as I could muster. "Come with me."

Chase bit into an apple and began chewing loudly. "You should go, dude. You've got a pretty girl and a sunny day. What the hell else do you need?"

"Yeah," I challenged him. "What else do you need?"

Cord only scowled and looked annoyed. He backed away from me and skirted around to the far side of the bed. "No can do, Saylor." The defiant resolve was written all over his face. He'd already chosen something that didn't include me.

I wasn't going to cry again. But I was going to get the hell out of there. I touched Chase on the shoulder. "Bye, kid. I'll come by tonight if I'm not back too late."

After nearly crashing into Creed in the doorway, I hurried out of the room without saying anything to Cord. He followed me.

"Wait," he took my arm. "I'll walk you to your car."

I shook him off. "Don't fucking bother."

"Saylor."

I ignored him.

"Saylor!"

Cord grabbed me around both arms and tried to hold me in place.

"Just let me go, Cord," I whispered, unable to do a thing to stem the flow of tears. "Just let me fucking go."

He pushed his forehead against mine and breathed heavily for a minute. But ultimately he released me without a word, just as I had demanded.

The drive to Emblem was horrible. I got out past Queen Creek and then began to feel a little sick. I pulled onto a dirt road surrounding a cotton farm and got out of the car. Miserably I collapsed in the dust and sobbed until my chest hurt.

After a half hour I'd worn myself out but hadn't found any answers to the ache inside. Cord evidently needed to submit to the dark nature of violence more than he needed me. He didn't say those words but he didn't need to.

When I got to my feet again I felt as if I'd aged twenty years. Then, when I remembered that I had failed to get my mother's wedding bouquet, I felt worse.

Luckily there was a Walmart along the way. Unluckily, they possessed a meager floral assortment. With a flash of brilliance I found the craft section and picked out something that I thought would do. There was still about a half hour of travel ahead but it was early. I made up my mind to drop in on my dad.

Emblem is an ugly town. As you're driving down the two lane road you see the state prison at the edge before you see anything else. It was a sprawling collection of low buildings surrounded by high fences that were topped with sharp wire. As I turned past the behemoth compound that hosted a light gathering of sign-waving protestors, I saw several men in orange jumpsuits standing on the other side of the fences. The men were too far away to distinguish their faces but I wondered about them. Presumably they had families and friends somewhere, people who cared for them. What had they done to get where they were now and did they regret it?

I'd grown up less than a mile from the prison. My parents had worked there for their entire adult lives. Yet it had somehow become scenery to me. I'd rarely thought about the collection of dire human events that were tied to its presence.

My father still lived in the house I'd grown up in. The neighborhood mostly consisted of families of correctional officers but it was one of the nicer areas of Emblem. I felt a trickle of doubt as I walked up the driveway. I hadn't talked to my father since the week I arrived in Arizona. He would have no idea that I might show up at his door today. I brushed off the hesitation. We weren't close but he would be pleased to see me. He always was.

A blowsy blonde answered the door with a cigarette in her mouth. "Yeah?" The woman, who must be my father's latest girlfriend, looked me over coolly, as if she'd already decided to dislike me.

"Hi," I tried to smile. "I'm John's daughter, Saylor."

She took a drag of her cigarette and scratched at the patchy exposed skin above her left breast. "Right, I recognize you. You might remember me too."

I looked at her more closely. She was vaguely familiar. Then it clicked. She was older, heavier, but she had the same face as one of my former classmates. "You're Marnie Hart's mom. How is Marnie?"

She made a face. "Knocked up and layin' down for a sorry loser out on parole."

"Oh," I said, rather at a loss. I never really liked Marnie anyway.

Marnie's mom was rapidly becoming bored. "Look, John's on third shift these days and he's sleepin'."

"Right," I fidgeted, feeling ill at ease. "Well I'm just in town for the day so I figured I'd say hi."

"Whatever," she shrugged and started to shut the door. "I'll tell him you were around."

"You do that," I muttered, already on my way back to my car.

I paused in front of the garage. The main door was closed but my dad had a longstanding habit of keeping the service door unlocked. I walked in, wrinkling my nose at the oppressive heat and the musty odor. It was filthy and crowded, as garages usually were. My dad hadn't parked his truck inside in years. I stared at the floor where once I'd had my first sexual encounter with Cord Gentry. It had been quick and dirty, almost a chore; nothing like what we had now. But it had set the stage for everything that happened later. If Cord hadn't taken my virginity on the floor of that garage I don't know if we ever would have found our way to each other later. Hadn't he said something of that nature the night we went swimming together? He'd leaned over and kissed me sweetly on the forehead after musing about the past and the future. I let out a ragged sigh and shut the garage door.

It was after noon and I was hungry so I stopped at the only McDonald's in town. Seated in a lonely booth, I sighed and called the glowing bride. She yelled at me for failing to answer her call yesterday but relaxed when I told her I had the bouquet. I sipped my soda and listened while she carried on about what a crappy job the hairdresser had done and shrieked at someone about color coordinated napkins.

"I'm already at the Roast," she said, referring to the seedy restaurant/bar where her wedding was to take place in a few hours. "I'm setting up but it's a pain in the ass so if you're not doing anything-"

"Sure, ma. I'll be there in a few minutes."

"Aw, baby. I can't wait to see you."

I rolled my eyes, knowing that was bullshit but unwilling to spend any time thinking about it. "Can't wait to see you either."

The older I got, the less I thought of my mother as 'Mom' and the more I thought of her as 'Amy'. I suppose some women just weren't meant to be mothers and Amy Cooper McCann was one of them. As I watched her from the doorway of Rooster's Roast, a dive that squatted off the main drag in town and had changed owners as many times as the years I'd been alive, she was patting her curled hair and fussing at the old man who was the tired current proprietor.

"There's the bride," I hailed, waving.

The look she gave me was brief annoyance immediately masked

by a smile. "My beautiful baby girl." I suffered a dry kiss on the cheek as she stared at me critically.

"So how are things, Saylor?"

"Good," I lied.

She looked behind me. "You come alone?"

"Yeah. Cord couldn't make it."

Amy gave a little snort of derision. The last thing I felt like doing was listen to her tear Cord down.

"So," I said brightly. "Where's the groom?"

As I expected, Amy's attention immediately shifted. "He's at home, getting ready."

"Where is home?"

She beamed at me. "I moved into Gary's place about a month ago."

Last I'd heard, Gary the Gnome occupied a custom built mini mansion at the north end of Main Street.

"How nice," I managed to respond.

"He insisted that I quit my job too."

That was surprising. "You left the prison?"

"Sure. I'm going to be a real housewife now. What is that?"

My mother was pointing to the bag in my hand which held the brightly colored purchase I'd made at Walmart.

"This?" I withdrew the contents with a flourish. "This is your bouquet."

My mother stared. "Those are fake."

"Well, yeah. I mean they're not fake. They are sub-real. They're actually better than real flowers. They won't wilt."

"You expect me to walk down the aisle with fake flowers?" Her voice had elevated to a high-pitched squeal. It was the same noise I'd heard from her the day she confronted me about the rumors that I'd had sex with Cord Gentry. It was snarling disgust mingled with disbelief.

"Sorry," I muttered, wishing for all the world I hadn't come out here.

For once though, Amy chose to let it go. She grabbed the fake flowers with a roll of her eyes and ordered me to fill the vase centerpieces with honeysuckle potpourri. I was actually happy to have something to do.

As I proceeded with my mother's wedding preparations I tried to push Cord out of my thoughts. I didn't want him there. But, as always, he just refused to leave.

26

CORD

"You should have gone," Chase scolded.

I'd found a deck of cards in the gift shop downstairs. We'd been playing War for an hour on Chase's food tray.

I kept my eyes down. "With Saylor?"

"Yes and you damn well know it."

"Nah, who would keep you entertained then?"

Chase shoved the cards away and crossed his arms. "Fuck that, Cord. I don't need you to babysit me. That's not why you're here now anyway."

"Really? 'Cause it sure feels like I've been at your side every possible minute."

He shook his head. "You're using me as an excuse."

I looked him in the eye. "For what?"

Chase tapped his head and gave me a glum smile. "I'm the smart one, remember?"

"Yeah, I know. You're a fucking genius."

He looked around suddenly. "Where's Creed?"

"In the shitter," I answered mildly.

It was a bald lie. Creed was off on a research mission. Now that we had both names and faces to attach to the assholes who'd jumped

Chase, we needed to figure out how to find them. I wasn't going to tell Chase that. He didn't need to know any more than Saylor needed to know. It would be dealt with. We would tell him when it was finished. It was what he would have done for us. It was how we Gentry boys had managed to reach the privilege of adulthood.

Chase yanked his hospital gown up and pulled the bandage off his abdomen. I flinched at the sight of the angry incision and at all the bruising surrounding it. He pointed to his injuries.

"I know this hurts you, Cord. I know it's eating the two of you alive. I sat here all fucking night trying to figure out how I would handle this shit if it were one of you instead of me." He sighed and tilted his head back, staring at the ceiling. "I think it's almost easier to be on this side. You can see things more clearly."

"I would argue that's the concussion talking."

"Cord, I'd go after them too if I was you. Let's imagine that we even know for absolute certain who's responsible. I'd want to rip off their fucking limbs and use 'em for firewood."

I glanced at the door. "We should stop talking about this."

"Why? You haven't done anything yet. I'm asking you not to. I'm fucking begging you not to." He leaned forward and clutched my arm. "Brother, pull Creedence off the ledge and come back down here, where there's an actual future. Go find that sweet girl who loves your ugly ass and bury yourself inside her until all the bullshit gets fucked out of your head."

"Tried that," I answered drily. "Only worked for a little while."

Chase sighed. "You told me something once, you know."

"I've told you a lot of things over the past twenty two years, Chasyn. What specific something are you referring to?"

"You said it the night before the three of us managed to scrape by and graduate from Emblem High. You know, we might not have deserved to graduate. The administration was petrified that if they didn't pass us we'd be back the following year but that's beside the point. We were talking about getting out. You said you needed to escape what it meant to be a Gentry of Emblem."

I remembered that night. The three of us had climbed the old water tower to glare down at the town below. We drank and bullshitted and made plans for what we were going to do. It was the first time I could remember looking out at the world and understanding that it held possibilities, even for us.

Chase watched me. I wanted to give him what he asked for. I just wished it wasn't so damn hard.

"Maybe," I said quietly, "there's no getting away from being a Gentry of Emblem. It's what we are. You know it. Remember that quote you spit out the other night? 'If you want to understand today, you have to search yesterday.'"

"And just what the hell do you think that means?"

"It means there's no getting away from your past."

Chase let out a hiss of air. He was getting angry. If he hadn't been hampered by an IV and a hospital bed he would have gotten right in my face.

"That's not what it means at all and you damn well know it. If there was no getting away from the past then Saylor McCann wouldn't have looked at you twice this time around. If there was no getting away from it then we wouldn't be able to wake up in the morning knowing there was still an evil son of a bitch living out there in the desert. Try again, Cord. What the fuck does it mean?"

I was silent. I leaned over and began to pick up the playing cards that had fluttered to the floor. A nurse poked a disapproving face into the room and told us to keep it down.

I held the cards in my hand and arranged them into a neat stack. Chase still awaited my answer. He wasn't going to stop challenging me until he got one.

"It means," I sighed, "that the reason Creed and I need to go out tonight and fix this is because that's what we've always done for each other. It's how we lived long enough to be here. If there hadn't been three of us to fight back then we wouldn't have gotten this far."

My brother shook his head in disgust, flopping back to the pillows. "You'll throw it away," he grumbled miserably. "You're going to throw away everything. Saylor. Me. Yourself. For what, Cordero? What will you get out of it?"

"Justice," I whispered.

"Oh yeah? Whose version?"

I couldn't answer that. I didn't even have a clear idea about what I was going to do. I remembered the bolt of fury that had shot through me when I looked into my phone and saw the faces of those men. I could well imagine how I would be overcome when I came face to face with them.

Creed walked in. He noted the tension in the room immediately and approached us with a question in his eyes.

Chase grinned at him. "You have a nice shit, Big C?"

Creed didn't return the grin. "It was all right." He cleared his throat. "We got some business, Cordero."

"All right," I nodded, rising from the chair.

"Someone fighting tonight?" Chase asked sarcastically.

"Yeah," Creed answered smoothly. "Someone might be fighting tonight."

"Dammit, Creed," Chase muttered. He was blinking rapidly, trying not to cry. I hadn't seen Chasyn cry since we were kids. It was painful, knowing that we were the ones making it happen now. It was the second time in a day I'd made myself a cause of misery to someone I loved.

Chase was an open wound. I was teetering on the brink of emotional collapse. Only Creed stood there, slightly apart, stoic and unmoved.

"Let's go, Cord," he said.

"You want us to get you anything, first?" I asked Chase, trying to keep the shakiness out of my voice. "I'm even willing to try to smuggle up a beer, although that moon-faced dude at the front desk has already been looking at me sideways every time I pass by."

"I don't want a fucking thing," Chase responded, replacing the bandages over his wound. It wasn't true. He'd already told me what he wanted.

Creed touched his arm lightly. "We'll be back, little brother."

"No," our brother answered bleakly, "you won't be."

Chase rolled over on his side, turning away from us. I dimmed the light on the way out and closed the door.

Once we were in the corridor Creed showed me a picture on his phone. It was a house with some sort of funky symbol hanging under the peak of the roof.

"Found 'em," he said, pointing emphatically as we made our way to the elevator.

"You sure?" I asked as the elevator door closed behind us. "So what's the plan? Roll through the front door with bats swinging?"

Creed gave me a hard look. "You said you were in this."

"I *am* in this. I'm just asking what the hell 'this' is?"

"We're going to make them answer. We're going to tear it the fuck out of their throats if need be. I can go it alone, Cord. I got no problem with that."

I scoffed. "Well I *do* have a problem with that. I'm with you, Creed."

The elevator opened into the lobby. A big wall clock caught my eye. It was six thirty. Saylor was in Emblem now, immersed in the misery of her mother's wedding celebration. As if on cue, my phone buzzed. Creed glanced back and waited while I pulled it out. It was a text from her.

"Miss your face."

I hit the reply button. Then I stared at the blank field until I realized I couldn't think of a single answer. Slowly, I put the phone back in my pocket.

"I'm ready," I said.

27

SAYLOR

My mother only stopped complaining long enough to say her vows out on the back patio in front of an audience of about two dozen guests, most of whom I knew and wished I didn't.

Gary, aka The Gnome, shook my hand and patted my ass in his first official capacity as my stepfather. Then he leered at me while licking the straw hanging out of a Long Island iced tea. It was uncomfortable; an optical violation of sorts. Gary had known my folks in high school. My mother turned him down for the prom or something. I don't know. I never really got the whole uncensored story. But I knew he was sort of a joke to her until she decided changing her mind could be more profitable. In addition to having served several mayoral terms he owned a local moving company.

As I watched him slobbering all over my mother I thought about how true to form his nickname was. He did look like a gnome. Only less attractive.

"Miss Saylor," said a voice as a hand gripped my elbow.

"Uncle Frank," I answered, somewhat displeased. My mother's half-brother was the epitome of sleaze. When my grandmother was lying on her deathbed five years earlier he stole some blank checks from her nightstand and cleaned out her account. After a few minutes of unpleasant small talk I managed to get away from Uncle Frank.

It was getting towards evening and a few people from town were starting to head inside. A group of men sitting at the bar caught my interest as I noticed my mother gesturing to them unhappily.

They were rough lookers. They wore leather jackets and took up a lot of space, not even troubling to dare anyone with their eyes to ask them to move. The petulant bride pouted over their presence but Gary just quietly prodded her to a table in the back.

It wasn't just habit that led me to check my phone. I was desperately hoping to hear from him. I wished I hadn't shoved him away at the hospital before taking off. Hesitantly I tapped out a text message.

"Miss your face."

I wasn't usually a drinker but I needed something although I didn't want my head to be too fuzzy for the drive home. I headed to the bar and ordered a beer.

The man to my left tossed a twenty on the counter and swiveled to give me a wink. He was huge, black-haired and adorned with tattoos and leather.

"It's on me," he said, pushing the beer over. I thought I knew him, or at least had seen him around. Emblem wasn't a huge town. There was something troubling about the way he grinned at me.

"Thanks," I grumbled and then heard my mother calling me over.

A few of the wedding guests were making use of the tiny dance floor. Uncle Frank had his hands around the ass of a woman who looked exactly like my elementary school principal.

Amy grabbed my arm and pulled me into a nearby chair. The Gnome stared at me from behind his mottled facial hair as his arm draped itself over my mother's shoulders. Amy patted my knee.

"Didn't get a chance to talk to my baby."

I shrugged, not really in the mood for token mothering. "You never do."

Her lips pursed. "You really messing around with Cord Gentry?"

"Not that it's appropriate post-wedding conversation, but yes, I am."

The Gnome cocked his head. "Which one is he again?"

"One of Benton's boys," my mother spat. "You know, those scabby triplets who were forever causing trouble."

"Oh yeah. Think my property value increased the day those little shits exited town." He gave me a nasty smile. "Now if only the rest of the Gentry trash would pack up their trailers and follow."

I glared at him while my mother giggled and then looked at me thoughtfully.

"What was the other guy's name? Your boyfriend in California? Rich, hot, total keeper from what you'd told me."

"Yeah, well I might have left a few things out," I said flatly.

She ignored the comment. Her voice, assisted by the buzz of alcohol, had grown quite loud. "So what the hell did you do to screw that up, Saylor? I mean you come crawling back to Arizona and bed down with a shitty Gentry. Doesn't sound like the earth shattering future you had planned for yourself."

My mother had quite an audience by this point. Even the men from the bar were watching.

"No," I agreed, "it sure as hell doesn't."

All of a sudden she got serious. "You're not pregnant, are you?"

"Jesus, Ma."

"No, Saylor. Shit, the last thing I can deal with is some snot-nosed little Gentry who wants to call me 'Grandma'."

I looked at that woman and felt no love. She was my mother so there would always be some connection, whether I wished it or not. But her view of the world had become so ass backwards that I knew even if I told her everything about what a shit Devin was she would still prefer him to Cord. She wouldn't give Cord a chance, not ever.

As my mother and her new husband cackled drunkenly and uttered filthy things about Cord's family, there were a lot of things I could have said. I could have started with what I had learned of Amy

McCann and Chrome Gentry. But instead I just stood and regarded them icily.

"You two fucking deserve each other," I said.

I exited out the back and climbed over the wrought iron fence surrounding the patio. I could feel quite a few eyes on me as I ducked into my car. It would have been a great parting shot. Except I couldn't leave because my car wouldn't start.

After issuing a series of rabid curses and vainly turning the key, I heard a knock on the window. It was the man who'd bought me the beer at the bar. I was able to get a better look at him as he hunkered down next to the driver's side window. He was broad and muscled with dual tattoo sleeves on his thick arms. He raised an eyebrow at me.

"Trouble?"

"A little," I admitted, then shook my head with a hiss. "Jesus, what a plot point. How many times does some poor chick get stranded by a bad engine?"

"Fuck if I know," the man responded smoothly and then called over his shoulder to several men milling around by the entrance to Rooster's Roast amid a collection of motorcycles.

"Pop the hood," he ordered me.

Several of those men he'd called over surrounded the car's engine and talked among themselves. Presently one of them came along with a pair of jumper cables and attached them to a nearby pickup truck. Within moments my car coughed back to life. I jumped out and stared into the depths of my struggling vehicle.

"It's a piece of shit," said the original tattooed man, "but it might do for you a little while longer if you change the battery and handle some minor maintenance." He tossed the jumper cables back to one of his buddies and then proceeded to climb into the passenger seat of my car.

"Come on," he directed. "You're driving."

I glanced around and then poked my head in the window. "Uh, listen dude. I'm grateful, but not *that* grateful. You get what I'm saying?"

The man gave me a withering look. "Look, I heard enough of that family reunion in there to know you're my cousin's girl."

I pulled back. "Cousin?" And then I had a flash of memory. It was of a boy who'd always seemed like a man to me although in all likelihood he'd only been about five years older. I knew his name. He was rumored to be the same kind of violent troublemaker as the rest of the family he came from. I vaguely remembered hearing that he'd joined the Marines. He had the overpowering build of the Gentry men but unlike the triplets he was black-haired and dark-eyed, more closely resembling his Mexican American mother. Cord had mentioned him before.

"You were Declan Gentry," I said.

"I still am, baby," he answered with a grin. "Now get in the car. We're going for a drive. Jesus, don't look at me like that. I already told you, I get it. You're Cord's girl and you seem all closed off and shit anyway."

Reluctantly I got in. "Where are we going?"

"Where we came from," he answered simply.

"Listen, I'm not trying to be a dick, but are you high?"

Declan turned to me and grinned broadly. I saw shades of his cousins in that arrogant, knowing smile. It made my heart hurt a little. Cord still hadn't responded to my text from earlier.

"Why?" he teased. "You trying to offer me something?"

"Uh, no. But why do you need me to drive you anywhere?"

"Because I did you a favor and now you're doing me one."

"Do you always speak in fucking riddles?"

"Ain't my fault you have trouble listening. Turn down Free Road. Keep on it until you're out of town. Then a left on Coyote." Declan stretched in the seat beside me and opened the window as I tried to concentrate on where I was going. He said something in a low voice.

"What?" I snapped.

Declan Gentry gave me a hard look. "I said I'm just trying not to end up like my father."

"And how was that?"

"Road kill, sweetheart."

A black cat scrabbled across the road. It appeared to be carrying a dead ground squirrel in its mouth.

"Oh," I said softly. "You're Chrome's son. Sorry, I'd forgotten."

Declan shrugged. "It's okay. He forgot too sometimes. I'm just not seeing so straight after sucking down a little too much juice. Not a good time to get on my bike."

"I get it." Free Road was a pot-holed two lane stretch which led southeast of town. There were no street lights out this way and the darkness settled fast. "So I'm kind of operating as your designated driver?"

"Cheaper than a cab," he nodded, "and safer than my buddies." He paused. "Besides, you can tell me all about the boys."

"They're your cousins. Why don't you just call them?"

Declan yawned. "Maybe when I wake up tomorrow I will."

I eyed his vast collection of ink. "You still a tattoo artist?"

He held out his avidly decorated arms. "How'd you guess?"

I studied him from the other side of the car. I was pretty certain this was the first conversation I'd ever had with Declan Gentry. He was years ahead of me in school and by the time I reached Emblem High he was long gone. He had a familiar kind of swagger about him that made me feel exceptionally lonely. Haltingly, I told him about Chase's injuries. I left out my uncertainty over Cord's quest for vengeance. He seemed to know there was more to it all than what I was saying although he didn't pry for more information.

I squinted in the descending darkness. "This is it, isn't it?" I asked. "Most of you Gentrys live out here."

Declan pointed. "I'm crashing in an ancient single wide about a half mile back that way. Belonged to my dad." He gestured in the opposite direction. I could discern the faint outlines of a small knot of neglected trailers. I braked to a stop and stared at the quiet desolation.

"So that's the place," I wondered softly. "That's where the Gentry boys came from." I'd never seen it before, never had any reason to come out this way.

Declan nodded soberly. "Yeah, and it's as splendid as it looks."

"Their folks still there?"

He sighed. "They're still there."

Declan didn't say a word when I turned the car off and stepped out. I needed to see it up close, the place of Cord's terrors, the place that both made him and broke him. I walked a few dozen yards, doing my best to step over unseen desert shrubbery that tried to catch itself on the hem of my dress. There was a faint light coming from a small window of the largest trailer, the one in the middle. I couldn't take my eyes off it as I moved closer. I pictured Cord, my sweet strong boy, running out of that ratty door trying to escape the horrors within. The vision nearly made me weep.

For a moment I stopped thinking about the Gentry brothers as grown men. They were boys who lingered on the playground long after dark because there was no one at home who cared where they were.

"Cord," I whispered, thinking of the defiant little soul who was intent on clawing his way, somehow, to survival. For the first time I was really understanding what it must have taken for him to get there.

I also thought about what Millie had been trying to tell me. She hadn't just been relating her own painful story. Our identities were defined in different ways. Ways that sometimes damaged us along the way.

There was the sound of a crash, like a bottle breaking, and a guttural male voice shouting something unintelligible. I glanced back at the car but Declan appeared to have dozed off in the front seat.

The high cackle of an insensible female chilled me to the bone. I stopped in my tracks and tried to guess what it must have meant to grow up here. My own parents were distant and self-absorbed but never cruel. I'd always had everything I needed to get a firm foothold in life. Cord, however, had truly come from nothing. I understood then the fear and anger of the brothers, the despair that came from believing that in the whole world they could only hope to cling to one another to avoid drowning.

There was another crash and a series of vile curses. Somewhere in there were people who neither knew nor cared that one of their sons had suffered a brush with death two days earlier. I closed my eyes, letting the soft heat of the night breeze sift through my hair as I felt the ghostly sadness of three little boys who had never known safety or a gentle hand. A tear rolled down my cheek as I whispered his name over and over.

Cordero.

The snap of the door brought me back to the moment. A big man crashed through it, cursing in a slurred voice. He threw something out into the yard where it missed me by only a few feet. I could see the thick outline of a body that once must have been muscled and impressive, just as his sons were. It wasn't yet dark enough for me to blend in. Benton Gentry noticed me.

"What the fuck you doin' out there, girl?"

I was frozen. I swallowed, feeling a real surge of fear as he began to advance, moving more quickly that I would have expected. I could feel the ferocity of his thoughts as he raked me over. This was not a reasonable man. This was the beast of Cord's nightmares. I needed to run, to scream, to do something other than stare dumbly at his malicious approach.

"I-I'm sorry," I stammered, belatedly trying to backtrack.

He grabbed me by the arms and shook me a little. It was awful. It was like Devin, only worse. Cord's father stunk of liquor and the rank haze of male sweat. He was terribly strong.

"Asked you a question, girl. Now we're gonna go out back a while until you can fuckin' answer."

Benton Gentry was yanked away by a shadow that happened to be stronger than him.

"The fuck, Deck?" he grumbled.

Declan stood in front of me, keeping Benton Gentry an arm's length away. "Go on, Uncle. My apologies; we didn't mean to take up a piece of your night."

Cord's father seemed to shrink slightly. "She yours then?"

"Yeah," answered Declan. He took a wad of bills out of his pocket and peeled a twenty off. "My treat," he said, passing the bill over to his uncle's greedy palm. "For any trouble we caused you tonight."

Benton's eyes narrowed. "You know how your Aunt Maggie gets the shakes when folks come up to the fuckin' place out of nowhere."

Declan nodded smoothly and peeled off another twenty. "I know," he said softly.

I cowered behind Declan until Benton began staggering back to his trailer. As he opened the door I looked up and saw the painfully thin silhouette of a woman standing in the doorway. She wore a shapeless shift that she seemed to be lost in. I couldn't see her face. I was glad I couldn't. I knew it would haunt me.

Declan prodded me. "Come on, Cord's Girl. Before he gets riled up again."

"Thanks," I coughed. "And it's Saylor."

"Where is there a sailor?"

"That's my name. Saylor."

"Oh," he shrugged with disinterest. "Well, thanks for the ride, Saylor. Why don't you get out of this dark hole and head home to your man? I'll bet he's wanting you tonight."

"I will," I answered, biting my lip in thought. "Hey, uh, Declan? What do you charge for a tattoo?"

He sighed as if he were getting tired of me. "Now you want a tattoo?"

"I need a tattoo."

"Well, that's a new one. No one really claims to 'need' a tattoo."

I sighed and described to him what I had in mind.

"Well," he grumbled, seeming a little embarrassed. "That's kind of the shit. Sure, it's easy enough. I can get it done in twenty minutes when I'm sober but I'm not exactly sober. It might not look pretty, Miss Saylor."

"It doesn't need to look pretty. It only needs to exist."

Ten minutes later I was sitting in a chair in Declan's crummy trailer while he prepared a needle for my arm. He seemed sharper, more professional, and at least halfway sober with his tools in his hands.

"Tell me," he said, staring down at my arm as he began to work. "Does Cordero love you as much as you love him?"

"I hope so."

Declan merely nodded and stayed quiet. The needle hurt more than I thought it would but I didn't mind. I didn't mind at all.

28

CORD

Creed glanced over as I took my phone out of my pocket. I stared at Saylor's last text message for a long while.

"What?" he grunted, his eyes on the road.

We weren't going anywhere, not really. We'd scoped out the frat house just north of the university and we were just driving around now, waiting for the daylight to fade completely. I didn't want to venture a guess what would happen after that.

"Nothing," I told him and shoved the phone back into my pants. It hurt picturing her somewhere down in Emblem, waiting for a response from me.

Creed was focused. There was a hard determination in him tonight that blotted out everything else. He didn't even ask what Chase and I had talked about or why our brother had sounded so defeated as we left him alone in his hospital room.

I punched the dashboard with irritation. "How long are we gonna drive in fucking circles?"

"All right." He pulled to the left and made a u-turn. "Let's start watching the place."

"What are we looking for, Creed? Do you really think you'll catch one or two of them coincidentally hanging out on the front lawn, waiting for us to come kick their asses?"

"Maybe," he answered with narrowed eyes. "Cord, I told you I'd take this. No need for us both to go down."

"One of us goes down and we all go down. That's the way it's always been. That's the way it always will be."

"Then quit your premenstrual bitching and roll with it."

Within five minutes we were sitting across the street and three houses down from the frat house. There was a light on in the front room but other than that there didn't appear to be much going on there.

"You sure that's it?" I squinted.

"That's it," he grumbled. He opened up the window and leaned outside slightly.

I'd always counted on my instincts and they'd rarely been wrong. Right now they were screaming at me to get the hell out of there. But one look at Creed's resolute face told me he wouldn't go with me. So I stayed. I stayed because I couldn't bear to leave him on his own.

But I was having trouble containing my agitation. After rifling through the glove compartment I came across an old spiral notebook.

"You got a pen?" I asked.

"You gonna write a letter or something?"

"Yeah, my last fucking will and testament. Now can I have the damn pen?"

Creed reached into the backseat and felt around the floor before coming through with a ballpoint pen. "Happy now?"

I didn't answer. I flipped to a blank page, and propped the notebook on my knees. The empty space on the paper was calling to the pen in my hand. Without a plan in mind, I began to lightly sketch, aware that my brother was watching me.

I'd forgotten what a release it was, to create something with my hands. I knew what to draw as soon the pen hit the paper. It was the only face in my mind.

"Saylor," Creed said, nodding to the emerging picture.

I kept going, filling in the details as best I could with the limited tools at hand. I'd drawn her in profile, with a pensive expression and her long hair falling around her face. It was the way she looked when she figured no one was noticing her. I sighed and dropped the pen.

"She told me she heard you sing."

Creed was startled. "What? Oh yeah. Her cousin's girlfriend brought out the guitar and asked if I would do something with it."

"Why *don't* you do something with it?"

He looked irritated. "You really want to talk about music right now?"

"No. I want to talk about you. We've told you a thousand times there's something to that talent you've got."

Creed shifted and exhaled, looking away again.

I looked at the house. Another light flicked on upstairs. "How do we know, Creed?"

"What are you fussing about now?"

"Dammit, would you at least look at me! We don't know that these are the guys. It's a big fat fucking guess."

"What the hell do you want, Cord? You want an ironclad guarantee? Maybe we should just wait around and hope that they'll turn themselves in out of a sense of civic duty."

I shook my head miserably. The minutes ticked past. A couple of guys wandered out of the house and got into a convertible. Creed tensed and stared at them closely but they weren't the ones we were looking for.

After a while I began to relax. There were probably a few dozen guys who came and went from that place every day. We were looking for two in particular, named Jay Pruitt and Henley Carter. It suddenly seemed very unlikely that they would just happen to roll up while we waited. I picked up the pen and began idly working on the sketch again. I figured after a few more hours of this I might persuade Creed to give it a rest for the night.

My brother sat up suddenly. "Well now," he said in a deadly tone, "here we go."

I looked up. The man exiting a silver Prius was Jay Pruitt. He whistled as he started up the walk to the front door of the frat house.

Creed had vaulted out the door before I could blink. In a flash I saw the ways this could go. He might tackle Pruitt, beat the ever loving shit out of him, possibly kill him, and likely receive an escort back to Emblem to sit behind the fences for a decade or two.

Or, whoever was inside that house might hear the racket and come storming out. Then there would be a front lawn hand-to-hand combat brawl that might land us next to Chase in the hospital, and still with a ticket back to Emblem.

Neither vision was tolerable. As Creed began barreling through the dark I knew I only had seconds to stop him.

I leapt out of the truck but he was already several yards ahead of me.

"Fucker!" he shouted and Jay Pruitt turned around.

His eyes widened as he saw Creed storming straight for him, with me close behind. Pruitt glanced desperately around for help and was on the verge of shouting when Creed caught up with him. Creed grabbed him by the front of his shirt and dragged him away from the house.

"Piece of shit," Creed was snarling as he shoved Pruitt into some bushes. Pruitt was making a strangled noise in his throat as he tried to get to his feet. He wasn't a small guy, but he knew damn well he wouldn't be a match for Creed. And he'd already seen what I could do in a fight.

Creed pulled back and I could tell he was going to unleash a crushing blow to the upturned face of Jay Pruitt. I could also tell he wasn't going to stop there. He was going to keep going until the guy couldn't fucking move. I knew how he felt. I'd felt the same way when I went tearing into Say's ex. I don't know how that would have ended if she hadn't stopped me. She was right to stop me.

His momentum was already underway and Creed didn't have time to pull back when I stepped in the way. I had twisted around so that the blow caught me on the right arm but it still hurt like hell because Creed was strong as shit.

When he realized he'd hit me instead of Pruitt he just stood up straight and stared with a baffled look in his face. I spun around and grabbed Jay Pruitt.

"Did you do it? Did you jump my brother like a cowardly bastard and fuck him up?"

Even in the dark I could see Pruitt's eyes were wide and petrified. He stammered. "N-no. I didn't do it."

But he couldn't quite keep the shiftiness out of his expression. I knew a liar when I saw one. He'd either done it or knew who had. I wanted to kill him myself.

"Go," I choked, shoving him away.

Creed shouted at me. "Cord!"

"Go!" I screamed at Pruitt as he scrabbled around trying to get his legs underneath him. In a few awkward lunges he was at the entrance of the frat house, banging at the door like crazy and shouting his stupid head off.

I pushed at Creed. "We need to get out of here."

He'd left the keys in the ignition. As I got behind the wheel and started the engine I could see a mess of angry college boys beginning to pour out of the fraternity house. I extended my middle finger out the window and sped away.

Creed was fuming. His eyes burned into me from across the seat. As we reached the lights of University Drive I rubbed casually at the arm where I'd taken his hit.

"That's gonna leave a mark," I said mildly.

"Pull the fuck over," he muttered.

"Let's just get back to the apartment and-"

"Pull. The. Fuck. OVER!"

I turned into an empty parking lot. It used to be a restaurant but now was boarded up and deserted.

Creed dove out of the truck and stalked away, cursing wildly.

"Hey!" I shouted.

He turned around and glared at me. He was furious. Both at me, and just in general.

"Creedence," I said gently, daring to take a few steps in his direction.

He spat on the ground. "We've always had each other's backs. Always."

I swallowed. "I know that. It's why I stood in front of you just now. I've stood in front of you before, you know. Both you and Chase, blocking someone else's threat. I know you didn't forget."

"And I've stood in front of you too, Cordero. I've taken hits that were meant for you and I was glad."

"Yeah, I know. Just like I'm glad now. I'm glad that I stopped you from doing something irreversible. We only get this one life, Creed. Just this one life. You want to be careful what kind of risk you take with it."

He turned away, scowling out towards the road with his arms crossed. I bent at the waist, breathing heavily. He was still out of my reach. I was no longer willing to jump into the black hole beside him, but I needed to reach out a hand and pull him back to safety. He'd done it for me before.

I stood straight and spoke his name softly. "Creed."

He didn't answer. Several yards away, the traffic continued to roar by.

"Do you remember the first week we got up here? We scraped together enough change for a single room in that roach motel by the freeway."

"No," he shook his head.

I smiled. "Yeah, you do. About the only things you carried out from Emblem were a few changes of clothes and that guitar you'd scored at the pawn shop."

"So?" he challenged. "So what? What the fuck does that have to do with where we're at right now?"

I sighed, remembering. "The only work we could find was under the table, shoveling gravel at a pit in in Mesa. We were eating bulk pasta for every meal, sleeping in a shithole and wondering how the hell anyone ever managed to make it out of the sand trap."

He was listening but still wouldn't say a word.

"Some creeper at the motel approached Chase with an offer to get into dealing. He was considering it. I was considering it. You put the brakes on and you were right. We'd already seen close up what that shit did to people, to our own mother."

I looked up at the sky. The stars looked back at me.

"It was a night like this. We were all feeling pretty low and wondering if we were going to wind up back in Emblem as a dead end Gentry after all. You grabbed your guitar and hustled us outside. You started singing. It was some of that old music you're so into. You kept going and people started coming out of their rooms to listen. And there, in that crappy place in the company of people who were no better off than us, it was a fucking beautiful moment. I was so god damn proud to call you my brother."

Creedence closed his eyes. "So?"

I grabbed him by the shoulders and forced him to look at me. "So can we have the same ending tonight? Please?"

He could have gone either way. He thought about it. It seemed like an eternity passed before he smiled. Then he grabbed me in a crushing bear hug. His voice was husky with emotion.

"Sure, Cordero."

We ambled back to the truck together. Creed wanted to drive and I let him. When he stopped by the apartment to pick something up I took my phone out and tapped out a message.

"Please come back to me."

29

SAYLOR

I'd done everything I needed to do in Emblem and now it was time to leave. Declan bid me farewell with a wave from the front step of his trailer. I saw the triplets, especially Cordero, in his smile.

There was only one way in and out of town so I had no choice but to pass the prison again. It was quiet now. The protesters had left and the rec yards were dark and empty. I knew inside those walls it was a different story though. It was a sad and chaotic bedlam of activity. I shuddered, wondering how my parents and their colleagues were able to stand it, working in there. I supposed after a while it just became common and boring, nothing even worth blinking over.

My arm was stinging. It felt like three hundred paper cuts treated with peroxide. It was a good pain though. It was the kind of pain that spoke of hope and desire; the epicenter of everything that mattered. It was something I'd once despaired of ever finding.

Emblem faded in my rearview mirror and I hurtled through the night, hoping my car held out long enough for me to reach Tempe. Tonight wasn't the time to get stuck on the side of the road somewhere. I felt slightly faint when I thought about Cord. I would have given ten years of my life to know that he was safe.

When my phone buzzed I figured it was Bray. I hadn't told him what time I'd be back but I knew how much he worried about me. I rifled around in my purse with one hand and pulled my phone out. The words on the screen nearly caused me to drive off the road.

"Please come back to me."

I had my finger on the button to call him but that's not how I wanted this to go. I needed to see him, to hold him, to revel in the way our bodies crashed together because that's how it was with us.

There were still about thirty miles of driving until I reached Tempe. I didn't know what to make of his message, other than the obvious. It left a few unanswered questions. Had he done something terrible tonight? I almost couldn't bear to know. It would be in his face when I saw him. The torment would show. He wouldn't be able to hide it.

I felt a cold sweat breaking out on the back of my neck as I dared to push the car fifteen miles past the speed limit. He would be at the hospital. There was still forty five minutes left to visiting hours.

The hospital parking lot was crowded. Finally I gave up and parked next to a dumpster by the perimeter.

I knew the day had taken a toll and I likely looked a wreck. It seemed like a silly thing to care about though, considering everything that had happened lately. Moreover, Cord wouldn't give a damn if my hair was out of place and my makeup smeared.

Hospitals never really got quiet. I supposed they were like prisons in that way. There were always dramas unfolding and needs to be met. As I walked down the corridor towards Chase's room I passed various people who were wrapped in their own emotional battles. I imagined that was the way of it for everyone, whether they said so or not.

The music was loud enough for me to hear as soon as I turned the corner. I stopped to listen, and smiled. A handful of patients and visitors were gathered by the doorway of the room. The hospital staff could have put a stop to it since technically it was disruptive, but they only smiled indulgently and let it continue for now.

They were all there, all three of them. Creed was seated with the guitar in his hands, playing avidly. Chase was in bed, shaking with laughter and holding his side. And Cord leaned against the far wall, singing along with Creed as they belted out the quirky lyrics of *The Joker*. They got to the chorus and elevated their pitch. I closed my eyes and thought about how perfect the song was there in that moment. The Gentry boys, they were perfect together.

When I opened my eyes Cord was staring at me. I took a few steps into the room and waited. Chase raised his eyebrows and glanced at his brother. Creed was so lost in his singing he didn't even appear to notice I was there.

When the song was finished people clapped and the nurses finally ushered everyone away since visiting hours were ending. Cord hadn't moved. He smiled at me bashfully as I went to Chase and kissed him on the cheek.

"Told you I'd be back today."

Chase grabbed me around the neck and gave me an affectionate squeeze. "I'm supposed to get out of here tomorrow."

"Yeah? That's good news."

Creed stood and gave me a short nod by way of greeting. Cord had crossed his arms and was looking me over with a glint in his eye.

"So," I said brightly, "I had a shitty day. How about you guys?"

I didn't miss the way Creed and Cord glanced at one another. It was Chase who spoke though.

"Shitty day all around, Miss McCann. Looking up now, though. What happened to your arm?"

"Oh, right." I glanced down at the clean bandage Declan had covered my tattoo with. I pulled it off to expose the permanent script on the inside of my wrist. The skin surrounding it was still raw and red.

Chase grabbed my arm, examining the tattoo, and then grinned. "'*Amor vincit omnia*'?"

I nodded. "I think it does. No, that's not right. I know so."

Creed peered at my arm, frowning. "Conquer love?" he guessed.

"'Love conquers all'," Cord corrected.

Creed let out a low whistle and snatched up his guitar. "Well, I'm gonna leave this little party and head out." He leaned briefly on the edge of the bed and his voice was unusually gentle. "Good night, little brother."

Chase yawned. "Good night, King Kong."

Creed started to walk out and then he turned around suddenly. He withdrew a piece of paper from his pocket and pushed it into my hand. I looked up at him and he smiled faintly.

Cord stood stock still on the other side of the bed. He watched as I unfolded the paper and saw my face staring back at me from the picture inside.

"Damn," I breathed. "Thank you."

Chase rolled over to his side and shut his eyes, waving us away. "Good night, everyone. Leave the premises. Go off to fuck or fight or whatever people are doing out there. Just remember that pretty soon Chase Gentry is rejoining the game."

He opened one blue eye and winked at me as Cord came to my side. Creed had already gone on ahead so we left quietly together. It was a long walk back to my car but we didn't speak the entire time. I handed my keys over to him. He took them without a word and opened the door for me.

When Cord started driving I figured he would just head back to the apartment. He seemed to have something else in mind though and when he parked on campus I realized what it was. It was easier to climb up the steep stairs of the art building barefoot so I slipped my sandals off and hiked up my dress for the trip up. Cord followed right behind. When we reached the top I couldn't wait anymore. I went to him and brushed my fingers across his cheek.

"Hey," I whispered.

"Hi," he answered, his arms already wrapping around my waist and drawing me close. His face was happy and relaxed. Whatever the plan had originally been tonight, the worst hadn't occurred.

"So how was Emblem?"

"The same."

"Is that where you got the ink?"

"Yeah," I smiled, thinking of Declan. I told Cord about it all and he laughed. There was something I hadn't mentioned yet though.

"I saw your folks," I said hesitantly and watched his smile disappear. "Do you want to hear about it?"

He shook his head and sighed. "No."

I hugged him fiercely. "I adore you, Cordero Gentry."

"You'd better. Because I plan on keeping you."

My heart jumped. "I think I like the idea of idea of being kept by you."

Cord pulled back a little and ran his fingers through my hair. "Then kiss me, baby. And once you start, don't ever stop."

There was nothing else to talk about tonight. It was all I wanted too.

EPILOGUE
CORD

"Damn, honey. Say that filthy shit again."

"You fucking own me, Cordero. I'm ruled by your huge cock and nothing else."

"And you like it that way."

"I love it that way. Oh god, I'm almost there. Can you keep going hard just a little longer?"

"I can keep going hard as long as it takes, baby."

It was the middle of the afternoon and we were screwing our brains out in our bedroom. Saylor shuddered and got even wetter as she tightened around me and yelled. She came longer and with more noise than any freaking female in history. It was hotter than the dirtiest porn flick. With a supreme effort I managed to hold back my release until she was all done.

"Shit," she whispered, melting into my arms as we rolled back into the bed together. I pulled her on top of me, loving the feel of her sweaty skin.

Chase banged on the living room wall with his fist to let us know he didn't appreciate the noisy afternoon theater. He'd been home from the hospital for two weeks but we were still forcing him to take it easy. It was making him increasingly irritable, especially when he was inadvertently forced to listen to neighboring bedroom acrobatics.

"Sorry," I yelled as Saylor giggled into my neck. I let my hand rest on her hip. "You got to head to work now?"

"Yeah," she sighed with regret. "Can't leave Truly alone with the famished masses. And you?"

I checked my phone. "I got about an hour before I need to show up."

When my cousin Declan had called following his run in with Saylor, I told him I was interested in his offer to show me the ink trade. Deck somehow got around everywhere and knew everyone. He got me in at a local shop on sort of an apprentice basis. Surprisingly, customers flipped over my designs and I liked the work. It wasn't the mass payout of a fight but it was steady and it was good. I couldn't go on forever getting my head knocked around, not when I had a reason to think about the future.

Saylor was being dreamy, looking down at her ring. I'd been almost embarrassed to give it to her. It wasn't the kind of ring girls showed other girls. It was nothing fancy; just a slim band of sterling silver with a few words etched into it. But holy shit did she go nuts over it. She cried and hugged me and then dragged me into the bedroom to fuck like crazy. I didn't call it an engagement ring because that was a stupid word that smacked of dull formality. But she was mine and someday soon we were going to stand up in front of anyone who wanted to hear about it and speak the words.

I pushed her hair out of the way so I could see her face more clearly. "What are you thinking?"

She smiled broadly. "I'm going to be a Gentry."

"You don't have to change your name if you don't want to."

"Are you kidding?" she laughed, kissing me, and then resting her chin on my chest. Her pretty green eyes twinkled. "I can't wait."

I pinched her ass lightly. "Historically, being a Gentry isn't exactly a point of pride."

"Well," she answered with stubbornness. "History is about to be transformed. I'll be proud, Cord. Proud to be next to you and proud to be a Gentry. It's who you are."

I heard Chase getting up and banging around in the kitchen. I figured maybe it was time we took the leash off and let him bang around something else for a change.

"You want to go out tonight after work? Us and the boys?"

"Oh, we're letting Chase out now?"

"Yeah," I grinned, listening to him curse loudly in the next room. "I think it's time to inflict Chasyn on society again."

Saylor paused. "You think Creed will come too?"

My thoughts darkened as I thought of my other brother. He still owed a big favor that could be called in at any time. Whether it took a day or six months, Gabe was going to come for his fighter. There was no doubt about it. When that happened we would just need to deal with it the same way we'd dealt with everything. Together.

"He'll probably come," I shrugged.

Saylor licked at my earlobe. "Will you come for *me*, big boy?"

"I just did. You forget?"

"No," she purred, getting all frisky again. "When we're out tonight I want to do something bad with you."

I spite of our recent workout I was getting interested. "Like what?"

Saylor had a vivid imagination. It served me well. She licked her lips and said all kinds of creative things involving my body and her body.

"Shit, you're dirty," I groaned. "In the best fucking way."

"That's why you love me."

"It's one of the reasons."

She flushed and glanced down, looking all serious in the way that always made my heart ache. "I'm so lucky," she whispered.

I grabbed her and held on tight. She was a damn miracle. She really was. Sometimes I didn't know how to tell her that but as she sighed in my arms I realized she knew. I'd make sure she never forgot it.

Saylor moved her palm to my chest and I closed my hand around hers, feeling the hard shape of the ring on her finger and thinking of the words that had been carved into its surface. The same ones that had been carved into her skin.

Amor vincit omnia.

Love really does conquer all.

We had taught each other that.

In this life it was the only lesson worth learning.

ALSO BY CORA BRENT

Gentry Boys Series
DRAW (SAYLOR AND CORD)
RISK (CREED AND TRULY)
GAME (CHASE AND STEPHANIE)
FALL (DECK AND JENNY)
HOLD
CROSS (A NOVELLA)
WALK (STONE AND EVIE)
EDGE (CONWAY AND ROSLYN)
SNOW (A CHRISTMAS STORY)

Gentry Generations
(A Gentry family spinoff series)
STRIKE (CAMI AND DALTON)
TURN (CASSIE AND CURTIS)
KEEP (A NOVELLA)
TEST (DEREK AND PAIGE)
CLASH (KELLAN AND TAYLOR)
WRECK (THOMAS AND GRACIE)

Also By Cora Brent

The Ruins of Emblem
TRISTAN (CADENCE AND TRISTAN)
JEDSON (RYAN AND LEAH)
LANDON (AUTUMN AND LANDON)

WICKED WEST REJECTS
HATEFUL
BRAVE (Coming Soon)
WISE (Coming soon)

Worked Up
FIRED
NAILED

STAND ALONE STORIES
UNRULY
IN THIS LIFE
HICKEY
SYLER MCKNIGHT
THE PRETENDER
LONG LOST
STRAYS
TILL IT HURTS
TILL NEXT TIME

CONTACT ME

I love to hear from readers! Contact me at corabrentwrites@yahoo.com.

www.facebook.com/CoraBrentAuthor

https://www.goodreads.com/CoraBrent

Amazon Author Page

Instagram: CoraBrentAuthor

TikTok: CoraBrentAuthor

Did you know that I have a private Facebook group where I post exclusive updates, teasers and ARC signups? Hope to see you there! Cora Brent's Book Corner